DRAGON DREAMS

The First Dragon Rider Book Two

AVA RICHARDSON

D1522565

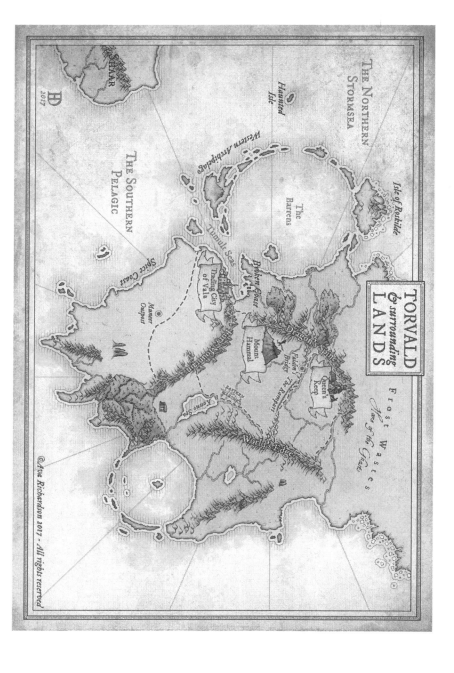

TORVALD
& surrounding
LANDS

THE NORTHERN
STORMSEA

Haunted
Isle

Isle of Roskilde

THE SOUTHERN
PELAGIC

Western Archipelago

The
Barrens

Tumult Seas

Spice Coast

Broken Coast
Vale

Trading City
of Vala

Maneri
Outpost

Mount
Hammal

Dragon's Spine

Paulin's
Bridge

Ox Rampart

Queen's
Keep

Winter's Edge

Sunra Sea

Eastern
Lagoon

Frost
Wastes
Sea of the Glass

THE FIRST DRAGON RIDER TRILOGY

Dragon God

Dragon Dreams

Dragon Mage

Cover Design by Joemel Requeza

www.relaypub.com

THE FIRST DRAGON RIDER

DRAGON DREAMS

AVA RICHARDSON

BLURB

Sometimes, the past is best left behind...

Char longs for peace and escape, preferring her dreams to the ugly realities of an uncertain age. As an illegitimate daughter of the North Prince, Char has always felt deep insecurity, but she must put that aside when Zaxx gives her the task of retrieving an ancient crown from her family's palace. If she brings him this crown, he says, he will allow the dragon hoard to choose their riders.

When her father sends for her to return home, fearing war, she senses an opportunity. But Char's dragon Paxala has grander ideas—she wants to become the greatest of all dragons and defeat the ancient Zaxx. But she can't do it without Char's guidance and aid. Employing patience and skill, Char will have to learn the secrets of dragon lore hidden away in her father's archives before Zaxx's suspicions turn aggressive.

With the help of her love, Neill, Char discovers the secret of the old queen's crown in her father's castle, learning a tale of dark magic steeped in blood. But when her father wishes to marry her off to the leader of the Wildmen, the fate of Torvald will depend on her difficult choice: accept the role she has always played, or learn to trust her own power.

MAILING LIST

Thank you for purchasing 'Dragon Dreams'
(The First Dragon Rider Book Two)

I would like to thank you for purchasing this book. If you would like to hear more about what I am up to, or continue to follow the stories set in this world with these characters—then please take a look at:

AvaRichardsonBooks.com

You can also find me on me on
www.facebook.com/AvaRichardsonBooks

Or sign up to my mailing list:
AvaRichardsonBooks.com/mailing-list/

PART I
THE MONASTERY

CHAPTER 1
CHAR NEFRETTE, THIEF!

The sweat trickled down my brow where I hung, clutching the rock walls of the cliff, and I could hear my heart thudding in my ears. Just calm down, Char, you can do this, I told myself, opening my mouth to try and breathe a little quieter. It wasn't just the fall that would kill me if I got this wrong, but I knew that if I made any noise at all, then I would probably get killed as well.

We would all get killed, I corrected. I was hanging from the sides of the sheer cliff, and clinging to the rocks by my fingers and toes. There the narrowest of rocky ledges under my soft shoes, but it wasn't wide enough to walk along. Beneath me the stone walls descended to the broken rocks of the dragon crater below, and I don't know why I had thought that this was a good idea.

"Pssst! Char, tell us what's happening out there," Neill's

voice came from behind me, and I managed to turn my face against the rock to see he was looking worried from where he and the others sat, huddled against the outcrop of broken rock behind me. Above the heads of Neill, Dorf, and Sigrid, the grey clouds started to fragment and rise as the dawn approached. That meant that we didn't have long.

"I'm clinging to a rock, Neill. What do you think is happening?" I hissed back. From my hip, there extended a thin line of rope all the way back to the rock that my three friends were hiding beside, and then to their hands. I had shown them how I wanted the rope to be held, and how they could loop it around their bodies or around a foot in case I fell.

At least my mother's mountain family had taught me that much, anyway, I thought. I reached out with my hand for a second time, my fingers prising at the nearest stub of woody truck of the gorse-type bush that clung to the rock wall.

Almost, almost… There! I gripped the sturdy wood with one hand, then moving my foot out along the thin ledge, and sliding my other hand and foot a few feet farther along the difficult transverse.

It was slow going, and the muscles in my back and legs burned with the effort, but I was nearly there. Nearly across. We'd been at this since the dark watch before dawn, when at first even Dorf and Sigrid's eyes had glittered with excitement at the prospect of sneaking into the dragon crater. This had been my idea: a chance to sneak in and try to rescue some of the dragon eggs from Zaxx. We now knew that Zaxx was actively helping the Abbot Ansall to cull the herd, and, in the scant few months since the battle against the Sons of Torvald, I couldn't stop thinking about the dangers that those eggs – and all of the young dragons in there – were in.

"Yeah, not so excited now I bet," I grumbled to myself, as I reached out from the scrubby tree trunk to the next outcrop of rock.

Crack. There was a sudden sensation of movement beneath my foot as the rock ledge I had thought was solid slab rock was in fact layers of compressed flakes. Oh no, I had time to think as my foot disappeared, and I lurched forward along the cliff wall.

"She's falling," I heard Dorf's terrified squeak of alarm.

"Skreayar!" There was a screech of dragon call from somewhere far above us—no doubt Paxala even though I had made it clear to her to leave us alone this morning, that the dragon crater was too dangerous for her. But I had no time to let my fears about her get in the way – I pushed out with my back foot, reaching with my hand towards the nearest rock—

"Ugh!" my gloved hands caught a rocky outcrop the moment before my body slammed into it, and I hugged my arms and legs around it like I could cling to it like a spider. Please don't splinter and crack, please... I begged the rock itself, but it held.

"Char? Char!" Neill was calling, standing from his position.

"No – don't move," I called back, scrabbling with my

hands until I could force my fingers between cracks and into the dirt behind my saving rock, hauling myself out to the much wider ledge I had been trying to get to. The rope I was attached to was tighter than before, but slack enough to let me flop over onto my back, groaning in exhaustion. I lay there for a moment, looking up at the lightening skies. The cold air felt chill in my lungs.

"Char is hurt? I can fly to her?" A reptilian voice said in my mind. Paxala's mind felt tense and skittish, and I could feel the concern seeping through her.

"No, don't," I murmured, knowing that the dragon would be able to hear my thought. "I told you to stay by the lake this morning." I frowned as I pushed myself up into a sitting position, pulling once on the rope for some more slack. There was an answering single tug at the rope, and then, when I pulled on it I found that there was much more give. I had told Neill how we had done such things in the mountains. One tug on the rope was 'okay, keep going' and two was 'halt!'

"How can Paxala sit by the lake while you go in there? Would you for me?" the young dragon chided me.

"Well, I guess that you are right. Just stay out of sight of the other dragons please," I murmured as I wound the rope several times around the large outcrop of rock, and then a couple more around another. That should hold, I hoped.

"Pssst!" I hissed back across the cliff, waving my hand over my head. In response, I saw the now-distant shape of Neill wave his arms, and start to progress along the way I had just come, but now with a guide rope to follow. I knelt by the rope, steadying it as much as I could with my hands as I watched him.

Neill was almost all healed from his scrapes and bruises of the last few months at the Draconis Monastery, but he still moved a little stiffly on his left foot. It made him cautious as he climbed, but that wasn't a bad thing. When he was halfway across he paused and recovered his breath, his face serious and grave as he carried on.

He has changed, I thought, watching him. Not only physically; growing a little taller and broader shouldered (but still nowhere near as tall as Sigrid) but he was also quieter as well. It had been almost a full season since the Sons of Torvald, Neill's very own older brothers, had attacked the Draconis Order in greed for their apparent power and rising popularity with Prince Vincent. Ever since then Torvald has seemed a little withdrawn and reserved, as if he was worried that something terrible was going to happen. That was part of the reason why I insisted that we do this now, rather than waiting any longer.

One of the Vicious Greens dragons had recently had a clutch of eggs, and we were heading into the dragon crater before break of day to steal them.

~

"Oof!" Neill crawled onto the ledge and collapsed just as I had against the stone wall.

"Congratulations." I gave him a moment to get his breath back, waving to the next person in line, Sigrid.

"That was tough," Neill groaned, rolling his shoulders with an audible crack.

"You should try it without a rope to hold onto," I teased, watching the long Sigrid cover the cliff much quicker than either of us had. "Still, you're right. We have to return with the eggs, yet. If only there was an easier way—"

"The tunnels?" Neill said as he stood to steady the rope on the other side of me.

"Have we got time to explore them?" I asked dubiously. Neill had told me about the tunnels, of course. He had told me that, during the battle for the monastery I had been dragged down beneath the monastery, to an opening on the mountain-side connected to the dragon tunnels that had allowed Zaxx the mighty Gold bull dragon (and leader of the crater) to worm his way to meet with the Abbot Ansall. That was when Jodreth the outcast Draconis Order monk had confronted the Abbot and challenged him to a magical duel. He had lost, and Paxala had carried him to safety.

The strange thing was neither Neill, Paxala, nor anyone else could remember where this cave and the tunnels were. I had asked to be taken back to them, to see if there might be a secret passage we could use to spy on Abbot Ansall–but all that had happened was that we had spent hours wandering aimlessly over the mountainside, finding nothing. It was odd, as if the sort of enchantment from those old folk tales and nursery rhymes had been placed upon it.

"Probably not," Neill agreed with a sigh. Whatever the answer to the mystery was, we did know that the Dragon Crater was riddled with tunnels and natural cave systems hollowed out for use by the dragons over centuries and millennia. That was how we knew one of the Vicious Greens had a clutch of eggs; she was seen making her way to the deeper, warmer, and soft-sanded caverns where brood mothers went to lay.

"Don't worry, Neill, next on the list after saving the eggs will be exploring the tunnels," I started to say, just as there was a scrape and a shout.

"Sigrid!" I couldn't stop myself from crying out, grabbing the rope and leaning my full weight into it to make it as taut as possible.

Sigrid Fenn, a daughter of the Fenn Clan of the Middle Kingdom had slipped at the same place on the ledge where I had, and was now clutching with both hands onto the rope as her feet dangled and kicked at the cliff walls. Bits of rock were chipping and flaking away, falling down the walls in a shower.

"Try to get a hold with your feet!" I hissed out, aware that somewhere below us the crater full of dragons was no doubt beginning to wake from their slumbers. We both held our breath, waiting for Sigrid to get her tiptoes onto the rocks, easing herself backwards towards the ledge they had come from.

Dammit, I thought. "Without that ledge there, it is going to make this journey a whole lot harder," I said tersely.

"A whole lot impossible for Dorf." Neill was frowning in worry, as Sigrid and Dorf exchanged hurried whispers. I could tell from their hand gestures and shaking heads that neither of them wanted to attempt to cross over now.

"That's okay," I said as loud as I dared, flapping with my hands and pointing at the floor where they stood. "Just. Wait," I said slowly and clearly, unsure if they even heard me over the distance.

"Looks like it's just you and me then," Neill said, as Dorf and Sigrid hunkered down by the rope bridge that we had rigged up.

"Yep, and this time we don't even have a dragon to ride…" I pointed out, leading the way down to the crater floor between the broken boulders.

There were dragon claw marks everywhere down here, deep scores clawed across the soft rocks, and smooth surfaces where dragons came to slough off their old scales. Tough, almost tropical little plants and shrubs dotted the ground which was noticeably warmer down here. One of the nearby pools bubbled and I was grateful the sound masked our crunching steps.

"There, up ahead." I pointed to the birthing cave that the green had chosen. It had a low entrance like the others beside it, although still higher than our heads, but much lower than most of the other greater caverns that the dragons used for their dens.

"Wait, I thought I heard something." Neill froze and I ducked to a crouch instinctively. What would happen if we were caught in the crater by Zaxx or any of the others? We had seen the way that the dragons tore apart the carcasses that the monks threw down to them every day. I was sure that we wouldn't last three breaths down here.

Why did I ever think this was a good idea?

"Because of the hatchlings," Paxala reminded me.

"Yes," I muttered under my breath. "Because of the hatchlings." If we managed to get to the eggs before they hatched, then there was a chance that we could free the young dragons from their captivity here, under the awful rule of Zaxx the Golden, and the Abbot. The Abbot chooses which dragons are going to die, that was what Neill had told me. Torvald had overheard the Abbot bargaining with Zaxx over dragons' lives. How could I leave a whole new generation of baby dragons in here, farmed as villagers might raise chickens or piglets?

"What did you say?" Neill whispered.

"Oh nothing." I shook my head. "Just talking to Paxala."

"Ah." He nodded, and a brief shadow flickered through his

eyes. He wished that he could hear her the way that I could, in my mind. But it was like this magic that the Abbot thought that some of us had. It was something that was natural and instinctive – and not something that I could control at all.

"Come on." I nodded, stepping towards the cavern, and walking inside so Neill wouldn't see my face.

It's not like he had anything to feel jealous about, though, I thought, a little annoyed. I guess that I was tired and scared because of where we were – it was making me irritable. Neill was the one whom Paxala had urged to get on her back, like a steed. It was Neill to whom most of the Draconis Order looked at in awe, fear, or surprise most days. He had been the first to do something that no one else had ever done in the entire history of the Draconis Order here at Mount Hammal. He had ridden a dragon.

It was dark inside, but not cold. Instead, the air was even warmer and dryer than in the crater, and there was no sound. I waited for my eyes to adjust to the gloom, and could see the hazy shapes of what I thought were rocks. I hoped that was all that they were anyway, as I didn't want to blunder onto a sleeping dragon just before dawn!

"Where are they?" Neill was whispering to me and I shrugged. Why did he think that I would be the one to know? Only because a dragon had bonded to me, didn't mean that I was suddenly an expert on all things draconic! In fact, that was one of the many reasons why I knew that we had to do this. There was still so much to know about dragons – did they really need to live with a mean old bull like Zaxx, or could they live quite happily on their own, as Paxala did? Would other dragons bond with humans if they had the chance to, as Paxala and I had?

And could we ride them...? I thought with the thrum of excitement I always felt at the prospect. Just as Neill had done. Just as Neill had shown us what we could do. We could stop this cruel farming that the Draconis Order seemed to be doing, and instead, we could have bonded dragons and humans - as friends, working together.

Still so much we don't know... I was thinking, as my feet scrunched on something softer on the ground. Dried grasses and leaves. The nest!

"Have you got the bags ready?" I whispered, and heard Neill grunt in the affirmative. They were little more than old canvas sacks I had begged from the stables, with softer velvet material that I had begged from Nan Barrow, the House Mistress and resident cook. I wasn't a great seamstress (my father thinking it more befitting for a daughter of the Northern Prince to learn how to shoot arrows than thread needles) but I had made it work. We now had three soft-lined bags, each of which might hold two or three eggs. I didn't even know how many eggs a dragon laid at a time, that was how little I knew.

"Okay, quiet now..." I hunkered down, taking a step

forward. The nest of the dragon was large, a vast mound of grass, bark, branches and dried foliage forming a round mound, in the center of which sat three large pale blue and speckled eggs. They were beautiful, the color of the softest summer sky – but they were not what had alarmed me.

Scrunch. The dried grasses crackled and crunched and I froze, my heart hammering in my throat. But nothing happened. Maybe there were no dragons nearby. I reached forward, patting the dried grasses carefully around me, reaching as far as I could until-

My hand hit something solid, smooth, and radiating warmth, as if from some inner flame. An egg! "Neill!" I hissed. "I think I've found them." I reached further, following the smooth curve of the egg to its nearest fellow, and then feeling the curve of another beside it. This one, too, was slightly warm to the touch and I was sure that I could feel a slight vibration coming from inside, like the beat of a heart that was already the size of my thumb.

Hang on. How big are the eggs? I moved forward (crunch-scrunch) to use both hands this time. The egg was almost the size of my entire torso. It was huge! What an idiot I was, I cursed myself – of course they were going to be large! For some reason, I had thought that they might be just a bit bigger than a goose's eggs, or the size of my hand. If they were this big then they would barely fit into the bags, and we could only carry one each…

"Hissssss…" There was a rattling sound from the darkness

ahead. Oh crap. I froze, not even breathing, my hands hovering over where I thought that the Vicious Green's dragon eggs would be. Could I slip my lined bag over one, turn and run? I wondered, waiting to see what would happen next.

Nothing. Whatever dragon had made that sound out there in the dark, they had either gone back to sleep or decided that I wasn't a threat. I moved my hands to my belt where the bag was tied.

"Sccckrrr…" This time, the dragon noise didn't come from deeper in the cavern ahead of us, but outside, and above us.

"Paxala?" I tried to 'think' at her, wondering if she had defied all of my orders and flown into the crater anyway. "Please, no, Zaxx will kill you!" I bit my lip, as suddenly there was another startled screeching from outside.

"Sessekrear!" Another dragon called, this time in a much higher pitch.

"Char?" Neill whispered, and when I turned to look back I could clearly see his outline silhouetted against the grey dawn light of the cave's entrance. "It's dawn. The dragons are waking up."

"I can hear that!" I hissed back at him, turning once more to the nest in front of me, and stopping in alarm at what I could see.

That was the snout of a very large, and very perturbed Giant White dragon that was raised from its slumber. The Giant Whites – the largest of all of the dragon species apart from Zaxx the Golden himself--made excellent brood-mothers. The Whites seemed to like taking care of, tending, and insulating the eggs of other dragons. She was looking at me with gold-green eyes that flashed an internal fire.

"Neill...?" I said slowly, my voice trembling.

"I see it, Char..." he responded, in just the same careful tone of voice, while outside more dragons rose their voices to join the dawn chorus.

The White's nostrils flared, breathing in the strange human scent that had invaded the birthing caves. I watched as her brows furrowed, clearly trying to work out whether we were threats or food.

"There now." I tried to keep my voice as calm and as low as possible, taking a step back down the nest.

Scrunch. As soon as my shoe crunched on the nest, the Giant White seemed to make up its mind that me plus nest wasn't something she would tolerate. Her throat inflated and filled like a bellows, and she opened her maw to make a long, warning and hooting noise that almost knocked me from my knees.

"Run!" I shouted, turning and leaping from the nest, my bag empty. In response to the Giant White's alarm call the dragons outside went silent for just a moment – and then erupted into a cacophony of shrieks that went up from every available cave and tunnel around us as we ran out onto the sand of the crater floor, moving as fast as our legs could carry us.

With sharp shrieks, the smaller Messenger dragons shot

out from their roosts in some of the tallest of scrub trees, flapping in alarm as they tried to work out whether it was the dawn call or something else that was causing the ruckus.

"The ledge!" Neill was saying, grabbing me by the hand, and yanking me up ahead of him. We clambered quickly, hand over hand as dragons behind us forced themselves out of their homes. Some of the wingless Earth Brown dragons who had been outside, basking in the steaming pools and mud holes at the bottom of the crater, raised their heads to croak at us in alarm. But it wasn't them that I was worried about.

"Here, this way," Neill helped me (even though I was the better climber than he was) and we crossed the area of broken boulders to the small ledge where we had tied the rope. Sinuous Blues were wending their way out of their caves, croaking at the first rays of sun that hit the rocks.

"We might just make it, if they begin their dawn call," Neill was saying, pushing me ahead of him onto the rope. Now, without most of the ledge underneath it we had to do a very undignified sort of hand-over-hand swing, something that made my shoulders scream in agony.

"Come on, come on!" Sigrid was clapping her hands to buoy us along, as we heard a deep rumble from below. The walls of the cliff itself shook, and the rope danced. It was Zaxx, emerging from his nest.

"WHAT IS THIS I SMELL? HUMANS?" The voice of the bull dragon hit my mind like a storm. It was like the internal joining of minds that I had with Paxala, only that the bull dragon could reach anyone's mind, human, dragon, bonded or not. I paused on the rope to look behind me – that was a mistake.

Down below us on the crater floor the vast maw of Zaxx the Golden broke the surface, nosing and pushing from a previously-concealed tunnel entrance, followed by the sunken scales of his ancient face, his deep-set eyes and swept-back horns of broken bone. His immense body followed. Rolls of skin that must have once been filled with muscle now hung like loose-fitting clothes, visible cords of tendons running beneath it. He was still a strong, powerful beast. The mightiest creature I had ever seen, for all of his years and cracked scales. Claws almost as long as I was pulled the beast to the surface, and I was reminded of a horrible worm or insect coiled around the heart of an apple, and it almost made me sick. The nostrils of the great gold were billowing and pumping, and his forked tongue flopped horridly into the air to taste where we might be.

"Char, come on!" Sigrid was saying, as I crossed the scrubby gorse bush and scrabbled for the ledge that took me back to her. "Take my hand." She leaned out, pulling me towards her and towards safety.

"But Neill is still out there," I said in alarm, looking back to see Neill already swinging from hand to hand along the rope, his fear lending speed to his movements.

"THE DRAGON-CHILD! THE BOY! THERE YOU ARE…" Zaxx tasted us on the air, swiveling his mighty head as smaller dragons started to crow towards the rising sun. Their calls were deafening as they followed an instinctive need to greet the sun, the object that gave them all of their energy and life.

"Neill," I said in terror, as Zaxx raised his neck, stretching it like a snake. "Cut the rope!" I hissed at him.

"What?" He paused in alarm, as Zaxx slithered and climbed the boulder field behind.

"Cut the rope behind you," I called again and the boy nodded, seeing what I meant to do. He drew out his boot knife, and, with one swift wrench, severed the rope that I had spent so long getting attached in the morning darkness. He fell like a stone, holding onto the rope as I pulled, jumping back, with Sigrid and Dorf at my side.

I grunted with effort as the sudden, heavy lurch of the rope dragged me towards the edge, but between the three of us, we managed to pull the rope up while Zaxx perched on the boulders below. Lucky for us, the great gold dragon hadn't warmed up yet from the sun. He was still sluggish and nowhere near his full speed or strength, his eyes drooping and blinking.

"THAT'S RIGHT, LITTLE HUMANS. RUN FROM THIS PLACE, BEFORE I CHANGE MY MIND AND EAT YOU!" Zaxx's voice resounded in our heads, as one of Neill's hands appeared over the edge, gripping onto the slab of rock, and then the other, to be followed by his pale and wide-eyed face. We pulled him on top of us, dropping the rope to scramble back over the broken lip of the dragon crater, and out, with stumbling feet onto the upper slopes of the Dragon Mountain itself.

I felt miserable. We had failed and that meant that there were at least three young hatchlings in there that would have to endure a lifetime of Zaxx's cruelty.

CHAPTER 2
PRINCESS OF THE NORTHERN LANDS

"We can try again in a few days or weeks, when the dragons have calmed down," Neill murmured at my side, trying to dispel the gloom that had fallen over me since leaving the dragon crater. We were trudging back to the monastery, our feet taking us up over the peak of the mountain itself and along the ridge line. Below us, the morning was spreading across the land, taking the fields and woods below from the darks of night to the greens of summer. Behind us came the excited sounds of the morning dragon call.

"Not if they stay like that," I muttered back to Neill. "It will take the dragons weeks to calm back down, and we might not *have* weeks."

"You think Zaxx might reject the eggs?" Neill asked.

I nodded. The older dragon could do what he wanted, and it was only by luck alone that I had managed to rescue Paxala after Zaxx had killed her mother for hiding her nest in the wilds beyond the crater.

"But it's not just that." I nodded to where Sigrid and Dorf where trudging ahead, clearly nervous and apprehensive of how we were going to sneak back into the Draconis Monastery without being seen. "It's them."

"Sigrid and Dorf?" Neill looked at our friends in confusion.

"Well, not *just* them, but people like them, you know. The other students. I overheard the older monks talking about trying to do what you did, riding the dragons," I pointed out.

Neill nodded. "Feodor told me." Feodor was the chief trainer for the Protector Monks; a bear of a man who had been a soldier in his youth. "He thinks it's a terrible idea."

"Well, he would, wouldn't he?" I pointed out, thinking of the scars that crisscrossed the monk's body from getting on the *wrong* end of a dragon. "And he would be right," I conceded with a groan, "if the monks go about it like they do everything else. They'll probably try to put a harness on them or shackle them, train them like horses or dogs, when they're not. They're not *steeds*." I was irritable, and my arms were still aching from the climb. "I think it only worked with you because of the bond that we share with Paxala, you know?"

Neill nodded, his face shadowed. "I know. The thought of Monk Olan, or the Abbot, or any of the other Draconis Order trying to train the dragons just terrifies me," he confided. "Someone will get hurt."

"Unless we can get access to those eggs and raise them with humans," I said. It was the only way that I could see it working. That was how it had worked with Paxala after all, wasn't it?

"Hurk!" There was a strange sound from up ahead, and I raised my eyes to see what had happened to Sigrid and Dorf, only to see that they had rounded the last bend in the mountain path and must be descending the narrow stone stairs back to the rear of the monastery walls.

"It's Dorf – he's probably hungry," Neill teased, and I playfully slapped him on the shoulder. Boys were so horrible to each other, I thought, even when they are trying to be friends.

"You idiot," I said to Neill, just as there was a sudden scuff from the rocks around us. I looked up, just in time to see a shape rising from the rocks. "Neill – down!" I gasped, as the shape threw something out over the air. It spun and hummed as it flew. A rope net!

The heavy weights attached to the ends of the netting hit me, knocking the breath out of me as I tried to throw a hand up to protect my face. I couldn't move, as the heavy rope whirled all around me, knotting itself together and tangling worse as I struggled.

"Char? You – release her now!" Neill shouted, and I saw his feet slipping on the shale and gravel as other shapes rose from the rocks around him.

"Shut him up," said one of our attackers, in a thick, guttural accent.

There were sounds of a struggle, and a sudden hiss as Neill, unarmed save for a knife, managed to kick one of them in places where he didn't want to get kicked. Meanwhile, rough hands grabbed me, turning me over and growling as I bucked like a fish, and lashed out with my own feet.

"Ow! Why, you little…" my would-be assailant snarled as I got a good stamp on his shins, and he hopped out of the way. "I thought you said she was a Princess?" the man snapped at one of his fellows.

Thud. "Got him." There was a loud thump and suddenly Neill stopped fighting with his attacker as I squirmed and rolled, trying to get my hands to my belt. I had a knife. It might be enough to cut the bonds…

"Char?" Paxala, already jittery and nervous after our confrontation with Zaxx, could be heard in my mind. I could sense her launching herself into the air above the lake. She was going to fly here, and save me.

"No, wait!" I tried to plead with her. What if she got hurt? But I already knew that there was nothing that I could say to stop a dragon that had made up its mind. My fingers found the knife at my belt and I tugged and tore at the rope bonds that held me, severing first one heavy strand enough to get a hand through the net, and then another-

"Hold it, Char!" A voice shouted, and I knew suddenly whose it was. "For heaven's sake, sister. Stop struggling –

24

we're doing this for your own good!" said Wurgan, my older brother as he bounded over the boulders to my side.

~

Wurgan, like me, took after my mother's side of the family. He was my true-blood brother, son of Prince Lander and our mother Galetta Nefrette, who was the Northern Prince's mistress. Despite both being born out of wedlock, our father had recognized us as was the mountain custom – and even his official wife, the Lady Odette Lander, acted as our stepmother. Wurgan was big and tall like most mountain men, with flame-red ginger hair and a heavy mustache.

He was also a complete idiot.

"What the hell did you do that for, Wurgan – these people are my friends!" I said angrily to him, endeavoring to keep my voice down in case any scouts from the Draconis Order were nearby. For a moment, I wondered if Wurgan, already a general in our father's army, had come to Mount Hammal with the armies of the north at his back just as the Sons of Torvald had arrived with theirs. *It seems that everyone wants something from the Dragon Monastery.*

"I'm sorry, but we have no time. I had to act now, or else I would lose you again into that place." Wurgan gave the monastery a suspicious look. He had never liked the idea of me going so far south to this place, and didn't trust the Draconis Order any more than Neill seemed to.

"But look." I pointed to the bodies of my unconscious friends. "Did you have to hit them over the head?"

"How was I to know that they weren't more of those monks, about to do something terrible to you?" Wurgan protested, as he sat on the ground and began unravelling the nets and ropes he had used to entrap us back into their carry sacks. We had moved behind the nearest of the boulders to stay out of sight of the watching walls of the Dragon Monastery, but I also knew that it wouldn't be long before the scouts would start going out, and people would start raising the alarm. We had been gone too long already.

"Shame you weren't here a watch ago, then you could really have seen something terrible about to happen to me," I murmured, as Neill groaned from his place by the side of the rocks.

"Char? Char – are you okay… Why does my head hurt so much?" Neill muttered.

"Ah, my deepest apologies, little man, it was a mistake please – I am Wurgan Lander, Prince of the Northern Kingdom." Wurgan winced, standing from his task to walk over to Neill and extend a hand down to help him up to his feet.

"Neill Torvald, Son of the Chief Warden Malos Torvald," Neill offered, holding his head and blinking, and worry and concern blossomed on my brother's face when it dawned on him that this was the boy I had written home about, the one who rode dragons, and the one who was my friend.

"Are we captured?" Neill asked unsteadily.

"No!" Wurgan said quickly, and I snorted in disgust. My brother could be charming, but he was also so transparent. *You're only being nice to Neill because he might have a dragon somewhere...* I glared at Wurgan.

"No," my brother repeated, as around us the other men of his troupe started to gather their things and pack them away. "But I am under orders to return the Princess Nefrette back to her rightful place in our father's keep."

"The Princess Nefrette...?" Neill looked confused, before suddenly realizing who my brother was talking about. "Ah, you mean Char."

"I'm not going," I said quickly and immediately, before Wurgan could get his hopes up.

"Sister! It is our father's orders," were the first words out of his mouth.

"Orders," I whispered. Not 'he cares for me' or 'he is worried about me.' No, it was 'orders.'

"Yes. You cannot stay here, it is impossible. The Middle Kingdom is collapsing, no offence, Torvald," Wurgan said as an aside to Neill, "but it is true. Word has reached even the Queen's Keep of what the Sons of Torvald attempted, and how Prince Vincent"—Wurgan made a sour face—"has reacted."

"What do you mean? How has Prince Vincent reacted?" Neill asked with a worried frown.

"You don't know?" Wurgan looked shocked. "You haven't heard? Prince Vincent of the Middle Kingdom, *this* kingdom we are in now, has closed all of the borders, and there have been sudden attacks on travelers up and down the country. It is clear to see who is behind it. The Dark Prince is seeking to rout out any who oppose his rule." Wurgan looked back at me. "I am sorry, sister, but our father has decreed that he cannot leave you down here in the Middle Kingdom, at the mercy of Prince Vincent. You are to come home with me and my men, now."

I shook my head once more. "Wurgan, I *won't,* and *I can't.*"

Wurgan folded his hands over his chest. That was a bad sign, and one that I knew well from my childhood. Our father had always said that we had inherited our mother's stubborn ways, in that we both would look at him and plant ourselves squarely into the ground like a mountain, refusing to budge on whatever we'd set our minds to. This was what the large man my brother had turned into was doing now. He was big and broad, with thick studded brown leather armor (not his full chain mail for this mission, I saw) and boots with fur tops.

"Char, I will carry you if I have to…" Wurgan growled, and I knew that he would as well. It was just then that a dragon-scream split the sky.

A shadow swooped low over the ridgeline, flashing over us and causing Wurgan and the rest of his men to tumble to the floor and roll to the shadow of the nearest rocks.

"Paxala, stop playing games," I said, as the young Crimson Red roared once more and landed, her wings causing a gale as her talons scratched at the rocks beside us.

"Medi, get me the iron arrows, quickly," Wurgan was saying, his face almost as pale as my hair as I tried not to laugh at him.

"You will do no such thing, brother." I said, looking over to Neill. We were the only two people who *hadn't* fallen to the floor and scrambled for cover as the mighty dragon had landed.

"Char? This one smells like you. He is your family? Why are you hurt?" Paxala sniffed and chirruped at me as I walked forward, reaching towards her with my hand.

"Sister? You are mad!" Wurgan spat, but fell silent as Paxala leaned her long snout down to bump at my hand affectionately, before looking up to make a low rumbling noise of warning at the other warriors.

"Wurgan, meet Paxala. Paxala, this is my fool of a brother." I introduced them.

"He smells like a goat," Paxala cocked her head at him, making me laugh. From their places by the rocks, Dorf and Sigrid were woozily coming to, wincing and groaning at all of the commotion around them.

"Sister, you… You *know* this dragon?" Wurgan managed to get himself into a crouch, but could not summon the courage to stand up and walk to where I patted Paxala's warm and smooth scales. *My friend.* I always felt better when I was in contact with her. She was like my sister, in just the same way that Wurgan was my brother – more so, even, because Paxala could share my innermost thoughts and feelings;

whereas sometimes Wurgan just looked at me as if he didn't even know where I had come from.

"Yes, Wurgan, I do know this dragon. And she is the reason why I cannot leave the Draconis Order with you, as much as I might want to."

"Leave? Char wants to leave me?" I felt the fear stiffen through Paxala as she slowly swung her head down to regard me.

"No, I won't leave you, Pax," I whispered into her great golden eyes. "I will never leave you."

"Zaxx is still strong here," Paxala reminded me. *"Any dragon under him is in threat. We cannot abandon them to him."*

"Then we must fight him," I whispered to her.

"Sister? Can you not *bring* the dragon with you?" Wurgan had managed a half-crouch, and I could see that he was looking in wonder at Paxala's strong legs, her complete armored hide, the spines and talons that were growing sharper and longer every day now. "What a magnificent beast! Imagine the terror we could strike into our enemies with it!" he said in awe.

"She isn't a beast," Neill said. "She's a dragon. She can probably understand just what you are saying about her, you know." And as if in answer to Neill's comment there was a loud *thump* from Paxala's tail against the rock.

"Brother, I am sorry, you will have to take this message back to our father: that I have work to do here, and you can see I have friends who will keep me safe." I patted Paxala's neck once more, causing her to rattle a throaty purr.

My brother frowned once more. "He won't like it," he said, shaking his head, but it was clear to both of us that there was no way that Wurgan and his small group of men were going to make us do anything, not with a dragon at our side. "But you have my word that I will tell father your message." He growled, looking hurt. "I just wish that you cared more for your people at Queen's Keep, sister mine."

"I do!" I burst out, feeling suddenly angry. How could he dare to say I cared any less for my father's home and my father himself, and all of the people up there than I did for my friends!? At that moment, I could have run forward and hit my brother just as I had done all through my childhood, with both of us ending up rolling on the floor as we fought, tearing clothes and giving each other bruises, but the throaty purr from the Crimson Red dragon above me had turned into a warning growl. Paxala was sharing in my anger.

"Easy, Paxala," I shushed her. "He is just being an idiot. It is what brothers and sister do."

"I think I understand – although I never knew my own hatch-mates, Char," Paxala said mournfully, but she at least stopped growling as we watched Wurgan and his warriors standing awkwardly in front of us.

"I have to give father something…" Wurgan started to say, attempting to look at me with that same look of displeasure that father used. It wasn't going to work on me.

"You can give him my assurance that I am doing the best for his realm, down here," I countered.

"Oh, for Stars' sake!" Wurgan turned on his heel, rolling his shoulders as he did so. I knew he was angry, and likely wanted to shout at me and drag me back to our father's lands as if I were just a petulant girl – but I could also see the worried looks of his warriors beside him. None of them particularly wanted to get on the wrong side of an angry dragon.

I waited for Wurgan to calm down. He was always like this. Hot-tempered, but with my father's gift for battle and strategy, and thus the ability to rein in his mood when it mattered. After kicking a bit of rock, his shoulders slumped a little. My brother wasn't a man who was used to losing.

"Wurgan" I tried again. "You have to trust me that I know what I am doing," I said, although a part of me wondered if I really did. "I'm good at this. I made friends with a dragon, after all!"

"Hmph." Wurgan grumbled, still shaking his head as he turned back to me. "I will lead the warband off the mountain, and we will head north to where there is a wood that is still pretty much wild," he said, thinking strategically. "There is an old water mill there, do you know of it?"

I nodded. "I do." It wasn't used by the monastery at all, but the wood was visible from the monastery walls.

"Then the warband and I will stay at the old water mill for a further two nights, before heading north once more. You may change your mind. You will be able to follow us and join up with us there."

"I would be able to follow you for a thousand leagues with my eyes shut!" Paxala's voice in mind whickered with laughter.

"I won't change my mind, Wurgan," I informed him, but he only shook his head at me, before he led his men away. I felt caught between two evils. Either betray my family and help out the dragons, or betray the helpless dragons and obey my father.

The air was still for a while as we watched my brother's group slip back into the hidden paths between the rocks, and behind us we could hear alarm shouts as Draconis Order scouts and monks spied the Crimson Red clearly visible out on the slopes of the mountain.

"Oh hell, we'd better get you back to the lake, and us back to lessons…" I murmured to Paxala.

"Before they make that painful shrieking noise again…" Paxala agreed in my mind, and for a moment I didn't quite know what she meant until I heard it for myself.

BWAAR! BWAAAR! It was the dragon pipes, the contraption made of brass tubes like an organ that was built into one of the towers of the monastery. The monks used it to try and scare and control the dragons when they got too rowdy, and right now I could see its effects close up on Paxala at our side.

To us humans, the pipes just sounded like a very loud,

strangulated goose perhaps, or a plains bison call. But to a sensitive dragons' ears, the sound was painful.

"Hssss! One day I will destroy it, I swear, that and the tower it lives in!" Paxala shrieked and, before I could say sorry she had leapt into the air, showering us with grit and sand as she flapped hurriedly over the ridge and out of the vicinity of the dragon pipes.

"Oh." I felt even worse now, but perhaps not as bad as my bruised and groggy friends who crowded around me.

"What was all that about?" Sigrid said as she held her temples.

"My brother wants me to go back home to my father's fortress," I muttered. "And Paxala wants to destroy the dragon pipes."

"And Zaxx wants to eat everybody!" Dorf said brightly, as if we were playing a game of competing bad news.

"Yeah." I nodded, wondering, as I trudged back with the others, how on earth we were going to succeed at anything. It wasn't even breakfast and already I had failed three times.

CHAPTER 3
NEILL, A SON OF TORVALD

"Torvald!" A voice shouted across the practice courtyard, and my heart fell. It was Olan, the monk who seemed to have taken over many of Quartermaster Greer's duties after Greer's unfortunate 'accident' during the battle (well, he had tried to kill me, and ended up falling out of the Abbot's Tower to the rocks below). At first I'd been glad, because Olan had disappeared in the days after the battle, having apparently been sent by the Abbot out to 'accompany' the Prince Vincent, though I daresay that really meant Olan was being used as a spy for the Abbot. But now Olan was back. The monk was small-featured, and a bit smaller than me even though he was a good ten years older. He had straw-colored hair and wore the heavy black clothes of the Order, and always vaguely reminded me of a ferret somehow.

"Brother Olan," I greeted him. It was a crisp summery

morning, but my body was aching from the morning's antics in the dragon crater. Char had disappeared as soon as we had got into the Dragon Monastery, claiming that she needed time to think, leaving Sigrid, Dorf, and me to rush to get breakfast before the monks realized we had been gone.

"Word is that dragon of yours was seen—" Olan began.

"She's not mine, she's her own," I said quickly.

"*That* dragon was seen outside the monastery walls this morning, and the pipes were played to drive her away. What do you know of this?" Monk Olan's booted feet crunched over the dirt and sand of the practice courtyard until he was standing almost eye to eye with me. I know that it was petty of me, but I reveled in the fact that I must have grown in the months Olan had been gone, and certainly since leaving Torvald lands so long ago. I think I was even a few inches taller and broader than him. He had to look *up* to me now.

"She's a free dragon, Brother Olan," I replied, trying to sound as nonchalant as possible. "She can fly where she wants."

"Do I have to remind you of the Abbot's proclamation, *trainee* Torvald?" Olan narrowed his eyes at me. I could see that he didn't believe a word that I said, not that I blamed him. The feeling was pretty mutual between us. "The Abbot has forbidden any dragon-flight over or near the confines of the monastery. If it happens again, then the Abbot will have to take steps to defend the monastery."

"Will he now?" I felt a flash of anger. *Was this little man threatening me?* I felt my chest swell with the injustice of it. The Abbot Ansall, so beloved by the Prince Vincent of the Middle Kingdom was responsible for selecting dragons to die! He was responsible for trying to kill Jodreth, and to possess Char, and a thousand other acts of petty cruelty. Why should such a man as that have such power?

"Torvald?" said a new voice, and I looked up to see Monk Feodor, entering the practice courtyard with Lila at his side, carrying the heavy leather kit bags for today's Advanced Protectors classes. There was a warning note to his voice, and I realized in my anger that I had taken a step forward towards Monk Olan, ready to strike him, and he was regarding me with a mixture of fear and glee.

He would win if I attacked him. He would be able to denounce me to the Abbot and have me thrown out of the monastery – not that there weren't enough voices already wanting to do just that, I thought. There was a knot of the older monks here who grumbled and rolled their eyes every time they saw me or any other student they thought 'inferior' to the Draconis Order's 'holy calling.'

But if I wanted to protect Paxala and keep my friend Char safe from the Abbot then I had to stay here. Stay a student. I took a deep breath, and stepped back, hating the petty victory I saw reflected in Brother Olan's smirk.

"Good day to you, *trainee* Torvald." Olan turned to go. "And bear in mind what I said. We would hate for that dragon to get hurt."

This time I had to bite the inside of my cheek to stop from physically snarling at him. I should be thankful that it was me he was trying to goad, and not Char who was bonded with Paxala – as I had no doubt that Char would have knocked him to the floor for that threat and gotten herself expelled in the bargain—and then what would happen to Paxala and the other dragons?

"Neill, are you alright?" Feodor muttered at me as he shucked the kit bags to the floor, waving to all of us students to start taking out their contents. Leather cuirasses and jerkins made of many strips of material over padding, and each section of the garment loosely tied together with string. He showed us how to put them on, before proceeding to help me to tie up my shoulder pieces (pauldrons) to the arms (greaves) and the chest. As he worked, he whispered under his breath.

"You need to be more careful around Monk Olan from now on," the man said. "He means you no good will."

"I think I can see that," I said, still seething from his threat to Paxala.

Thud. There was a light cuff to the side of the leather cap that I had put on. Ow!" I said. "What was that for?"

"Mind your backchat, Torvald," Feodor growled. "You can get away with it on me, as I grew up amongst soldiers, but the other monks will have you up for disciplinary for using a tone like that."

"I didn't *do* anything," I protested, not caring if the other students heard me or not. "It was Olan who was threatening me!"

"Shh!" The larger monk trainer grabbed me by the shoulders and none too gently spun me around on the spot until I was facing him. He looked angry, and an animal part of me realized that Feodor was *much* bigger and *much* more experienced at brawling than I was. "And you'll keep that to yourself, young Torvald," he muttered, holding me by the shoulders still, and lowering his face as he looked me in the eyes, waiting for me to blink and look away. As soon as I did he released me, but whispered, "Things have changed since the battle. The Abbot and the other monks are edgy. There hasn't been a battle up here for ten years or more, and now you come along riding dragons and your brothers are knocking on our gates?"

"I didn't ask them to—" I began, but Feodor silenced me with a scowl.

"I'm doing this for your own good, Neill. The students might think that you are something special, but the monks see you as a threat to their power. So, stop acting all big and tough, and keep your head down for a while, will you?" Feodor growled, stepping back.

I hung my head and scuffed my boots on the sand. Things *had* changed since the battle, I couldn't deny it. We had seen the dark magic that the Abbot could summon (with the help of his acolyte Mage-trainees like Char), and the world had seen just what sorts of men my brothers were – angry, violent, aggressive. It was how the older monks viewed them and would mutter darkly about "the *brutes* of Torvald" and, I hated to say that I even agreed. Before, the Sons of Torvald had been known as fierce and effective warriors, but a certain pride and respect had always seemed to go hand in hand with that (or maybe I believed that because my father insulated me from the views of the villagers and townspeople). Now, however, it was obvious that everyone knew what I had always known in private: that Rubin and Rik were violent, greedy, and demanding. It made me feel tired, and didn't feel like a vindication at all.

But had I been acting differently since then? I knew that the other students often regarded me strangely, like *I* was the one who had sprouted wings and flown around the monastery. Dorf hadn't stopped asking me how I had done it, or what it felt like. I don't know, was the honest answer. It just sort of happened, and what made the whole situation even stranger was that it wasn't even *me* who was particularly close to Paxala. Olan and the others seemed to think that she was 'my' dragon - but she wasn't. *Wait until they find out that Char can hear Paxala in her own head. That will really freak them out*, I thought.

Feodor was checking the other leather suits of the students around me when I looked up and, from their watchful and wary stares, I had to admit Feodor was right. The students did look at me as though I was something special, and I guess the way that I had sized up to Monk Olan only made it clear that I was beginning to act like it too.

I can't afford to let it get to my head, I realized, as I reached down to pick up one of the wooden staves that we would be using for practice. My father, Malos Torvald, was still out there, injured, and my brothers Rubin and Rik were still seething from their defeat and my apparent treachery when I had flown the dragon against them. They were in danger, and they were also a threat.

I had never felt so conflicted in all of my life. Was I no longer a Son of Torvald now?

"Hey, Torvald," sneered a voice, and I looked up to see Terence, the ruddy-haired son of Prince Griffith of the Southern Kingdom. He stood with Faldo and Archibald, his own little gang of henchmen amongst the Protectors. We didn't get on, and he relished any opportunity to remind me that I was a Gypsy-blooded bastard. "Looks like you're not so high and mighty after all, huh?" he sniggered, nodding to Feodor and the recent obvious dressing down and cuffed head that I had received. "Isn't your dragon going to come save you?"

"Oh, shut up, Terence." I rolled my eyes, and then rolled my shoulders as I practiced a few lunges and swings.

"Or what, you'll set your dragon on me?" Terence said airily, to a peal of laughter from his fellows.

I bloody well should do, just to wipe that grin off your face. The thought of seeing Terence wet himself in fear if the mighty Crimson Red landed in the middle of the courtyard almost took away my bad mood. As did the realization that even just a month ago, I wouldn't have had the confidence to think of such a thing, even if it wasn't going to happen. Terence and the others knew as well as I did that, at first sight of dragon-flight, the dragon pipes would sound, driving Paxala away. The Abbot had stationed someone permanently up there, scanning the horizon for signs of what he termed 'rogue dragons.'

I scuffed my feet on the floor, and practiced another thrust with my practice-stave.

CHAPTER 4
CHAR'S MISSION

I hurried down the spiraling stone steps bearing a heavy load of tomes and grimoires—a few of which would have to be chained to their shelves, so rare and valuable and new they were-- ready to return to the Monastery Library, housed in what must have been either old wine cellars or, more disgustingly, old catacombs. The air was dusty and my footsteps echoed as I made my way down to the low-ceilinged libraries where we Scribes and Mages were supposed to spend most of our time, reading, translating, transcribing, and studying at the long work tables set up between bookshelves. I would much rather be up on the mountain with Paxala – or even out there in the practice courtyard trading blows with Neill-- even though I couldn't land a sword blow against a semi-trained student, it seemed!

But at least being down here gives me time to think, I

agreed as I hit the bottom of the stairs at a run, and down the narrow stone corridor to the wooden doors. They were heavy as I pushed them open, but instead of the hushed silence of acres of books and ink housed in a complex maze-like network of high and wide wooden shelves, what met my ears were the muted whispers of students.

"Oh, hi," I said to the small throng of students already waiting in the lantern-lit lobby area of the library, huddled beneath one of the stone arches that crisscrossed the room, and boxed in by the heavily laden shelves packed between the pillars.

"I'm sorry I'm late?" I tried, seeing a gaggle of pale faces looking back at me in alarm, only, it soon turned out that it wasn't for me that they were alarmed. "Where's the tutors?" I asked the congregation, getting shrugs and blank looks from most of them, until wide-eyed little Maxal Ganna, son of one of the most erudite Draconis Order monks who had ever lived, stepped forward, looking in almost every respect like a small bean or unsprouted seed.

Maxal Ganna was also, like me, a Mage in training, and also like me, was always getting lumped in with the Scribes when there weren't any special Mage meditations and exercises to perform

"The Abbot came and took them away," Maxal said in his ever-serious, grave voice. I don't think I had ever seen that boy crack so much as a smile. "But he left us with more work to do."

44

There was a collective groan from the rest of the students – about thirty of us in all perhaps. We'd been having a lot of 'chores' these last few months, which had so far meant cleaning, shelving, picking vegetables, tending the garden, cleaning equipment, and of course, feeding the dragons. One of the few exciting jobs left was hauling up the big sacks of meat to the top of the crater and throwing them down to each group of dragons, starting with Zaxx the Golden, of course.

"Why do we have to do *more* chores?" It seemed that the rounded Dorf, who had barely seemed to recover from this morning's adventures, seemed fed up with them. "If it's more mopping and sweeping, I swear I will scream…" he said with a sigh, although I knew that meek-mannered Dorf Lesser would do no such thing.

It's since the battle, and Paxala. I knew. The monks didn't know what to do with us. Were we all troublemakers? Should they expel us? Or could we be an asset to them?

"Oh, this one doesn't seem too bad, Dorf," Maxal ameliorated, pointing to where there were more stacks of books and scrolls on one of the nearby tables. "The Abbot said we had to shelve all of those in their correct places in the Library, to keep us out of mischief."

He did, did he? I wandered over to deposit the books on the tables, actually glad that I didn't have to run into the Abbot. I hated to be near him, now that I knew he chose dragons to be killed for no good reason. "What are they about?" I looked at the first cover of the top book, seeing that

45

it was made out of some fine-scaled material, and inset with gems. When I flicked open the cover it was written in strange hatch marks and squiggles that I couldn't read.

"Are they new?" Dorf said, looking considerably brighter at the prospect of handling new books. He had a thing for books and maps.

"Yeah, new in today I think." Maxal was the first to join me at the table, opening the covers of a few to show pages full of strange languages, or else woodcut images of dragons and wyrms from long ago. "I think they are from the south, the furthest south, where the dragons are wild?"

That made sense, I thought. The Draconis Order was the world's repository for information on dragons, and they collected works from all across the Three Kingdoms to add to their collections. *And beyond,* it seemed.

"We have wild dragons up north as well," I pointed out. No one seemed too eager to be doing a study of *them,* I wanted to say, probably because our midnight blue and purple wild dragons were much smaller than the Middle Kingdom dragons, more vicious than the Greens, and almost as fast as the Blues.

"I think that there must be wild dragons everywhere," Maxal said, suddenly interested in the new line of inquiry. "It might only be in the Middle Kingdom where the dragons have become able to uh…" his voice suddenly trailed off as he looked warily at me.

"Able to be ridden?" I raised an eyebrow. Was Maxal

thinking of Neill and Paxala? "Or do you mean almost *tamed*?" I added with a bit of a growl to my voice. Paxala was *not* a domesticated dragon, not in my eyes – and neither should any of those dragons in the crater be!

"No – I didn't mean that at all," Maxal said quickly, looking concerned. "It's just, my father and my uncles – they were all Draconis Order too, you know – they always told me that dragons shouldn't be touched, should only be approached at by the ordained monks…" His words petered off as he saw me glaring at him.

"And *I'm* not good enough, is that it?" I said, not full-blown furious, but annoyed at the backward attitudes that the very monks who were supposed to be studying these noble creatures harbored.

"No, I mean, of course not," Maxal blabbered. He really hadn't meant to cause offense, I could see. He had grown up in a very sheltered environment. "All I mean is that Neill is the first person to ride a dragon, and it's unheard of. It goes against everything that my father taught me," he said, and I was about to tell him surely that was a good thing, when we were rudely interrupted.

"Never mind," Dorf burst in, seizing the first couple of books. "I wonder what they say? How do we know where to shelve them?"

"We'll have to look at the pictures of those in any language we can translate, and try to work it out from there," Maxal said, looking glad for the distraction. He was a nice kid actually, but he was too eager to believe in the words of the monks and their books. But Dorf liked him, and Dorf didn't seem to have a mean bone in his body.

So began our long morning of shelving. Maxal became our unofficial tutor as he spoke more languages than any of us, and he helped us find the secret affiliations and associations of each book. I picked up a tome called *'Remedyes for Drag-onnes'* and wandered off into the large area, looking for the nearest names to this author, Azur Laird.

I was quite happy in my task actually, managing to forget for a little while what Wurgan had said to me as I wandered the peaceful aisles of the Library. I didn't have to think about the weapons and wars of the Three Kingdoms, or of the secret plans that my father wanted me to take part in. I could see why Dorf liked it down here. There were no homicidal monks, tyrant-dragons, or bloodthirsty soldiers anywhere in sight. I had just found the book's place next to the other dragon reme-dies and herbologies, when Maxal Ganna appeared again, silent and watchful.

"Maxal," I greeted him. "If it is about earlier, then don't worry. I was just tired and irritable. I'm sorry for snapping at you."

"No, you were right," Maxal said. "The Middle Kingdom dragons shouldn't be tame, but they are easier to approach than any of the other dragons. That, uh, is actually why I wanted to talk to you. It's about the Abbot," he said carefully, looking behind him to make sure that he wasn't being followed.

"What is it?" I said. "Is it about Mage classes?" Another thing that had stopped since the battle where the Abbot's nightly meditation study sessions with us Mage students. Maxal was one of the best magical students here, it seemed, and so like me must be wondering what was happening.

"Maybe, I don't know," Maxal said. "But when I got here early for class, I found the Abbot and some of the other tutors delivering the books there, and then the Abbot told me that we were to be doing shelving today."

"Okay…" it all sounded fairly boring so far, I thought.

"But then I overheard the Abbot saying to the others that the meeting was about to begin and that he didn't want anyone to be late. It seemed a special meeting, something important for the future of the monastery perhaps?" Maxal looked up at me with worried, large eyes. It was then that I knew that Maxal really *was* on my side, along with Dorf and the others. Maybe he had seen the way that the Abbot and the other monks had treated me for being half mountain-folk (and a woman, at that)! Or perhaps he had seen the way that I cared for Paxala and…

"They went towards the gemstones section," Maxal said, pointing to a part of the Library that I rarely ever visited. (What use have I got of rocks?) "If you hurry, and are quiet you might be able to find out what they are talking about. Just follow the lanterns."

"Oh, by the skies, thank you, Maxal." I nodded, shoving Azur Laird's *Remedyes* into the boy's hands as I wove through the aisles and shelves quickly.

~

As Maxal suggested, I followed the murky radiance of the glass-shuttered lanterns hanging at the sides of the Library shelves. Their use was limited due to the threat of fire, so if there were any lit, then it was a sure sign a monk had passed this way.

The sounds of the students filing, scuffling, laughing, and whispering faded into a low murmur behind me as I jogged, thankful that I had worn my soft-soled leather shoes today, and not my boots. I went so far I began to think I had been mistaken, or gone past where Maxal had intended. There was almost no sound, and I could not even say for certain if this deep into the stacks I were even still in the same catacombs as the rest of the Library.

How long have the Draconis Order been collecting knowledge down here? I thought, shocked at the enormity of what they had accomplished. There must be something in all of these shelves that would tell us more about the dragons, and how to bond with them, I thought, just as I heard a murmur.

"...I am telling you, it cannot be done!" a loud and angry male voice said. It was followed by a hissed voice that I couldn't make out, and the shuffling of feet. The meeting was near. I hunkered down, creeping across the aisle to get closer until I knelt in a dark, unlit aisle apparently *behind* where the Abbot was having his meeting.

"But look at this," said a voice. It was Rothan, a monk who I had seen helping Feodor out occasionally. Tall, grey-brown haired, with a deeply lined and wrinkled face. "The explorer Versi—"

"Versi was a fool," spat the voice of Abbot Ansall himself. I froze. "A vain, spoilt child who probably made up what he saw to keep the old queen's grandfather giving him money!" The Abbot spoke as if he had known this 'explorer Versi' fellow even though the old Queen Delia had died a long time ago, and certainly her grandfather had too.

I held my breath as I eased myself forward, scanning the bookshelves for a gap. I found a glow of light coming through from the other side of the shelf beyond, and carefully moved one of the books to peer through the crack it left, into a small 'study plaza' beyond. This one had a central wooden table and the familiar wooden benches, but the monks gathered there were too important to sit. Instead, they stood around the shelves or else leaned over the table (as Rothan and the Abbot Ansall were doing), pointing and gesturing at passages in books and scrolls. I tried to count how many were there, but the angle of my peephole made it almost impossible to see. I guessed there were at least seven or ten of the fully ordained monks, but I only recognized Rothan, the Abbot, and Olan. I bit my lip, breathing shallowly and slowly as I watched and listened.

"Maybe so," Rothan continued. "But the explorer Versi clearly states here that he observed tribal children in the far south on the backs of dragons, until the dragons reached maturity. So it can be done. Humans *can* ride dragons."

I knew it! I had to stop myself from gasping out loud. What was happening between me and Paxala was natural. It was a bonding that had been happening between dragons and humans for centuries! Surely the Abbot would have known about this before, I thought. Why wasn't he overjoyed at the news? Why wasn't he trying to teach the students how to approach the dragons?

"And what else happens when the dragons of the furthest south reach maturity? The ones known as Great Lizards, are they not?" the Abbot spat.

Rothan blinked, rifling through the book pages. "The explorer Versi doesn't say…"

"No, he doesn't. Because he never studied the Great Lizards of the furthest deserts, did he? Nor did he ever see them? But here," --the Abbot slapped a sheath of heavy parchments on the floor most filled with odd squiggles and curls-- "in here are some of the written accounts taken from an oral tradition of stories of the furthest tribes. They tell of how the Great Lizards started *hunting* when they reached maturity. And that they hunted *humans*." The Abbot sighed.

"You see? I knew it – the boy and the Crimson Red are

freaks. Anomalies. It cannot be replicated," one of the older monks, the first speaker, said. I had to bite my lip to stop my anger from spilling out in a shout. Neill and Paxala weren't freaks. They were special.

"Perhaps," the Abbot said measuredly, walking across my peephole of light and into full view. The Abbot Ansall was an almost skeletal, tall man dressed in the finest black robes of his office, with a wiry beard and a bald head under a black skullcap. He tapped the explorer's account with the black and ivory-handled cane that he always carried with him, his icy-blue eyes narrowing as he stared at Rothan.

"Whatever you may think of Versi's brave exploits, the man was a fool. I am the only one here who has communed with the Great Zaxx the Mighty, and it is from Zaxx himself which my knowledge comes. Zaxx is ancient. Perhaps the oldest. He knew the family of Great Lizards, he knew what they did. They *farmed* humans. They befriended these backward desert tribes, letting their children play together with their hatchlings and when time came for the young hatchlings to learn how to eat – then what do you think happened?"

I closed my eyes at the horror. It was the sort of thing that cruel Zaxx would do, to play along with being friends, only to turn and eat anyone weaker when the mood took him. The horror of what the Abbot was saying was almost too much, and I had to look away. But Paxala wouldn't do that. Paxala couldn't do that! The affection and friendship we shared was real, I knew it, and through the bond that I had with her, I could feel her thoughts and feelings for me, as fierce and as loving as a sister.

It's the other way around, I wanted to scream at them. *It's the Draconis Order who are farming the dragons, not the dragons farming us!*

"So, you see, the boy is a freak," the Abbot Ansall said. "The boy is confused if he thinks he has any kind of friendship with the dragon. Sooner or later, the dragon will turn around and attack him, and maybe all of us. What will that do to the delicate balance of power inside the crater? What will mighty Zaxx the Golden do? And so, now we have to do as *I* have always commanded: we *totally* control the dragons. We feed them. We make them dependent on us. We decide how many there are, and *we* keep Zaxx the Mighty happy."

"So that he might shower us with wisdom," breathed one of the other monks in the plaza, making me feel sick as the other monks repeated it instantly.

"So that he might shower us with wisdom," they said almost as one, making me feel uneasy. It was almost like the monks were brainwashed to believe Zaxx the Golden was not just a god, but a *pet* god.

"Indeed. So, we will not be throwing our students into the crater to be eaten," the Abbot Ansall said genially, sounding for all the world like he was being beneficent and wise. "Instead, we shall choose some of the smaller, weaker dragons – let us start with the Earth Dragons-- and we shall apply harnesses to them. We shall train them to obey our orders, not as friends or as equals, but as beasts. For the dragons are mighty and they are noble, but we must overcome them and wrest their knowledge from them," the Abbot said. "I know, I know my brethren – this is not a truth that you wish to hear, and yet it is true. You all know as well as I do that the dragons only respect strength. That Zaxx is their leader because he can dominate them. *We* must dominate them. *We* must become the 'bulls' of the crater for them to give up their secrets. We have here a great store of knowledge about their ancient species, and we shall use it."

There was a murmur from the group, and I wondered if it was agreement or unease -but it certainly wasn't outright dissension as the Abbot continued.

"Just think of what we can achieve," Ansall raised his voice a little, taking on that same theatrical tone that he used when trying to inspire us students. "The new Dragon Age will be glorious! From these walls will pour great beasts with their masters and trainers using them to protect castles and to attack our enemies. Think of what great industries and achievements we could bring into the world, if we had a dragons' size and strength to shift rock, to dig, to melt metal? Who would ever stand against the Draconis Order, or the Middle Kingdom? We would be the center of the world!"

I shivered where I sat. What the Abbot Ansall was proposing was a nightmare vision of dragon servitude, and a new age of prosperity and wealth for him and Zaxx alone.

But there is hope... I moved back to the peephole between

the books, seeing that the monks were agreeing and clapping, shuffling the papers and the books back into their rightful places. *Explorer Versi,* I tried to follow the movements of the tall monk Rothan as he put the tomes that he had gathered away. *The explorer Versi might have seen a way that humans and dragons could bond, even if he didn't understand what he was looking at...*

I desperately wanted to ignore the small worm of doubt in the back of my mind, but I couldn't. My thoughts kept on pointing out that—according to the Abbot—all those southern tribal kids had ended up as meat for their friends' bellies. Those dragons were different from Middle Kingdom dragons, I hoped. Didn't Maxal himself say so just earlier? Middle Kingdom dragons were friendlier. They wouldn't turn on us just because...

The meeting was breaking up, and I froze as the monks packed away all of their things and shuffled back out into the narrow avenues, whispering and muttering among themselves as they left. I waited, counted to ten, and then waited for a further three breaths before going back to the space between the books.

A shadow moved across the space and I bit my tongue to stop from gasping in fear. *Ansall.* The Abbot had waited after all the others, standing and looking around the little study-space. I thought for sure that his ice-chip eyes bored into mine as his gaze searched the shelves for something, before shaking his head to himself. Had he heard me? Had I betrayed myself somehow?

"Nihil." The man growled, snapping his fingers and the flame in the lantern suddenly snapped out, plunging my eyes into darkness. I held my breath and waited, as his footsteps clicked heavily and precisely, heading back to the more commonplace areas of the Library.

I stayed in the dark for a long time, before I could pluck up the courage to sneak around the shelves, and search for the memoirs of the explorer Versi.

CHAPTER 5
GOADING DRAGONS

I was awoken by the deafening sound of the dragon pipes rattling the window shutters. I groaned, it was still dark outside.

"What time is it? What is going on?" Sigrid muttered from her bed across from mine in the cold tower room we shared. She was always unwilling to leave the warmth of her cot, and instead waited for me to get the fire lit.

"I don't know," I grumbled, sucking in my breath as my feet hit the cold flagstones. "The pipes are much earlier today than they are usually…" I was cut off when the noise blasted again.

The monks usually only played the pipes to subdue or rouse the dragons in the nearby crater, as the sound hurt their sensitive ears. Did that mean we were under attack? Instantly, my mind reached out to the Crimson Red, my friend - *Paxala?*

I was still unsure if she would even be able to hear my thoughts, thanks to the rousing clanging of the dragon pipes, but in answer I got a warm, fuzzy impression of the cave in which she had made her home in the wilds on the other side of Mount Hammal.

"What is that racket?" The great Crimson Red thought at me, her mind heavy with irritation.

"I don't know…" I said, half to Paxala, and half to the Fenn girl I shared a room with. I hurried to the window. Outside in the courtyard below there were monks with torches and others pushing handcarts filled with bulky hessian bags and wooden boxes.

"What is going on? Is there an attack? What are they doing?" Uncharacteristically, Sigrid joined me, scowling down at the monks as the dragon pipes in the Astrographer's Tower above pealed and rang. We watched as one of the black-robed monks hurried to the door of the boy's tower, torch in one hand and bell in the other.

"I guess those dragon pipes mean we all have to get up," I groaned, grabbing my clothes from the stool by the side of my bed. Underneath them was a very old leather-bound book, barely bigger than my hand and filled with spidery black writing I could only barely make out. *I should probably just hide this for now…* I looked at the room, wondering where I could hide it without any of the Draconis Order monks finding it. No, I settled for slipping the slim stolen volume of *'Versi's Voyage'* (written by the explorer himself) into my jerkin. I

59

couldn't risk the Abbot discovering I had checked the book out, let alone that I was studying it.

"Ready?" I asked Sigrid.

"No." She grumbled, but was pulling on her own leggings and robes by the time that our own monk entered the girl's tower to roust us.

~

"Pssst, Neill – what's going on?" I shuffled next to him through the gaggle of tired students standing in rows in the courtyard, while the monks in front of us unpacked packages and boxes from the equipment sheds, and stacked them in the courtyard. Neill was looking almost as tired as I felt, blinking in the torch light and frowning.

"I don't know," he offered. "But I know those are the Protector's kit boxes." He pointed to a stack of wooden crates that held the leather cuirasses, the studded arm and leg greaves, the padded helmets, weapons, and bandages that the Protectors needed in their training, or else used on the walls. I nodded, but couldn't help feeling confused. The monastery was split into three training 'streams' one of which were the Protectors (warriors like Neill and Lila), Scribes (like Dorf and Sigrid) and then the Mages (like me and Maxal).

"So, this is going to be a Protector's Class? But why is it happening so early in the morning -and why are the rest of us being forced to take part?" I couldn't help asking, though I knew there was no student who could answer.

"Neill? I've got a bad feeling about this." I muttered, only for it to be confirmed moments later as the Abbot Ansall, little Monk Olan, and the giant-like Monk Feodor marched out from the main house. It was clear to anyone that Monk Feodor was fuming, and trying to keep himself apart from the others as much as possible.

"Students! What a great day this is about to be for you." The Abbot didn't have to raise his voice particularly high for it to cut through the cool air. "Today you are going to be led up to the dragon crater by our Chief Dragon Handler and Advanced Trainer for the Protectors, Monk Feodor." --the Abbot beamed, as there was a sudden cough from Monk Feodor-- "where you will receive your first instruction on the handling and use of dragons."

"What?" Neill hissed under his breath beside me, and I could only share his apprehension.

No one at the monastery knew how to 'handle' and 'use' dragons. Not even me, and I had helped raise one from an egg. Certainly not the other students around me, half of whom were punching the air in reckless delight while the other half were looking terrified. I agreed with the second half – especially after our previous morning's misadventures.

"Neill?" I whispered to him as the monks led us through the rear gates and up to the mountain beyond. "We need to do what we can to keep these students alive." He nodded, his face ghostly pale. "It's up to us."

We trudged through the shale and grit of the mountain path, gorse bushes spiking through our leggings, and students whispering in apprehension or excitement. Behind us the dragon pipes blared, their tones creating a shriek across the dark skies. The Chief Dragon Handler Feodor led us up the way we would take as if we were going to feed the dragons, but then, unexpectedly, he turned at the entrance to the high boulder field, where Feodor did something at the face of one of the rocks, and there was a grating sound as a boulder rolled away from a wide tunnel. He waited at the mouth of the tunnel as we filed past him. I exchanged a look with Neill. Could this be the tunnel entrance he'd told me of, where Abbot Ansall had taken me the night of the battle?

"Students? I want you all to walk through to the larger chamber below and *wait* there. Do not make a sound, any at all!" he said to us over and again, until it was time for me and Neill to file past him. "Torvald, Nefrette, out of line and with me, *now*," he growled. Even though it was dark I could hear the impatience in his tone. We waited by his side as the other students filed past us into the dark, and we three were the only ones out on the dark mountain alone where even still the dragon pipes blaring call reverberated.

"Hmph." Feodor growled at the sound. "Right now, the pipes are probably the only thing keeping the rest of those students alive, and god knows what will happen at dawn," he

62

said, and I was shocked by his honesty. "You two, I want you to explain to me right now how you managed to befriend that Crimson Red of yours, or else a whole lot of people are probably going to die today."

Neill opened and closed his mouth helplessly, before looking at me.

"Nefrette? It was you behind all this, was it?" Monk Feodor stared hard at me.

"I, I don't know how to befriend a dragon. It just sort of *happened* with Pax," I said in a low, urgent whisper.

"Pax?" Feodor's brows furrowed in confusion, and then, as comprehension dawned on him I saw his eyes widen. "That's the Crimson Red's name? She told you her name?"

"Yeah." I nodded. I still didn't know why others couldn't hear Paxala.

Monk Feodor took a step toward me and said, very quickly, "Never, *ever* share that name with any of the other monks. No one you cannot trust entirely, understand? I have heard in the old legends of dragons sharing their names with humans, but it was only the rarest, bravest humans who became true dragon friends." Feodor seemed to be thinking quickly. "And that is not something I can hope that every student down there will become." The light of the torches glinted off of the white tracery of his scars. "The dragons in the crater look to humans for their food, but also as competition. If Zaxx for a second believes that we are entering his domain to compete for the loyalty or mastery of his brood, then he will attack us, and we're doomed."

"Char? Can you summon Paxala?" Neill said urgently, before I could protest, however, it was Monk Feodor who squashed the idea.

"That Crimson Red is barely two, maybe three years old, though isn't she? She hasn't got the size, skill, or weight on her to even damage the bull dragon. No, Char, I forbid it. If you want to keep that Crimson Red alive, then please *don't* call her here." The trainer growled in frustration. "The Abbot has got it into his head to try and *control* the dragons in the crater now, to use them as you rode the Red. Neill – but not as a dragon friend but as a dragon *tamer*." Feodor cracked his neck and I stared at the scars that scored his body; one entire arm from hand to shoulder, and up over the shoulder to his neck in thick rivers of ridged white scar tissue. He had told us that he had 'earned' that scar the last time that the Abbot had some great idea to work closely with the dragons (although I don't know exactly what it was, much to my annoyance), and I could only imagine how apprehensive the monk must be feeling right now. "I know how dangerous that can be," Feodor said in a low voice.

"The eggs," I said quickly. I was taking a gamble whether I could trust Feodor or not, but on Neill's wary nod, I pressed on. "I think you have to raise the hatchlings from egg, or soon after as I did with Paxala. And the explorer Versi writes about young children bonding with young dragons…"

"So, you think it *might* only work with the youngest of dragons." Feodor nodded to himself, before looking up at the greying skies. "Thank you, Char, that gives me something to work with at least, buys us some time. Now get down there with the rest of the students, and do what you can to stop them getting themselves killed!"

"Aye, aye, sir," Neill said quickly, turning to jog down the torch-lit passageway into the mountain.

"And Char?" Feodor caught my arm as I turned to go. "I just wish that you had told me about this young dragonet of yours earlier. I could have helped."

Could you? I wondered, catching myself on a moment of wistfulness. It would have been nice to have a friend back then, back before Neill showed up and befriended Paxala. In fact, it would have been nice to have *any* friends in the monastery back then – aside from Nan Barrow. But, looking at the big man I still felt a little apprehensive. Would he have been able to keep the newt a secret? Or would he have told the Abbot on me? I had no way of knowing, now.

"I'm sorry, sir," I mumbled, before he gestured with a nod that it was too late now, and we hurried after the others.

I made my way through a wide passageway carved in stone, following Neill as we headed at a steep angle down into the rock. Torches lit the way as we passed underground cross-roads, these other passages unlit.

"Where do all these tunnels go?" I whispered to Monk Feodor behind.

"Never you mind that, Char," he said darkly, before the tunnel widened out into a sandy-floored cavern with a thin crack at one end, through which a greying predawn light filtered. It was dry as a bone down here, but it was also as hot as a summer's day.

"Hear me students, through that crack is one of the entrances to the dragon crater," Feodor said. "I want you all to suit up in Protector's gear, and I have instructions from the Abbot that you are to be in groups of three, two students with goads, and one student with these iron harnesses." Feodor gestured to the hand carts that a group of silent monks were unpacking as he spoke.

From the wooden boxes came heavy leather jerkins, arm and leg greaves, and leather caps that would do nothing to protect our heads from a dragon bite. Finally, the monks laid the eight-foot-long metal goads in two piles on the ground. Terrence immediately picked up a goad experimentally, shoving its wide metal barbs forward, as if catching a dragon leg, arm, or neck. Next to them sat piles of heavy, clanking iron chains.

"Char...?" Neill looked at me in alarm.

"I know, this is madness," I hissed.

"The *idea*,"--Feodor continued as we dressed ourselves,

layering as much scorn and sarcasm into the word 'idea' as was possible--"is to use the goad to pin the dragon down, and then one more student uses those heavy iron chains to lock around their necks, like halters for horses." Feodor looked at the silent, cold-eyed, black-robed monks who had helped push the carts down. Were they all the Abbot's henchmen? Would they brook any rebellion from us at this madness?

"But," Feodor continued. "I want every student to be as careful as possible, and if, *for one second* you think that the dragon will not respond well or I tell you I do not like what you are doing, then *instantly* drop your tools and make your way as fast as you can back here. Understand me, everyone?" He glared at us all. I think it was then that the sheer insanity of what we were trying began to sink in with the others. Dorf looked pale with fright as did Maxal, but Lila beside me looked fierce.

I have to do something, or else this will be a bloodbath. "Sir?" I struck up my hand and broke the fearful silence. "I want to volunteer to go first."

Feodor held my gaze for a moment, before nodding. "Very well. Perhaps it is only right that the students with apparently *any* experience of dragon-riding goes first. Torvald, you're with her," he barked at Neill, who nodded.

"And Lila," I said impetuously. *She's the only one besides Neill I would trust to be able to either run or fight at my side when an angry dragon attacks.*

Monk Feodor nodded once more. "Agreed. You three are

67

the first group. Pick up your goads and chains and follow me. The rest of you students wait here."

"But, sir, this isn't fair," Terrence called out in his high, outraged voice. "I'm the son of a prince, I should get the honor to go first."

"Terrence Aldo, it is precisely because you are a true-blooded *son* of a prince of the realm that I am leaving you here," Monk Feodor snarled back. "Do not be so eager to die, Aldo, and wait here with the others."

I watched as Terrence made the calculation that Monk Feodor thought my life (also as a daughter of a prince, but a bastard one) was more expendable than his was. I felt that familiar sting of anger and frustration, but knew that Feodor was just trying to find a way to save lives. Enough time for old rivalries, Char, I counselled myself. Who cares what Terrence Aldo and the Southern Kingdom thought of us northerners? Right now, I had to stop my friends from dying.

We hurried, half scrambling and half climbing through the gap in the cavern wall to emerge into the gloomy greying light of the sandy, warm, boulder-strewn crater outside.

"Right, well, the dragons will still be mostly groggy from sleep, and hopefully any of those that are awake will be subdued by those caterwauling dragon pipes," Feodor said doubtfully, before turning to me. "Nefrette? You said that you've done this before, what do we do?"

I was shocked by the older monk's sudden faith in me, and I looked to Neill.

"You can do it, Char," he whispered.

This might save a dragon from Zaxx, I thought. If I can encourage another young dragon to flee the crater with us, or stop the other students from getting themselves eaten…

"The mother caves," I said, feeling both anxious and excited. Maybe I could actually do some good here. "There are some younger dragons in there." I picked up one of the goads, and Neill picked up the other beside me, leaving Lila to carry the chains. I knew instinctively that it shouldn't be either me or Neill trying to learn how to connect with another dragon. We already had done so over Paxala.

"There are some yearlings in there, under one of the Brood Whites," Feodor said, leading the way carefully past the boulders and through the green, jungle-like giant ferns. I noticed that he wore heavier leather armor, studded with bits of metal, and he had strapped to his back a round buckler shield, and a metal mace at his belt. He had not come dressed to make friends with a dragon, but to protect his students from one.

It was impossible to think of anything being still asleep around us with the dragon pipes reverberating and echoing throughout the crater. For a moment, I got a sense of how it must feel to be a dragon, with this oppressive yammering beating down on them, grating on their ears, even as we reached the low-lying caves where the brood dragons lay. This area of the crater seemed less populated than some of the others, with fewer Messenger or Earth dragons and almost none of the larger breeds.

Perhaps dragons know to stay away from a brood mother, I thought, biting my lip. Unlike humans. I had once seen my father try to help one of the tough little mountain ponies through the birth of her foal. My father, the Prince Lander, was like that, as were most of the Northern kingdom; practical, and resilient. The mare had refused all aid and kicked him full in the chest, before taking herself off to the corners of her stable where she birthed the foal herself without any help.

"It isn't from fear the other dragons stay away," Paxala's voice suddenly broke into my mind. *"It is from respect."*

My heart plummeted. Respect was almost precisely what we weren't doing. I considered asking Paxala how we might show respect for the brood mothers, but then I realized-- Paxala knew what we were doing. Would she endanger herself to help me if—when-- things went awry?

"Wait, I'll see which cave she is in." Feodor snuck forward, unslinging the shield and holding it across the front of his body as he edged to the lip of the middle of three caves and peered in.

Two screeching blue shapes sprang out from the caves, each small by dragon's standards (about the size of a small stable). Feodor gasped as he hit the floor and rolled out of the way, and we were looking at the two, inquisitive faces of sinuous, long-necked blue dragons, barely a year old. They hissed and tasted the air with their long tongues, reaching their heads forward and back.

"Which one, Char, which one?" Neill was saying, holding the goad awkwardly in front of him. I couldn't blame him. This was an insane way to try and make friends with a dragon.

"The younger," Feodor said gruffly, pointing to the dragon on the far side of him. "Just see how close you can get, don't frighten them!"

They're both terrified already. I took a step forward, raising my goad out as Neill did the same a few meters away from me. "I'll try and hold the front left foot," I said, hating myself as I said so.

"Front left," Neill agreed, as just behind us Lila readied the chains into a loop.

This couldn't be happening. What was I doing? This wasn't the right way to make friends with a dragon, I thought, taking a ginger step forward. But it was the best I could do with the situation the Abbot had forced us into, I reminded myself. If we could succeed today, we might manage to make things better for at least a few of the dragons.

As fast as lightning the older blue lunged forward, seizing the goad I held before I could even approach its younger sibling, clamping it in its long jaws. I couldn't help but see the creature's needle-sharp fangs as it clutched one end of the goad, and shook its head.

"Woah," I hollered as the young dragon yanked me forward a few meters.

"Char-" Feodor gasped.

And then I was thrown back, the metal goad falling from my hand as I tumbled over the ground. I heard a snarl from nearby as a shadow fell over me.

There was grunting and a scuffing of feet and I rolled onto my knees to see that both Feodor and Neill had rushed to stand between the older blue dragonet and me. Feodor had his shield held aloft (puny against even a yearling) and Neill still held the goad warningly in front of them.

"Er, friends?" whispered a girl's voice. It was Lila. She was still standing across from the youngest blue dragonet with the chains, and she was cut off from us. *Oh no.* This was now no longer a dragon training mission, but a rescue mission.

"What do I do?" Lila was whispering, holding the chains in front of her at the youngest dragon, as we tried to fend off the slightly larger.

"Char – run back to the others. Get help," Feodor hissed, but I knew getting more students would only enrage the dragons more.

"No. Lila, listen to me." I remembered what the meeting last night had said about the explorer Versi and the southern desert tribes. "You have to drop the chain. Slowly."

"What?" The Pirate girl said. "Are you mad – this is the only defense that I have!"

"The dragons are scared. They'll never do anything but attack if they're scared," I said. "You have to trust me, Lila, the larger blue is protecting its sibling, because it thinks we're going to attack it."

Which we were. A hot shame ran through me. *Damn the Abbot and his crazy ideas. He probably didn't care if we succeeded or failed. He could count our mission a success, whether we captured a dragon or became an offering for Zaxx —live bait for the Abbot's plans.*

"Are you sure about this, Nefrette?" Feodor said. "We might be able to defeat one young dragon between us."

"No! Please trust me – Lila, drop the chain and step back. Show both dragons you don't mean them any harm," I begged her, as even the youngest dragon towered over my friend, ready to pounce.

CHAPTER 6
NEILL, AND ZAXX'S MESSAGE

*S*he's going to die. Panic clutched at my heart as I risked a glance at Lila. The other side of the sandy crater could not feel farther away.

"Steady boy, watch the eyes," Feodor said through gritted teeth from where he crouched in front of me. We had naturally fallen into one of the advanced maneuvers he had taught the Protectors just last week, with him kneeling before me with a raised shield, and me standing behind with spear held in the air. It was a maneuver from his soldiering days, the man had said, designed to take out cavalry. I wasn't sure what good (if any) it would do against dragons.

"Char...?" I said nervously, looking at the older blue dragon. It was puffing its long throat muscles, trying to summon the fire that I knew that some of the older, mature dragons could create. I hoped that this was not the time that it would suddenly realize how to do it.

"Lila, you have to trust the dragon in front of you," Char was hissing at our friend.

"Trust it do what, eat me?" Lila almost shouted. She still gripped the chains Feodor had given her, but she had lowered them to just over the floor. Lila Penna was from a proud Southern Raider people – what Terrence and his father would call Pirates as they spent half their time on their fast and narrow boats, heading northwards up the coast, involved in endless disputes and skirmishes. Asking her to give up her weapons was like asking these dragons to be humble.

But then I saw something incredible happen. Char rolled across the floor towards Lila, before slowly pushing herself up.

"Char? What are you doing – get out of there!" Monk Feodor was growling in front of me. I could see the white scars all over the back of his bald head and neck rippling as the muscles underneath them tensed.

"It's okay, Lila, shh… It's going to be okay," Char was saying, holding both unarmed hands out, one towards the dragon's snout and the other to Lila. It would almost be comical if it hadn't been so life threatening, as it reminded me of just the way I would try to get between my brawling brothers.

"Char, what do I do?" I heard Lila whisper.

"Try to relax," Char was saying. "She's scared. They both are."

"She?" Monk Feodor growled, moving back and forth on the balls of his feet.

"They're both female," Char said. "You can tell by the markings below the ears."

"You can?" Feodor marveled and I wondered how the heck Char had learned this but then the dragon made a feinting lunge and I came back to the moment, gritting my teeth in frustration. I didn't like having Char out there with Lila, at the mercy of the blue dragonet, but even if it was only a yearling, with dawn fast approaching and the rest of the dragons about to wake up, I knew that it was our only chance. Char cooed at the youngest dragon soothingly, and beckoned Lila to do the same.

The youngest dragon made a high-pitched chirruping noise, just like Paxala did when she was interested in something. I watched as she cocked her head to one side, and then darted her neck forward then back, forward again and back.

"What? How is she doing that?" Feodor whispered to me.

"It's Char," was the only answer I had.

To me it looked like Char was conducting music. She moved her hand gently, beckoning to the youngest dragon all the while talking to it; a soft murmur of words that didn't stop for a second. I had seen horse whisperers do the same thing at fairs on my father's land.

"Lila, come here," the Princess of the Northern Kingdom called, and Lila took a halting step forward beside Char.

"What do I do?" the dark-skinned girl muttered as she looked up in wonder at the blue dragonet. It was barely a few feet away.

"I don't know," Char said, taking a step back. "I think she has to meet you first…" Another step back and Char had left Lila alone in front of the younger dragon, the chain forgotten on the ground behind.

"Look at you, girl, look how strong you are already," Lila said in awe. The beast, who appeared to like being complimented, lowered her snout to gently snuff the air above the girl.

"That's it…" Char said, continuing to step back until she got to us. "I think it's going to be okay. We should leave the older sister too," she said, and amazingly the Monk Feodor agreed, giving me terse whispered instructions to step back slowly and to slowly lower the goad. The older blue dragon watched our every movement, but seemed to approve of what we were doing, as she stopped bellowing her lungs.

"Ha! Look at those teeth you have, you are a fierce princess yourself, aren't you?" Lila was congratulating the youngest blue, reaching up an open hand.

"Skrip-pip," the blue chirruped once more, lowering its snout to rub it against the Raider's palm like a cat.

"There. She's done it. Nefrette's done it!" Feodor was

saying in amazement, and we all felt relief blossom around us like spring.

Until it was broken by the blare of the dragon pipes.

BWAAR! BWAAAR! Instantly, the dragonets flinched and shook their sensitive heads, hissing at the skies, and then at us as they reared up on their back legs. They didn't understand what was going on, or why.

"The pipes," Char cursed. "They're hurting them."

Lila scrambled back from the rearing Blue, and there was a rumble from the ground beneath followed by the approaching crunch of heavy, monstrous feet. Lila's eyes went wide as she realized the same thing I did: It must be one of the brood mothers, or perhaps Zaxx himself. None of us had any illusions that we might be able to perform the same soothing tricks with and angry mother or the bull dragon.

"Right, all of you – get back!" Feodor shouted, and we needed no encouragement to race past the giant ferns and boulders to the crack in the crater wall where the other students would be waiting, watching. Monk Feodor was the last to run behind us, and I got to the small gap in the rocks to help first Lila and then Char, who looked at me oddly.

"I don't need help, Neill!" Char snapped.

I felt a flash of stupidity. "Oh yeah, of course…" It had just seemed like something that I should do – to protect them. Not that either of the tough girls needed it.

"WHO DISTURBS US! WHY THIS RACKET!? WHAT INTRUDERS DO I SMELL?" The voice of the great golden

bull erupted into our minds, and I couldn't stop myself from shouting in pain. It was like a fierce gale suddenly blowing through my thoughts. There was a thrashing from the ferns and plants and a rumbling of rocks as his golden body burst from one of the many hidden caves nearby.

"Get into the tunnels, quickly Torvald," Feodor shouted, turning to raise his tiny shield and metal mace in the air. I did as I was told, clambering through the rock, but even as hands grabbed my arms and pulled me through, I could see on the faces of the assembled students that they too could hear what Zaxx was shouting.

"AH. SO, IT IS YOU, COME TO DISTURB MY CHIL-DREN AGAIN, IS IT? HAVE YOU NOT FELT ENOUGH OF MY TALONS ON YOUR BODY, MONK?"

"We are on the business of the Abbot Ansall, Zaxx..." Feodor was saying through gritted teeth as he stepped back towards the tunnel.

A sudden crashing sound, and I swear that I could even see a hint of gold through the small tunnel walls.

*"YOU KNOW THE COMPACT, MONK. THE ABBOT DOESN'T RULE DOWN HERE. THIS IS **MY** DOMAIN, AND IF I SEE YOU OR ANY OF YOUR LIKE HERE AGAIN WITHOUT MY PERMISSION – THEN I WILL EAT YOU. I WILL EAT ALL OF YOU IN YOUR STONE HOUSE UP THERE."*

There was a sound of rending earth and rocks, and Feodor fought his way through the tunnel as the walls shook and boulders closed off its entrance to the bull dragon's domain. We waited for the growls of the shaking earth and the dragon's anger outside to subside before Feodor looked at us all by the glow of the flickering torches.

"I think that the lesson is over for today, students," he said wearily, looking older than I had ever seen him before.

"Well done, Torvald," Terrence Aldo sneered at me as we trudged back up through the tunnel to the slopes of the mountain outside. "Now you've ruined the chances of anyone else ever riding a dragon," he said loudly, adding to his gaggle of students that accompanied him everywhere. "The Gypsy probably did it on purpose, you know, so that he wouldn't have any competition…"

"Shut up, Terrence," I said, glaring at him until even the pompous son of the Southern Prince fell silent. Today wasn't a day that I wanted to get into another pointless argument with him. Not after what I had just seen and heard. *Char can do it. She can help people connect with dragons – but how can we do that when Zaxx will rip us all to shreds?*

"Neill," a voice said at my side as we emerged into the first light of day. It was Char, smiling as she jerked her head, directing my attention behind her, to the expression of rapt wonder and pride that spread across Lila Penna's face. The girl looked lost and entranced, marveling at her own hands – the ones that had touched a dragon.

CHAPTER 7
VERSI'S VOYAGE

I sat on the low stone bench at the back of the Kitchen Gardens. It was just before the dinner bell, which meant it was one of the few times Sigrid, Neill, Lila, Dorf, and I could come together. We younger students had a free watch before the madness of the evening dinner, and so it wasn't *too* unusual to see gaggles of us in odd places.

"...The youngest children seemed to be better at picking up a natural affinity for the dragons, and there were many times when I would walk down to the oasis to see children no older than five or ten playing 'chase' with dragons just a few months from their shells..." I read aloud from my stolen book, *Versi's Voyage.*

"I don't believe it," said Sigrid, frowning as she looked over my shoulder at what I had just read.

"I do," said Lila with a broad smile on her face. She had

changed since her encounter a couple of days before with the young blue dragon. She no longer scowled quite as much, and she had even greeted me with a smile when I asked her to come along to our 'dragon meeting.'

"We have to keep anything we do here a secret, for the moment," I had impressed upon her, knowing she would likely do anything to return to the crater and to be able to spend time with the blue yearling again. Dragons have a way of getting into your heart, and staying. Our meeting was about one thing: how we were going to get more students to bond with dragons as I had done with Paxala.

"We should know the consequences of what will happen if the monastery tries to use the dragons *without* bonding with them," I said out loud to the group, having to raise my voice a little over the clang of pots and shouts from the kitchen beyond.

"Zaxx will attack anyone who interferes with his dragons," Neill said darkly. "And he may attack the dragons who reach out to us as well."

"Oh no!" Lila said with a gasp. "You mean he might go after my dragon?"

I had to nod, though secretly I was pleased Lila had said '*my dragon.*' It was time that she knew. "Lila, Sigrid, Dorf… There's something else you have to hear." I took a breath, looking at their round and worried faces. "The Abbot is colluding with Zaxx to decide which dragons to kill."

"What?" Both Dorf and Lila said at once.

"I know, it sounds crazy, but Neill heard it himself, and Monk Feodor as much as told us that was the case. For some reason, the Abbot demands certain dragons to die, and we think Zaxx attacks the dragons he doesn't like or who resist him--with the Abbot's help. The Draconis Order isn't here to protect the Dragons, it's here to farm them." Even saying the last sentence felt terrible, and the words threatened to twist in my mouth.

"Farm them for what?" Dorf asked, his face pinched and scared.

"I'm not sure as yet," I said. It felt like we didn't have all of the pieces of what was going on here. "But think about it: we know the monks feed them and so they don't go out and hunt – or only very rarely. That keeps them in the crater. And the monks use the dragon pipes to subdue them when they're being too rowdy – and decide which healthy dragons should die. That doesn't sound like they're celebrating or learning from the dragons at all, does it? It's what you do to dangerous cattle." I felt sick.

"That's awful," the Raider girl was the first to say, and I found myself smiling grimly. She understood now, just as I and Neill did, that these dragons were in danger, and we were the only ones who could help them.

"We have to do something," Lila said.

"Yes, we do. We are." I nodded to Neill, who was giving me a grim smile, before clearing his throat and taking over.

"There are tunnels all the way through Mount Hammal,

and I know there is another way into the crater, because just before the battle with my brothers I saw Zaxx and the Abbot in there. We just have to find it. That's why we need all of you-- next time we're not going to try and climb down into the crater. We're going to try and find a way through the tunnels," Neill said.

"Next time?" Lila asked, and I remembered that we hadn't managed to invite the Raider girl to come with us on our first abortive attempt to rescue some dragon eggs.

"We snuck into the crater, in the early morning," I said to the girl, watching as her eyes sparked with enthusiasm for the idea. "We're going to try and rescue some of those dragon eggs, and get them away from Zaxx and the Abbot's control."

"Yes!" Lila said, looking at her hands as she must be remembering the dragon she had met.

"With Zaxx in them as well?" Sigrid said doubtfully.

"Yes." I nodded. *Please don't let me down now, Sigrid!* "I need you," I said to her a little quieter, and Sigrid pouted in that characteristic scornful Fenn way, before nodding.

"Okay. I'm in. This is much more exciting than studying anyway." She sighed dramatically.

"And me," Lila said automatically. "I'm not afraid of Zaxx."

"You should be," Neill pointed out before I could hush him.

"Tonight," I said. "We meet here, and we go out to find the

tunnels again. I think I know the way in, but I don't know *how* Feodor opened the door."

"Why don't we just ask him?" Sigrid said. "He seems the nicest of the teachers so far."

No way. "Too risky." I shot down the idea, as the other faces of the students looked at me. "Feodor has been a monk here for a long time, how do we know whether he'll side with us? And…" I hesitated, remembering the hypnotizing powers the Abbot Ansall had over me. "And I remember what the Abbot made me do." *Like defending the tower from Neill, my friend – even drawing a sword against him!* "If Feodor falls under the Abbot's power, then our plans will be ruined…" I looked up to find Neill giving me a concerned stare. It made me embarrassed for what I had done, and that made me angry. "It won't happen again," I said, as much to Neill as to the rest of the students.

"I can look in the libraries for anything," Dorf spoke up, surprising me. "I can always sneak food from the kitchens later, after we get back, as Nan knows me," he said with a guilty smile. "And no one here knows the libraries as well as me apart from Maxal."

Ah, Maxal, I thought. The small spooky kid was another one who we should have invited, despite Neill's suspicion of him. Maxal had helped me find the Abbot's secret meeting. And he was also one of the most powerful dragon Mages-in-training in our classes before. He could be a good ally – if we could rely on him. "That's a point, Dorf – do you think we can trust him to keep his mouth shut?"

"Maxal is my friend," Dorf said simply. It seemed good enough reason to me, especially combined with the way he'd pointed me to the Abbot's secret meeting.

"But he's a Mage-in-training," Neill said abruptly.

"So am I," I pointed out. What was wrong with Neill? Why was he suddenly arguing with me? I watched as the boy whom I had thought was my friend looked at his hands and then at his boots, before he finally spoke.

"I know, but after what the Abbot did to you the last time… he hypnotized you," Neill said through gritted teeth. "It was terrible. You wouldn't listen to me, you didn't know that I was your friend… and if he did that to you, he could do it to Maxal."

"It's okay, I don't think the Abbot will do that again," I said, a little shocked at how hurt Neill had been feeling.

"You don't think the Abbot can do what again?" A new voice broke into our conversation, and I looked up, over the giant winter kale and the straggling shrub of pea plants to see none other than spooky Maxal Ganna standing there, regarding us seriously and warily.

～

How long has he been standing there? Has he heard our plans? I thought in alarm.

"Ask us to go back into the dragon crater to harness the dragons," Neill cut in, standing up from the stone bench. We students weren't allowed to carry any weapons, but Neill's relative size and broader shoulders already made it clear that he could overpower the little boy should he want to.

Neill... I wanted to stop him.

"What are you all doing here?" Maxal said, one pale hand picking a pea pod from the nearby plant and carefully opening it with a slit of his thumbnail down the body. Where others might eagerly pop the delicious bright green orbs into their mouth, Maxal only looked at the splayed contents as if it were a creature or a machine whose inner workings he was examining.

"We're just talking," I said, standing up and not realizing that I still had the stolen book in my hands.

"Ah, *Versi's Voyage,*" Maxal said, his wide eyes looking out at me from the pale, shaved-bald head. "It was my one of my favorites too, for a while. Can I read you the best bit?" He offered a hand, and I heard a low warning cough from Neill beside me, but what could I do? If he decided to keep it or run off with it or tell one of the monks I'd taken it, I was sure that Neill or I could catch him.

"Sure," I said, handing over the book, and watching as the boy eagerly flipped through the pages skim-reading this and that passage until he found the entry that he wanted.

"Ah yes, here... 'The lights were low, and the sun had only just gone down when they lit the sacrificial bonfires. I waited with the matrons and elderly folk – annoyed at first that they thought that I, Versi, was either too elderly or too infirm to join in this special ritual, but as the tribe seemed to think that I was a traveling madman then perhaps it was no great shock…. Just as the last rays of the sun fell, the youths chosen for the coming of age ceremony were led out and told to run down through the avenue of bonfires, holding their own torch aloft, calling out their challenge… We all stood with baited breath, waiting for the moment. In a rush, one of the youths began his race towards manhood, hollering and hooting as he ran, and, in wonder I heard an answering shriek from the dark airs above us, as a shadow detached itself from the cliff and swept over our heads on giant wings. I waited to hear the scream, but there was none. Only a momentary gasp and the torch fell to the floor out there, past the bonfires. The boy was gone. The dragon had taken him.'"

Maxal looked up at me with wonderment in my disturbed face. "I don't think I understand it," I said awkwardly, remembering what the Abbot had said, about the Great Dragons of the south eating humans. Is that what Versi had just seen? I couldn't believe it. Not Paxala. She would never…

"Did that boy just sacrifice himself to the dragon as food?" Sigrid asked with a disgusted look on her face.

Maxal shrugged. "Some people think so. That's why no one reads Versi anymore. They think that he was glorifying in dragon-worship, and a traitor to his own kind."

"*Some* people think so?" I pointed out. "What do the others say?"

"Oh, I don't know. Some nonsense about humans and dragons flying off into the sunset together," Maxal said awkwardly, looking embarrassed at the poetic notion. "My father always thought I was a fool for believing as a child that the dragon just picked up the human and they became the best of friends. But it does remind me…" I saw Maxal look thoughtfully at Neill, "What your dragon did to Neill during the battle, she landed, allowing Neill to clamber on, almost as if she were choosing Neill, and not Neill commanding her…"

But that is what they can do… I thought, looking at Maxal with a new light. Maybe he did see dragons in the same way that I did, despite being from a Draconis Order family. That passage gave me an idea… I suddenly had a mental image of all of the good dragons of the crater, flying over the heads of the students, and then, as fast as lightning, one might swoop down, *choosing* the particular human that it wanted to work with. What if there had been a way in the past to allow the dragons to choose their humans, and for their humans to ride them? Could we replicate what Versi saw – but only using it as a means to bond a dragon and a human together?

"Well, yes, very nice description, if a little creepy," Neill said, plucking *Versi's Voyage* out from Maxal's un-protesting fingers. "And why are *you* out here in the Kitchen Gardens, can I ask?"

"I'm here to give a message to Char." Maxal's smile

collapsed in on itself, and eager, dragon-dreaming boy became once again the spooky, serious, and grim youth once more. "It's from the Abbot. We're to have our first Mage's meditation after dinner tonight but he wants me to bring you to him straight away, Char..." Maxal looked at me with wide eyes, frowning with worry, as if he felt nervous giving me this message. Did he not want to hurt my feelings? Was he scared of what reaction I might have? Or was it just that we were having our first training since before the battle? But small Maxal ducked his head and muttered to his feet.

"Uh... We'd better be going," he said, casting a look at the collection of students, still sitting in the garden around us. "I'll wait for you at the garden gate," he said awkwardly, and left. I felt a momentary flash of sadness for the small boy. He seemed so alone – but I also didn't know how much I could trust him.

"Char, don't go..." Neill stiffened at my side.

The temperature in the garden seemed to have suddenly dropped. I was scared. Scared of what Maxal might reveal to the Abbot. Scared of what the Abbot would do to me, and how much worse my punishment might be if he learned I'd taken a library book on top of everything else. If he could make me take leave of my senses before, then what would he do now that he knew that I defied him and had flown a dragon and continued to break his rules?

Nothing. I felt the warm buzz of thought in the back of my mind that came from Paxala. I could feel her stretching long muscles and shaking herself from her slumber. *"I am here, and I will stand guard tonight. If I feel the Abbot's dirty little mind anywhere near yours, I will come and tear the tower to pieces, looking for you."*

Well, I could hope that at least she wouldn't tear the tower down with me inside it, but I guess that there was also little I could do to stop her. For now, I had to obey what the Abbot said, or find a way to refuse, I thought. I had to stay here, to protect Paxala and the other young dragons. I had to learn as much as I could that would help me do that. *Or at least keep the Abbot unaware of what I was really up to...*

"Neill?" I said, both a request and an apology.

"I'll feed her," he said with a sigh, not that it was a chore but because he didn't want to leave the monastery with me up in the Abbot's Tower.

"You mean the Crimson Red, the friendly dragon, don't you? Can I come?" Lila asked excitedly. Her enthusiasm almost swept away any hesitation I felt. It was good to see someone else so happy just at the mere thought of seeing a dragon.

"It's okay, Neill," I murmured. "It will do Lila good to have more practice around dragons. Take her with you when you feed Pax." It was settled, and I turned and walked out of the Kitchen Garden, leaving my scheming and plotting friends to carry on the mission without me.

CHAPTER 8

THE SCROLL

"It'll be okay," a voice said at my side as I stood at the foot of the Abbot's Tower, and I realized that it was Maxal, still standing there after leading me here, despite the fact that he had not been summoned early along with me. He gave me a small, encouraging smile and I realized then that there probably was a lot more to the boy than meets the eye. I remembered him looking so small and alone, walking away from the others before I had caught him up. It made me feel bad.

"Do you...you *like* the dragons, don't you?" Something—a hunch, perhaps-- made me ask him outright.

Maxal looked at me with careful eyes, not saying anything at all, but he nodded.

"Then, when this is over – come speak to me," I whispered, and Maxal nodded seriously back at me, as I made my way inside, alone.

I hadn't been up here since the battle. That was almost a season ago, and no students had been allowed up here since that night and the tragic 'accident' that had claimed the Quartermaster Greer's life (actually it was Neill trying to defend himself from a homicidal Greer, but no one else knew how the Quartermaster had managed to fall from the heights). I would be the first, and the heavy import of the Abbot's summons was not lost on me as I spiraled up and up and up the narrow stairs, the window slits revealing the dark mountain and the purpling sky outside so that I felt like I was climbing into the night itself. Finally, my feet hesitated near the top, where the simple wooden door stood ajar, and light and freezing air washed over me.

"You may enter," said the cold, thin voice of the Abbot from inside, and I stepped around the door to see that the room had changed only in small ways.

The cold and bare stone flags were still there, as was the Abbot's desk, and the stack of wooden stools upon which we had sometimes been allowed to sit during our Mage classes. The room occupied the very top of the tower, and used to have floor to ceiling high wooden shutters that opened out onto the wild skies beyond, but nothing more. They had gone, replaced with a single metal bar across the window. It wouldn't stop someone climbing out, but it would stop someone tripping or being thrown out in a brawl.

The Abbot stood beside one of these barred windows, heedless of the cold air. I had the sudden, insane urge to run up behind him and push him, to make all of this stop right now, but by the time I blinked to clear the anger away he had turned, as fast as a snake, and was looking at me with his crystal-sharp eyes. "Nefrette," he said, not as a greeting or as a question, but instead as an accusation.

"Abbot," I replied, attempting to keep myself proud and still, though he could probably see my fear. I had seen this man summon black lightning storms out of clear skies (with the help of us magician students, it has to be said), as well as summon and extinguish flame from apparently nowhere.

"Every time there is trouble in this monastery, Nefrette, I look up to see that there is either you or the boy at the bottom of it," the Abbot said wearily.

What am I supposed to have done now? I bit the inside of my cheek a little nervously. *Apart from plotting the liberation of all of the dragons in the crater and stealing library books.*

"But now it seems, Nefrette, the trouble that you have caused comes from *outside* the monastery." He stared hard at me as I stood in silence. Did he mean Paxala? Had he found out where her lair was?

"Sir?" I asked nervously.

"This," the Abbot said with a wave of his hand, indicating a roll of paper with multiple ribbons and seals broken across it. "Is a missive from none other than the Royal Prince Vincent, regarding *you.*"

"Me, sir?" My blood almost went cold. What would the

Prince of the Middle Kingdom, my uncle, want with me when he had never once in my life shown any interest in me?

"Yes. *You*," the Abbot said with great regret. "It appears that there have been skirmishes in the near highlands, near the town of Faldin's Bridge, you know it?"

My heart thumped. "I do, your grace. Faldin's Bridge is the main border between the North and Middle Kingdom." It was also the place that my father, Prince Lander, said that we must never lose control of if we wanted to survive – it was one of the largest and easiest crossing points of the great river that separated my father's Northern Kingdom from my uncle's Middle.

"There is war coming, Nefrette –I'm sure even you can see that. The warlords are jockeying for power, and *your* father is probing the defenses of our noble Lord Vincent…"

I doubted that immediately. My father might be a hard man-- a harsh and a stern man some might say-- but he would never willingly seek to start a war, I was sure of it – would he?

"And so, the Lord Vincent has taken it upon himself to ask us, the Draconis Order, to do what we were meant to be doing here. To calm the relations between the Three Kingdoms, and to remind the princes and warlords just what we are trying to accomplish. *You*, Char Nefrette, against my wishes, are going to be sent to the Northern Kingdom as a part of a delegation of treaty with your father, where you will plead and bargain with your father for peace. Do you understand?"

I coughed in the sudden shock. I didn't understand. My

heart felt immediately torn between returning home, and leaving the dragons—Paxala-- behind. "But, but sire – my training here hasn't even been completed…"

"You do not have to tell *me* that, Nefrette," the Abbot said, squinting his eyes at me. "But I must say that I am a little relieved that you will not be interfering with the education of the other students here, at least for a few weeks."

"But, Abbot…" I tried to say. I wondered what had caused this, why was Prince Vincent sending me away north so easily? Was it a part of negotiating this treaty with his brother, my father? What game were they playing, with my life as the bargaining chip?

And how could I leave Paxala and the other dragons behind? I thought in alarm.

"I do not quite see why you are so upset, Nefrette. You are returning home for a while. Or do you care for our company that much?" The Abbot sneered, every word dripping with sarcasm. "You will have an escort of course, of the monks that I can trust to instruct you during your absence-"

And who will report back to him, no doubt.

"-and I do not need to remind you, child, that whilst you are away the other students here, your friends might I add, will have to pick up your slack. If I discover that you are disobeying your tutors, or are bringing shame to our liege, lord Prince Vincent, then, well…" The Abbot didn't continue, but instead turned to sigh sadly as he looked down at the Main Hall below us where my friends and colleagues ate right now.

"This monastery works only when we all work together, don't you think? Towards the same goal. If there is one rotten apple then the whole batch can get spoiled."

The threat was clear. If I chose to disobey the Abbot or Prince Vincent by remaining here – not in the monastery but out on the mountain with Paxala maybe – somewhere I could continue my plan to sneak into the crater, then I would bring down punishment and revenge on the heads of my friends here – Neill, Sigrid, Dorf, Lila; and now perhaps even Maxal Ganna.

"Do you understand what I am telling you, child?" The Abbot shot me a look.

"Yes, your grace. I understand perfectly," I said through gritted teeth.

"Good. You will be leaving tomorrow."

Tomorrow? I thought in alarm. I had to see Paxala. I had to see Neill, I thought in alarm as the Abbot continued speaking.

"…There are some dried apples and water on the table, see that you eat before our lesson begins. Ah look, little Maxal and the others are coming." The Abbot simpered as the shapes of the other would-be Mages left the doors of the Main Hall and made their way to the bottom of the tower. I could have growled at the Abbot if I had thought that it would do any good. He had clearly known that I wouldn't have time to get dinner after his little lecture and the Mage meditations began again, but I managed a couple of bites from the meagre, sour provisions he'd provided. Truth was, I wasn't really hungry anyway, my mind still in turmoil.

How could I leave Paxala? How was Lila going to cement her bond with the young Blue without my aid? What would happen to the other young dragons while I was away?

The other students filed in slowly, some surprised to see me there, taking their places where they had stood around the room before the battle. Maxal shot me a warning look, but didn't say anything as we waited instruction.

"Clear your minds, students," the Abbot began as always, but I found it impossible. Frightful fantasies and nightmares of monks throwing chains and lassos onto baby dragons filled my mind, along with dark shadows with torches surrounding Paxala's hidden cave in the middle of the night. Could I refuse to go? What would happen then? Had my father *really* been starting these skirmishes at Faldin's Bridge, one side being declared the North, and the other the Middle? Why would he do that now? It was no surprise to me that there *would* be tensions between my father and my uncle. There had been stories of skirmishes before, of caravans going missing, and trade embargoes levied in response. There had been the constant sending-back and forth of diplomats and counsellors. *But a war?* There was a lot of talk of a civil war brewing amongst the students. Their parents' letters had been full of questions about the Sons of Torvald battle, and what it portended for the entire Three Kingdoms. Was *that* why my father would harass the borders and demand my return before the Middle Kingdom tore itself apart?

In a way, that idea made me feel a little comforted, in an anxious way. My father had only ever looked at me as a pawn before now anyway – did this mean that he cared for me? My heart sank as I considered a much more likely scenario: That all this was happening because I'd refused to return home with Wurgan. Or had the Abbot somehow learned that I'd tried to help Lila befriend the young Blue, and now he was trying to stop us?

The meditation class was long, tedious, and taxing in a way that concentrating and standing for long periods leave a deep ache in the bones. The Abbot didn't seem to have changed his tactics at all since we'd last trained—before the battle. He opened the shutters to leave our bodies cold, and made us stand or crouch for long periods in awkward positions because, as he said, 'discomfort purifies the mind.' When it came time to start rehearsing the mental images once again - the crown, the dragon's tooth, the flame, the sword –my mind couldn't conjure their images. Instead I thought of Paxala, and Neill, and the other dragons. At several junctures during this process, when my body was shaking with exhaustion and my mind was numb with brain fog, I felt a sort of buzzing headache and a pressure around my ears. It was almost similar to the feeling before a storm, of heaviness and approaching threat, and when I looked up I saw the Abbot regarding me carefully.

"You're not trying hard enough!" the Abbot burst out after the last feeling of invisible pressure, before snarling at the skies outside. "Clearly, your time away from lessons has made your thinking sloppy and weak! You will return to practicing your images, every morning and every night, and we will meet here once every week to see how you have progressed. Now, get out all of you," he said with a snap, pointing his finger at the door which swung open of its own accord.

We were only too eager to pile down the tower steps and make for our beds, and I could see from the faces of the other students that they were just as worried and as tired as I was by the Abbot's erratic behavior.

"At least he's not doing nightly classes anymore," a voice whispered shyly beside me as we crossed the practice court-yard. It was Maxal Ganna, his brow was furrowed. I nodded. He had a point. Before the battle, the Abbot had made us take this meditation class every night after dinner, but now it would only be once a week—though of course, I wouldn't even be here to practice.

Did that mean that the Abbot was weaker than he was before? Had Jodreth managed to injure his magical power somehow? Or, I thought in alarm – were the Abbot's other schemes keeping him busy? Could the treaty negotiations be just one part of a larger plan the Abbot was making? We had to know what the Abbot was up to, but there was no way that I could do that if I was hundreds of leagues away to the north. *Maybe that's exactly the point.*

With a heavy heart, I trudged up the girl's dormitory tower to my bed. I didn't practice any of his silly meditation images, either.

CHAPTER 9
THE CROWN

"Pax?" I whispered into the night. I couldn't have slept even if I wanted to, and the Abbot's ultimatum this evening just made it all the more difficult. I had waited until it was deep dark before carefully sliding from my cot and getting dressed, sneaking out of the room to pad softly down the stairs, across the courtyard, and out through the Kitchen Garden gate and onto the mountain slopes beyond, hurrying over the rocks and boulders, heading for the deeply wooded ravines on the far side.

"I am here," I heard her in my mind, as a dark shadow swept across the brilliant night sky. Paxala was being silent – even I hadn't heard her swoop past me.

"You're getting good at hiding," I congratulated her. But would it be enough while I am gone? Why should she even have to hide? I thought in despair.

"Char is going?" A note of alarm sounded in the reptile's thoughts, as there was a light thump as she landed in a clearing ahead of me, turning with a swishing tail.

"I don't want to, but if I don't – the Abbot will start hurting the students," I said miserably, telling her just what the Abbot had demanded that I do the very next day.

"Then Paxala will come with Char," the dragon announced, dipping her head above mine to nuzzle at the top of my head.

"No, Pax, I wish that you could, but the Northlanders… they see dragons very differently than even the Draconis Order." I tried to explain to Paxala how the wild mountain dragons were nothing like the Crimson Red here before me. They were smaller, vicious, and boiled like writhing snakes together out of their hidden places in the mountains, ripping the flesh from anything that moved. My father Prince Lander had ordered that they be shot on sight as even a small brood could destroy a flock of cattle in moments. "It wouldn't be safe for you to travel North," I said urgently. I had to get her to understand. "I need you here, I need you looking after Neill and the others. The hatchlings."

"No. Where Char goes, I will go," Paxala said once more. *"You are mine, and I am yours. That is the end of it."* She jerked her head forward then, bumping me in the chest to push me none-too-gently. Being reprimanded by a dragon – even a friendly dragon – could sometimes hurt.

"Oh, Pax." I sighed. What was I going to do? How could I

encourage her to stay here, without me? Or, if she did follow the entourage, could she remain out of sight from my father and his troops in the north?

Zaxx. I thought darkly. That was the problem. With Zaxx still in that crater there ruling over every helpless dragon then no one would be safe. No dragonet, no hatchling, and certainly not Paxala here. I knew that even if I *did* manage to convince the Crimson Red to stay here at the Dragon Mountain without me, then there was still nothing that I would be able to do to stop Zaxx from attacking her. Zaxx had already killed Paxala's parents, and when he discovered that Paxala was flying free then the old bull might even think that she was a threat to him.

How could I leave Pax here, unguarded?

"Char need never worry about Paxala!" the Crimson Red scoffed. *"I will be with her wherever she goes, anyway."*

"But then what about the young Blue that Lila is befriending?" I asked in desperation. "Who will protect her from Zaxx? Or from the Abbot?"

Pax shook her snout, huffing sooty air into the sky. She had no answers to this conundrum, and through our mental connection I could sense her growing frustration. *"Human problems!"* she said severely, lashing her tail to take out a nearby sapling. *"Char wants me to stay to look after the young dragons, but Char doesn't want me to fight the bull? Humans make everything complicated, when it should be simple."* Paxala growled.

"But how could it be simple?" I breathed, feeling trapped.

"You stay. We live in my cave. We fight the bull." Paxala growled pragmatically.

My heart fell. "I wish that I could, Pax," I said morosely. "I truly wish that I could – but if I don't go, then my father might start a war. A human war is a terrible thing. Many hundreds die. My brother could die. Our friends here could die."

"Everyone dies eventually, Char," the dragon said dismissively, and I realized how very different a dragon's take on the world was from a human.

"All you can choose is how to hunt, when to sleep, and who to fight – today," Pax said as I felt her turning to take a bound and then a leap into the night sky.

"Pax, wait…" I groaned, knowing I had upset her. Maybe it was for the best that she was annoyed with me, I thought with a heavy heart. At least then she might not follow me when I traveled north with the other monks.

But the thought of leaving her here with the other monks and the Abbot was too much. *No.* I had to find a way to fix this…. With no better plan in mind, I jumped to my feet and turned towards the dragon crater.

There was a rattle as scree slid from the side of the cliff and fell down in the dark. I could only be glad that it was night and that I couldn't actually see how far it fell as I clung to the rock.

I was once again climbing down into the dragon crater, using the same path that I had taken before with Neill, Sigrid, and Dorf, but this time without ropes. It was strangely easier to do this on my own, and in the dark – as I was no longer scared for their lives; only my own.

My anger and fury at what the Abbot was asking me to do outweighed my fear. However, I had to at least save one egg from the clutches of Zaxx before I was sent north. *Perhaps I could even take the egg to Paxala to keep warm*, I thought, aware that the plan was a reckless one – I was going into the crater alone, without friends, without back-up, and on the same day that Zaxx had roared his threat at us. But I also knew that it might be the only chance that I might get.

My father might not allow me to come back, if this were some part of a complicated peace deal between him and Uncle Vincent. My father must have been incandescent with anger when he realized that I was not returning north with brother Wurgan and his men, and this might have been his way of ensuring that I did come north – perhaps he'd threatened Prince Vincent that he would attack Faldin's Bridge if he didn't get his daughter back? That didn't sound like my father, but times were chaotic now.

My foot scraped once more on the narrow ledge of rock underneath and I heard a cracking sound.

There! I reached the far ledge, holding myself against the rock for a moment as I caught my breath and hauled myself over the edge to roll, panting, to the safer shelves of rock. Below me there came the soft whuffling noises of sleeping dragons as the Earth dragons turned and rolled in their slumbers. As quietly as I could, I crept past the boulder field and down to the crater floor itself. It was warmer down here, constantly hot thanks to the warm springs and steams that seemed to rise throughout this mountain. Giant ferns that were twice my size dwarfed me as I jogged first this way, and then that.

There was a low-pitched groan as what I had thought was a fat, low boulder turned over in its sleep, revealing short, crocodile like arms and a wingless and broad body. I froze, my heart in my throat. It was another Earth dragon. They didn't go into the caves below at night, as Zaxx and the other dragons regarded them as little better than animals. I still knew that their grunts and howls would bring the interest of dragons down on me though, as I tiptoed carefully around him, watching as his nostrils flared, dreaming of my scent.

"Char? What is Char doing?" Paxala's voice resounded in my mind. Through our connection, I could sense her alarm as she wheeled and turned in her flight. She had flown far to the north on the cooler winds, and I guessed that she must have been trying to scout the way ahead for when she would either follow or carry me to my father's keep.

"I am in the dragon crater," I thought back at her, amazed at how easy and clear this connection between us was becoming. I felt through her mind the clear chill of wind on her body, the scent of fresh crisp snows in the north, and even the scurry of rabbits and voles on the ground beneath her passage, hurrying for cover. I wondered if we were bonding closer, the dragon and I, or whether it was my natural magic becoming stronger and allowing this deeper connection. *What was it Feodor had said, something about being a dragon friend?*

"Char must leave the crater. Now!" Paxala breathed into my mind, shutting off our connection so abruptly that I recoiled from her command. I stumbled a little on the path, and ignored her. I had no time to think about what Paxala wanted me to do, or to wonder about Monk Feodor's old legends and superstitions.

I had to save at least one more dragon while I had the chance.

My steps took me to the edges of the mothering caves, where I could see the low openings and even hear the wheezes of the White brood mothers inside. Knowing this hadn't gone so well last time, my plan was now simple. No sneaking, no panicking. Just run in, seize an egg, place it into my soft hessian sack, and escape. The brood White might wake up, she might roar and chase me – but she would also be lethargic and slow given her size and the fact that it was the middle of the night, and cold. Dragons need heat, I reminded myself – all apart from the wild northern mountain dragons it seemed, which somehow survived in the snows up there. But I wasn't in the north, and down here I had a chance to get out and at least halfway across the crater before Middle Kingdom dragons could follow.

I tried not to think about what would happen when they did. With any luck, the brood Whites might not wake up at all, as no dragon it seemed--aside from Paxala-- coped well at night. They are sun-blooded creatures, powered and filled with the warmth of the sun – or so I had read, which didn't explain the fact that wild mountain dragons spent most of their time at cold altitude. Obviously, dragon texts didn't cover everything there was to know and understand about the creatures.

This has to work, because if it doesn't... I loosened the velvet bag from my shoulder and took a step forward. If it didn't work then everything I had done over the past two years —disobeying the Abbot, hiding and rearing Paxala in secret, risking my life – all of it would be for naught. Zaxx the bull would still be in charge down here, and eventually the Abbot and Zaxx together would find Paxala. There had to be more *free* dragons in the world if we were going to counter the fell evil of the Draconis Order and the Dragon Mountain.

Now resolved, I took a deep breath and, just as I ducked to go into the cave, I saw high up on the ridge of rock above the mothering caves a great, golden eye.

~

"YOU, GIRL. I THOUGHT I DREAMED YOUR SCENT," Zaxx the Golden's voice washed through my mind, so loud

and dominating that I fell to my knees, and somewhere there was a mournful hooting of a very far away Crimson Red.

*"SO. YOU **DO** HAVE ANOTHER DRAGON OUT THERE, THAT YOU ARE HIDING FROM ME?"* Slowly, dreadfully, and awfully, the overhang of rock that I had taken for a ridge line unfolded itself, dislodging smaller pebbles and sand as the mighty head of the Golden Bull peeled away from the true crater walls beyond. In the dark I couldn't make out all of the dragon's body, but the star light gleamed like liquid lamp oil on scales. The air was filled with smell of soot and ash, and I heard the crunch of trees and the scrape of mighty talons as large as ponies as the rear legs of the bull stepped down.

"You cannot have her!" I shook my head, my heart hammering in terror even though I knew I would never, ever, allow Paxala to be hurt.

"I CAN SMELL HER THROUGH YOUR MIND, YOU KNOW," Zaxx said, and the sudden horrible pressure of the Golden's mind flared against my own, breaking my walls and petty barriers, threatening to push all that was Char Nefrette out of the way.

'Focus on one image. Maintain the center' flashed through my thoughts. Any other time it would have seemed somewhat obscene, but it was the teaching of Abbot Ansall that saved my mind. I remembered his lessons in resisting the pain of the cold and of the strange positions we sat in during meditation. The image of the crown or the sword or the dragon tooth was meant to dominate everything, drown out every pain and

discomfort until it was all that there was. I used the technique to drown out the noise of Zaxx's mind rifling through my own – but I used the image of Paxala, flying fierce and proud through the night sky.

"Ah. So you have a little skill with the dragon magic then," Zaxx purred at me, turning his head first one way and then that as he regarded me in the way that a bird might regard a potential meal. This time the bull's thoughts were pushed to the edges of my mind and were not as loud as they had been before.

"All magic is dragon magic, you see. There are no Draconis Mages, and there are no dragon friends. Just dragons, and the magic that flows from us to you," Zaxx said contemptuously. I didn't understand, but as long as the bull was reveling in the sound of its own voice then he wasn't eating me or any of the others, so I was happy to let him continue.

"And now, Char Nefrette, it is time. I made an ultimatum to the scarred monk that were any to interfere with my broods once more, the monastery would suffer. You will have to decide, Char Nefrette – do you wish your friends, or the Crimson Red to die tonight?" I watched as Zaxx the mighty licked his scaled lips with a forked tongue.

"Neither!" I bellowed without thinking. "How could you kill your own dragons like this, or the innocent people who are only trying to learn from you?"

"It is the way of the world, child. Dragons eat humans.

Humans eat cows. Or are you suggesting that I just eat you instead of the others?"*

Zaxx's head hovered in front of mine, his teeth almost as high as my body and as yellowed as old bone. I would barely even be a morsel to the old creature. I could beg for my life, I thought. I could offer Zaxx the Abbot instead, or Monk Olan, or the entire Middle Kingdom to save mine, Paxala's, and my friends' skins.

No. I won't do it. Instead, I summoned all of my anger in just the way the Abbot had taught us and threw out my hand as I had seen the Abbot do. "Flamos!" I said out loud, watching as light flared in the dark.

There was a deep rumbling sound, and a breath of scorched air, and I realized that Zaxx the Golden was laughing at my defiance. I had magicked little more than a flash of flame, that was instantly snuffed in the night air.

"Oh, you are tough, little human. Few Mages and seers would attempt to take on the mighty Zaxx the Golden in a battle." The rumbling continued, and Zaxx raised his snout high above me to sniff at the air. I felt crushed already, certain of my defeat.

"I am impressed with your bravery, girl. I will delay your punishment and instead set you a challenge. Bring me the crown of the old queen and you, the Crimson Red, and your friends may continue to live. But fail me, and I will have to kill them all. Agreed?"

"No," I shouted angrily into the night. "I will do nothing for you!"

"It wasn't a question. A dragon never asks permission, Char Nefrette. That is something else you will have to learn if you ever want to understand us." Zaxx chuckled, ignoring me as he climbed back onto the shelf of rock above the mothering caves. I was defeated, and I knew it. I would have to do what Zaxx said if I wanted those eggs to survive, and my friends, and even Paxala.

Where was I going to find the crown of the old queen? I thought miserably, my feet heavy as I trudged back across the dragon crater to the place I had climbed in.

PART II
THE NORTH

CHAPTER 10
FALDIN'S BRIDGE

This was it. *This was where the North began,* I thought as I looked out from aboard my mount. The stubby mountain pony was barely tall enough so my feet didn't touch the ground, but the monks had insisted I ride instead of walk, like I was precious goods for them to transport from one place to another.

The irony of being treated like royalty now, outside the monastery, by the very monks who had called me 'bastard' behind its walls was not lost on me.

We stood on the rise of land that led down to the river valley settlement that was Faldin's Bridge. In the center, spanning the river, was a town of sorts – really more of a large wooden town surrounding the old stone bridge that crossed the river. On the far side, the ground was rough, and rose suddenly in tumps and hills, and was scattered with a dusting of snow.

This river, and this bridge marked the edge of Prince Vincent's Middle Kingdom, and the start of my father, Prince Lander's Northern Kingdom. We had left the Dragon Monastery many days ago, and I felt a pang in the center of my chest where my heart should be every moment. I wondered how the others were doing. Had they even attempted stealing the dragon eggs? Were they alive? Did it go well or badly? I worried. I had to admit I missed them. They were my only friends; moonish Dorf; caustic Sigrid; fierce Lila – even little Maxal.

And Neill. How could I leave him down there to guard Paxala and continue on, all on his own? As if his life wasn't hard enough. It felt to me like I was running away – even though I knew that I had no choice but to be here. Like I was abandoning everyone who needed me. I didn't relish returning north right now – even though I preferred the mountain air, the more direct and brusque ways of the people; I couldn't find any joy in returning to my father's court at this time. It felt like I was returning to being just a child somehow.

'Paxala?' I reached out once more with my thoughts towards my dragon-friend, but, just like all the other times, there was nothing. Maybe my connection only worked at close distances. Or maybe it only worked on the sacred Dragon Mountain.

Of course, there was another option as well – that perhaps Paxala had given up on me. She had been annoyed at me for leaving, and perhaps that was just how dragon friendships worked? Who said that the dragon had to stay friends with you for life? I thought miserably. My teeth chattered.

"I thought you Northlanders liked the cold, Nefrette?" grumbled Monk Olan, frowning through a rat-like face at the cold. He had been sent with us as Abbot Ansall's emissary, but so far, he had deigned to speak to me about three times on the whole trip.

There were a few agreeing chuckles from the other three monks around us, all wearing their black, red, and purple traveling robes with long staves.

"We do." I glared at Olan defiantly, shrugging off the coarse woven shawl that I had draped over my shoulders. "It's only the softer southern kingdoms that don't appreciate good mountain weather," I said icily, allowing myself to feel a moment of triumph as Olan's face screwed up tighter in fury. He knew that he couldn't insult me, not now, not with my father's pennants and flags clearly visible on the other side of the bridge. My father had brought a warband down from his distant tower-keep, and now I could see them clearly encamped on the far sides of the bridge, their round-framed canvas yurts sprouting my father's white and purple banner above.

I wonder if you came down to see me yourself, father – or whether you sent Wurgan again, or another captain. Still, it was good to see the banners of my home, even if they brought with them some very mixed feelings.

Father never wanted me to stay at the monastery, I thought

dismally, as Olan kicked his own little mountain steed roughly with his heels. Father had sent me there because he thought that he had to, in order to have a 'seat at the table' as he put it. But he hated the monks and their strange ways. Still, I was glad that I had gone, all the same. Even with everything that the Abbot had put me through – I was glad of going. Because I had met Paxala. And Neill.

"Come on, ya' old goat, come on!" the monk snarled suddenly, breaking my musings and hurrying our troupe down to the town below.

On this side of the bridge-town there was an entirely different sort of encampment however; long tented marquees with elaborate displays of banners the color of gold and red and yellow and royal blue. *Prince Vincent's entourage.* I thought with a shudder, noticing how, behind the grand, almost festive display there were also tents and tents in small groups around campfires. Soldiers. Lots and lots of Prince Vincent's soldiers, and even now, there were some of them on tall steeds waving their hands at us, indicating that we were to ride straight through the gates to the scrape of village beyond.

Here we go, I thought. I had never felt more like a pawn in an elaborate chess game as I did at that moment. I didn't even know what the Abbot and Vincent were expecting me to do here, other than placate my father just by being on this side of the border.

~

"It's them! The Dragon Monks..." I heard the whispers from the peasants clearly over the sullen clips of the ponies' hooves as we passed. Faldin's Bridge didn't have so much a set of gates as a wooden fence, and we had been waved through not by the Faldin's Bridge people, but instead by tall and fierce men and women in full plate armor: knights of my uncle, the Prince Vincent.

So, my uncle has seized the town then, had he? I thought in bitter alarm. I had been right: this was nothing but a power-play between my uncle and my father, and it looked like Uncle Vincent had all the cards.

"...don't look at them directly in the eye, they'll put the dragon curse on you!" a peasant woman scolded her daughter. The pair stood at the verge of the simple street, and I tried to smile at them to show them that not everything that came out of the Dragon Monastery was creepy and strange, but the daughter gasped in terror. Monk Olan chuckled and that was when I realized he was pulling a scary face at them.

Is the Draconis Order so feared throughout the Three Kingdoms, I wondered as hooves clattered up ahead, and mingled with the stamp of marching feet.

A group of soldiers emerged from one of the narrow side streets, dressed in full plate armor like the gate guards, and carrying long pikes. Behind them rode a cadre of fully-armored knights, and, in the center of *that* was none other than my Uncle Vincent, the thin and pale-skinned ruler of the Middle Kingdom, dressed in midnight finery.

"Niece," he greeted me after the different cohorts of protection had finally arrayed themselves (the pike men spanning across the bridge entrance, pikes lowered to the north, and the mounted knights in a gaggle around him).

"Uncle." I nodded. It was odd calling Prince Vincent that, as we had never even met in any family way. Prince Vincent might be the ruler of the Middle Kingdom, and the nominal overseer of our grandmother, the old queen's legacy, but to me he was nothing more than a name on a seal. He had certainly never expressed any interest in me, the bastard child of his northern brother before.

"It is such a pleasure to see you again." The prince nodded at me and poured honey over his words. "Please take these gifts, on behalf of the Middle Kingdom, to your father and tell him that I look forward to hearing from him," he indicated to where servants had laid out wooden crates and chests on the ground, which I guessed must contain the sorts of riches and wealth that princes give to each other: fine bolts of cloth, dyed with rare and expensive dyes, gold bullion or coins, or maybe even some of the rare artefacts that happened occasionally as gifts: heirlooms of the Great Queen – an engraved dagger, a set of books, an ancient banner maybe.

"As you wish, sire." I bowed my head, wishing this would be over as quickly as possible.

"And niece? I do hope that you inform your father of all of the good that you have been doing down there in my Dragon Monastery, and just how we loved having you be part of it."

Your Dragon Monastery? I thought in anger. It was luck alone that the sacred Dragon Mountain was on Middle Kingdom land, surely! What about the Abbot's pledge that the Draconis Order remain neutral in all of this?

"I will tell my father of everything that has befallen me," I lied, but knowing those words would have the effect of unsettling the Dark Prince. He squirmed in his seat for a moment, and then scowled, before replacing the look of discomfort with a fake smile.

Good. In fact, I had no intention of telling my father hardly anything. How was I to tell him that I could communicate with a dragon just through the power of my mind alone? It wasn't too long ago when people had been burned for such strange and occult claims out in the wilds. And how was I to tell father of the mistreatment at the hands of the Abbot? Or of the constant danger we have been in? Or of Zaxx's threats? I gritted my teeth at the thought. Of course, I couldn't tell my father those things. He would never let me back to the Dragon Monastery afterwards, and that would mean that I would never see Paxala, or my friends again.

My dismay and heartache must have shown in my face, as Prince Vincent interpreted it as his personal success. He grinned at me.

"I must thank you for your most dedicated efforts in the service of the crown, Char Nefrette, and please, I bid you free and safe passage through these lands," he said loftily, as much for the benefit of the watching peasants, soldiers, and monks as for me.

"Go on, girl, get going," Monk Olan whispered to me as servants ahead of us picked up the gifts, and the knights formed an avenue for me to trudge through. "And we'll have the pony back, too," he hissed, nodding to one of the monks to take the reins. I was past caring about the Monk Olan's capacity for cruelty. Instead, I nodded, slid from the small horse and followed the servants through the avenue of weapons, into a corridor, and then rattling and thumping on what could only be the wide river bridge. Each board was made, it looked, from a split tree-trunk, with iron braces and supports holding them together. It was a wide and a long bridge, and soon myself and the servants were walking alone across the flat and cold river, towards the far side.

"Sister!" There was a shout, and a figure waved two upraised arms at me.

Wurgan. I caught sight of his bright beard and hair as he started to jog across the bridge, his closest warriors beside him. He wore a tight fitting studded-leather suit of armor, lots of strips of cured hide nailed and sown together to form an almost impenetrable shell. *You're taking no chances with our uncle then,* I saw in a weary sort of depression, dismayed at how little love there was between any of our family.

Despite my morose heart, I still managed a wave as he raced up to me, seizing me in his muscle-bound arms and swept me into the air with a fierce hug.

"Brother," I tried.

"You are safe, sister. You will be safe with us now." He was laughing, grinning at his fellow warriors who were holding their rounded shields around us warily, looking across the bridge at the Middle Kingdom soldiers.

"But will I be safe with you?" he joked, looking up warily at the heavy overcast skies above us all, clearly wondering where the dragon was that he had last seen me with not a few short months ago.

"You're remembering the dragon-- Paxala?" I said. "Yes, you will be safe. You were always safe before, you know. Sort of." I pointed out as he set me down again, and ordered his men to take the gifts back to their encampment.

My general brother frowned, making the sign to ward off bad luck with two fingers. "I don't think anyone is ever safe around a dragon, little sister," he said steadily, before nodding back. "Come on, father will be pleased to see you."

"Father is here?" I gasped. That was the last thing that I had expected to happen, as I knew my father to be ever the tactician, and risking his life so near to the frontline between the two Kingdoms could be disastrous.

"Of course, Char," Wurgan said as we walked companionably back to the other side of the river, and into the brightly lit, feasting encampment of the North. There was a line of warriors standing guard with half drawn bows and great axes, but other than that, the camp seemed to be in the midst of a celebration. The smell of roasting meat made me remember just how hungry I was, and just how little the monks ate on a daily basis. 'Good for our moral character' apparently, or so the Abbot had said.

"Yes, father has been worried sick about you down there in that accursed priest's-hill." Wurgan shuddered as he walked through the collections of yurts wooden palisades.

"It's a monastery, Wurgan. A monastery on top of a sacred mountain, not a priest's hill," I said in exasperation.

"Still," my brother pointed out. "It's unnatural, that's what it is."

I doubted very much that my father had even noticed where I was, until it had seemed that the Prince Vincent could use me as a hostage, I thought to myself. My father had a history of not being there as far as I was concerned. He was always out on some campaign or another, or involved in high-level committees, or else trying to entertain either his official wife Odette or his 'mountain wife' (our mother) Galetta. Wurgan had been lucky enough to share in my father's passion for warring and soldiering, and thus also shared his life that way – but me? I was a woman, and therefore, even though it was the northern custom that women could be soldiers and just as proficient as men, my father still thought best that I be married off, schooled just enough to garner such a profitable union for the kingdom.

In other words, my father has always seen me as a liability, I thought sullenly as Wurgan laughed and waved at his fellow captains and henchmen that they had achieved a great victory, in 'rescuing' his sister from 'the clutches of the evil monastery.'

Maybe he was right, I sighed, thinking about the Abbot and Monk Olan back there. They were certainly evil, I thought dismally.

~

"Daughter!" my father said in his clipped and exact way, just as always. He hadn't changed, not seeming to even age, I saw as I greeted him and the audience of his assembled counsellors with a bow.

"Father," I said guardedly.

My father was a tall man. Apart from my other uncle, the prince of the Southern realm Prince Griffith, the sons of Queen Delia had that thin, rangy sort of build to them. Although that was where the similarity between them stopped dead, I thought. My father was a contained and restrained man, but whereas Vincent had jet black hair with a shock of white, my father had short hair, clipped close to the skull. He was the older of the three brothers, and yet he was not the successor to the throne. That was because old Queen Delia – in her apparent wisdom – had chosen to separate the realm into the three kingdoms to save the brothers from murdering each other.

And by the look of the two warbands camped on either side

of Faldin's Bridge, it doesn't seem to have worked at all! I had never met her, the old queen – who was also my grandmother.

He wore, like my brother Wurgan, simple woven leather armor, still with his sword at his side and gloves on his hands. My father was never awake without a weapon to hand, as he had spent long years fighting the more dangerous mountain folk, or else protecting the north from the wild mountain dragons. His counsellors greeted me with cheers and smiles, and I nodded at them; all warriors or ex-fighters from one mountain tower or another.

"Come," my father beckoned me over to the nearest tall iron-work fire holder, where he ordered a clay goblet of mulled wine pushed into my hands. He watched me, his eyes glittering as a hawk as I drank. *Ever the strategist, hey father?* I bit my lip, trying to stop the rising feeling of despair in my heart. *Why did he always make me feel so useless, like I was just a 'foolish girl'?*

"I should say how glad we all are to have you back, safe, from that place," my father breathed, keeping his voice low and soft so that the other counsellors wouldn't hear over their own feasting and loud reveling. Behind us in the tent there were other warriors and messengers moving back and forth, loudly singing the favorite sagas or songs of the north.

Liar, I thought. If you were really happy to see me, you would have hugged me.

"Thank you," I said all the same anyway. "But it wasn't so

bad, really." I hesitated. How much could I tell him about Paxala?

"Perhaps. But we have heard reports. The attack by the Sons of Torvald last season?" my father said lightly.

"It was dealt with," I said.

My father nodded, not saying anything for a moment, before he cleared his throat. "These are strange times, daughter. We stand not a league away from my brother, and yet we cannot even share a cup of mead together. Our armies are at each other's throats, and every month there is another attack by the bandits of Prince Vincent on my territory."

"You know this?" I asked sharply. It was no doubt that there was no love lost between north and middle kingdoms, but to directly accuse them of civil war...?

"These bandits were trained. They operated in units, they knew how to use pikes and bows, and fight my cavalry. Always attacking a town, burning the gates and the storehouses, and then retreating. It is no question." My father gritted his teeth. "That is part of the reason why I needed you here, safe with me....*and* your dragon..." he added the last part delicately, watching me as he said it.

"She's not mine," I said quickly. "The dragon, Paxala..."

"Paxala," my father repeated, tapping his shaved chin as he stored the name for future machinations. "Yes. Your brother said that the dragon came when you called. I was hoping even, that you might bring her with you when you came."

Oh damn! I thought in annoyance, remembering how

Feodor had told me not to share a dragon's name. But he was my father, wasn't he – surely he would have our own best interest at heart…

But maybe not, I considered as I saw my father's calculating gaze as I was sure he must be thinking about Paxala and me. My heart lurched. *I thought you wanted me, safe, just for myself.* "I cannot command her," I said finally. "I'm not even the one who got her to carry a rider, it was Neill…"

"Ah, yes, the Torvald boy. The lesser son of Malos Torvald, correct?" my father said.

I nodded.

"And the dragon would obey *him*?" My father looked into the flame.

I felt a wave of exasperation surge through me, almost making me want to cry. How could he be so callous with me? Could he not even pretend to be a normal father? "No," I said heavily. "Dragon's don't *obey* anyone. They barely even *listen* to anyone. If you were hoping to start your own dragon monastery, then I can't help you I'm afraid, father…"

"Not a monastery, no," my father said, frowning just slightly. "I have no time for mumbling Draconis Order monks and priests, talking about universal oneness or inner flames or whatever that fool Abbot Ansall says. You know me, daughter, I believe in cold, hard steel. I believe in soldiers. I believe in strength, and looking after your own. *That* is why you are here, because now we can look after you, and you can help look after your kingdom," my father said finally. "And I don't

130

much like your tone of voice when you speak to me, young madam."

And who will be left to look after the dragons then, if I do not return to the monastery? I thought in dismay, as my father nodded to Wurgan.

"See that she gets a tent, food, and a guard on her door," he called, and my brother nodded, motioning for two of his most trusted warriors to escort me out. As they did so, my father leaned in to say to me in a low voice.

"I *am* glad you are back, my daughter. But from now on, things will change. Starting with tomorrow, when we will decide who you will be marrying."

What. Marriage was the last thing on my mind. And I couldn't believe it was on my father's mind, with Prince Vincent staring at him across the river. Unless...

"You just brought me here to trade my virginity for an alliance? Is that it, father?"

My father blinked rapidly. "Of course not, Char. But we have to consider these things, especially as the times are so dangerous right now."

Wouldn't that be a good reason *not* to have a marriage ceremony? I thought as my blood started to boil. I knew what he was doing. He was seeking to forge some sort of alliance with my hand in marriage. It made me feel sick.

"No, father, I won't do it." I said resolutely.

"You will, Char," he glowered, settling his shoulders and crossing his arms in that way Wurgan had learned from him. I knew that he would be immovable when he was like this. But then again, so was I.

"I won't. There's nothing that you can do to make me," I said tartly. "And besides, I have to go back to the monastery!" I blurted out as the warriors indicated that I follow them. I ignored them. "I have my dragon still there, and I need to be the one to look after her. How could I ever bring her here if I was miles and leagues away?" I didn't—couldn't—tell father the rest, that I had to get the old queen's crown and deliver it to Zaxx, or else everyone I cared about—I realized the truth of it with a start, that those I loved most were not my father or even my brother or my clan—would die.

My father's eyes narrowed, and I could see that he was considering my idea that I could get a dragon to bring to the north. That would be a powerful tool in his arsenal.

My father made up his mind, however. "There is no reason you cannot return to the monastery at the head of a guard escort, as a wife of one of my clan chiefs, and demand that this dragon of yours be handed over, is there?"

"Well, apart from the fact that Vincent would never let a northern armed escort across his lands—" I started to say, before there was a short, sharp clap from my father, effectively ending the discussion. His warriors stepped forward to either side of me. "Enough of this nonsense, Char. You're staying in the North, now." My father clapped his hands and turned back to the other counsellors and war captains, and I was dismissed. If it hadn't been for these two guards standing right there beside me, I would have run there and then. Not that I wanted to train how to be a Dragon Monk, but I wanted to see my friends Paxala, Neill, and the others. This was a mistake. I realized. Paxala had been right, I should never have come. I was making all of the wrong decisions, I thought miserably. If I hadn't agreed to come, then I wouldn't have tried to sneak into the crater, I wouldn't have been cornered by Zaxx, I wouldn't have his ridiculous threat hanging over my head...

But there was nothing that I could do about that now, I thought. I was trapped here. My father just wanted to use me in his strategies and wars. I felt gutted. Tomorrow, I promised myself, even as my hands shook. I'll make father see sense tomorrow. That he had to let me go. He had to let me return to my friends and to the monastery.

CHAPTER 11
NEILL, GROUNDED

I t should have been easy. That was what I kept telling myself, over and over again for the last two days. I mean, I could ride a horse, and I could ride the little mountain ponies they have on Dragon Mountain – how difficult was riding a dragon going to be? Especially since I'd done it before, without even really meaning to.

Very difficult, it turns out.

"Skreap-pip!" Paxala chirruped once again at me, standing over me as I groaned by the side of the meadow where we had stopped. In fact, where I had begged her to stop. The problem wasn't so much the flying (as all I really did was hold on for dear life), it was more the 'getting Paxala to do anything other than what she wanted' part of it. So far she had flown straight towards Char and the monks several times, but each time I had begged her to at least *try* and stay hidden. Just for now, just

until we had a chance to speak to Char on her own. If we could ever get her alone, my innermost self grumbled. So far, there had never yet been even a moment when Char wasn't accompanied by one of the monks, or now, her father's guards.

I was certain that Char was going to know that we were there. But somehow, despite all the odds, we never saw her little band stop on the road, or look up at the skies. I wondered if Paxala was keeping herself quiet in her mind as part of her strategy to stay hidden, or if maybe the dragon was just too scared to attempt communicating with Char.

"We'll talk to her tonight, I promise," I gasped, my knees feeling like sea-foam as I lurched to my feet, still rubbing the cold water over my face. It was night time, and I reckoned we were only a few hills away from Faldin's Bridge. We had watched from on high as the troops had approached, converging on the river town from afar and looking as though a battle was certain. Paxala had seemed jittery around them, bold and brash, flaring her wings and puffing her neck muscles as though she could challenge them all.

"We have to be quiet, secret," I said again to Paxala, who just cocked her head and looked at me in amazement as if I had gone totally mad. *Maybe this was a stupid idea.* I rolled my shoulders, trying to loosen the stiffness throughout my body. "We're going to have to develop saddles, or harnesses or something if we're going to do this," I said out loud as the dragon preened her leathery wings.

I wasn't even quite sure what 'this' was that we were

going to do at all. *Char told me to get the others ready to bond with dragons,* I remembered our last words, *and that she was going, but would be coming back as soon as she could.* Paxala had been distraught of course, and I had been getting out of the monastery grounds before the crack of dawn and after lessons and had even spent a couple nights with the Crimson Red, sleeping curled up against her warm-as-coals belly to try and let her know that Char being gone wasn't the end of the world.

"Srrip?" the young Red raised her snout and pointed in the direction of the village, on the other side of the trees. We had landed as close as I dared, but now I thought we were too close, and I still didn't quite know what we were going to do when we arrived. Challenge her father for Char? Take Char back to the Draconis Order? I didn't know Prince Lander, but I'd heard from my father that he was a tough man. My father admired him, in a way of traditional enemies.

'We would have been friends, I think,' he had told me once, in his gruff and steady growl. 'He is a strong man, and he looks after his people. The sort of king that the Middle Kingdom deserves.'

But he didn't seem to me to be the sort that would give up his daughter easily to me, a warlord's son, and even to a dragon, no matter how important it is, I thought with a sigh. Char had told me about Zaxx's request, that the bull Gold dragon had wanted the old queen's crown for some reason, and if Char could return with it, she would. Were the legends

136

true then, that the dragon had a hoard down there in the middle of Mount Hammal? That Zaxx the Mighty slept on a bed of gold so vast that it could buy the entire Southern Kingdom, every house, ship, and strip of cloth on every person's back who lived there?

"Then why would he need the old crown as well?" I sighed, shaking my head as I sorted through my things. A few scrolls and some journals Dorf had found for me about the old queen's crown, some food Nan Barrow had packed for me, the short sword, leather cap, and heavy black cloak that marked me as a trainee Draconis Monk. I put the cap and cloak on, vaguely thinking that the plan I'd been certain would materialize on the journey here, never had. The best I could come up with was that I could sneak into Faldin's Bridge, pretending to be some kind of messenger. I picked up one of Dorf's scrolls after I had dressed, reminding myself of how important this quest had to be.

"After her husband's death, the Great Queen Delia decreed that a new crown should be made, a joining of her husband's warlike crown with her own circlet, and that it should be set with mighty gemstones of rare beauty and power, and that her best alchemists, silver and goldsmiths, and seers should all work to make it. The crown took a year and a day to make, with rare gemstones being found from deep in the earth and sought for throughout the lands. Later folktales say that the Grand Crown gave the queen the power to command the

elements and to always rule wisely, such were the powers that it was said to have been blessed by…"

"Well. At least we know what it looks like, huh?" I murmured at Paxala, who was urging me to go and find Char.

The next scroll was even less illuminating.

"Upon her death, the Great Queen Delia's will distributed twenty-seven mansions to her favorite courtiers, her personal flagship was sailed to the Southern Kingdom, where it remained anchored off of Knife Bay for a further ten years, and her dresses were sold, and the monies raised spent on the benefit of the poor of the land. Such was the depth of sadness at her death, that no advisor, seer, or priest could bear to look upon the Great Crown that was the symbol of her wisdom and power, and there are different accounts of what happened to it. Belvedere the Unsteady claims that it was cast into the sea, whereas Athanasius the Small writes that it was stolen by one of her sons, and hidden away until such a time as the kingdoms were unified once more. Although the mystery surrounding the exact whereabouts of the Great Crown of the Great Queen has never been solved, it has perplexed scholars throughout the generations…"

"So, in short it could be anywhere, too," I said out loud. "And Zaxx expects us to find it and bring it back to him, otherwise…"

"Sssskrech!" At the mention of the tyrannical bull dragon's name, Pax suddenly reared and spat a tiny plume of soot.

"Okay, girl, okay. I won't talk about him again. Let's not

think about it, shall we?" I patted her side, glad for the interruption to be honest. The other option was to think about what Zaxx had told Char – that he would kill someone, one of us students, or a young dragon, or Pax herself.

Which is why I had to get Pax out of there, and off of the mountain, I thought, feeling the large Crimson Red's breath start to slow as she calmed herself down.

There was a crunching sound from the very edge of the clearing, out there, in the trees. My heart hammered, even as Paxala swiveled her head and took a deep snuff of the night air. Oh no, we've been discovered, I thought, looking up at the skies above. It was a starry night, which meant that we couldn't escape into the clouds with any ease. We would be seen, and then shot down.

Paxala was making small, shaking movements, her body quivering in anxiety of excitement. I put my hand to my short sword, wondering if I was good enough to face a grown, fully trained knight of the realm – and then I saw it – a dark shape out there, moving through the trees, swathed in heavy clothes. Were we being spied on?

"Srip-ip!" Paxala chirruped at the figure.

"Shhh – we cannot let them know you are here," I urged her, not that she paid any attention to me.

At the mere sound of the mighty dragon, the figure froze in the dark, and then, very slowly, started to trudge straight towards us, and then started to jog, and then run…

"Halt!" I shouted, sliding my weapon from its scabbard

just as the small and shadowed figure broke from the tree line and threw itself straight at the dragon. What was this person doing?

"Pax," a familiar voice said, and I was looking at the pale and overjoyed face of Char as she wrapped her hands around the snout of the much larger Crimson Red, closing her eyes in satisfaction.

"*Schrech!*" Paxala purred at her, nudging her with her forehead to the floor with a not-so-gentle thump, and then playfully patting her fallen sister with one giant paw, as if she had been hunted.

"Char, by the heavens – how did you know we were here?" I whispered. And never mind just that, I thought, how did you sneak away from your father's encampment?

"I had a dream." Char said in a sleepy, cozy voice as she hefted the dragon's paw from her chest with a groan, before jumping to scramble up onto Paxala's shoulder, where she started to scratch around the dragon's ears. I watched, grinning, as Paxala's eyes drooped and threatened to close as, with a groan and a mighty thud, she flopped down to one side (almost dislodging Char perched on her shoulder, but not quite) as she purred at the attention.

Huh. She never did that with me.

"I was in one of my father's tents, not sleeping really, when I dreamed that Paxala was flying out here, above me, and that she was calling to me."

I felt a prickling in my teeth, and that haze of pressure that came whenever the dragon and the girl were sharing thoughts, and I knew that Paxala was talking to her directly.

"She says that she was," Char smiled happily. "But it's harder out here, farther away from each other, and farther away from the Dragon Mountain." A frown crossed her face for a moment. "But I can't leave my father right now. He'll go to war against Prince Vincent..."

"You don't have to!" I said excitedly, picking up my pack where it had tumbled to the floor, and taking out the different scrolls for her to look at.

"Neill, it's pitch black. Even the initiates in the monastery library have candles!" Char grumbled playfully, and, in response Paxala coughed a brief spark of flame, to set alight some fallen branches.

"Pax! You can make fire?" Char looked delighted, once again seizing the dragon around the head and shaking her as if she were a cute dog. "What a clever girl you are," Char baby-talked to her. "How long has she been making fire? I didn't think that she could yet? Dorf told me that she might *never* be able to, as not all dragons could make fire at all." Char was clearly overjoyed at this new development.

I didn't know. If it was some new skill that the Crimson Red had developed since Char had left, this was the first time that I had seen it.

"This is excellent news, because if she is on her way to making fire, then she might just become strong enough to defeat Zaxx..."

"Ssss," the Crimson Red hissed angrily at the sound of the bull dragon's name, and even the night air felt a little colder somehow.

"Never mind that right now," I said hurriedly, not wanting to upset either the dragon or Char. "Look at these." I pointed her through the different passages of the scrolls by the flickering light of the embers. I watched as Char read them all slowly and carefully, moving her hand through the passages until she got to the legends of what happened to the old queen's crown. I watched as her eyes widened, and her face took on a mask of wonder. It was good to see her looking hopeful, although I had no idea why she could be after everything that we had been through both last year and this, but maybe things might be about to go our way after all.

"My father's castle is called the Queen's Keep," Char said. "They said it was because the old queen was the first to build it, way up in the north and the west to keep an eye on the mountain passes."

"You see?" I whispered. "The Great Crown – your own father might have it, look, it says so right here!"

"Or it might be at the bottom of the sea, don't forget," Char pointed out, the shadow of indecision and fear infiltrating her face once again as a cloud crossed the face of the moon. "Or with Prince Griffith, a few thousand leagues to the south."

"Skreych!" chirruped Paxala, and even I didn't need the strange dragon bonding that Char had to understand what she

must have said. The south. We could fly to the south, if we wanted. We now had a dragon, and that meant that we could go anywhere.

"Yes, Paxala, thank you, you are a most brave wyrm," Char congratulated her. "So, it is settled. We will all travel north with my father, and when we get to Queen's Keep we will look for the Great Crown."

"And if we don't find it?" I urged.

"If we don't, then I guess that I will have to find some way of excusing myself, because we will have to fly a few thousand leagues south to Prince Griffith's lands," Char said with a shrug, although there was something in her eye. A hesitancy. Was she scared?

"We can do this, Char. I know it." I smiled at her.

"Yeah, I hope so," Char said, but I could tell that there was something bothering her. It must just be Zaxx's threat, I thought as she continued. "But you two have to stay out of sight, please," Char said urgently as she stroked Paxala's ear. "You don't know what my father is like. He's not mad, or cruel like the Dark Prince, but he's…" Char scowled. "He's cold. Like the mountains. He only looks for the benefit of his kingdom and his people."

"That would make him a good king," I pointed out, echoing exactly what my father had said of the Northern Prince.

"Yes, but a terrible father," Char said. "And if he saw you and Paxala here? Well, he wouldn't see you, Neill, as my friend, but as a Son of Torvald of the Middle Kingdom. He would think about ways to influence you, or capture you, or what it would mean for his power over Prince Vincent. And if he saw Paxala…" Char shook her head sorrowfully. "He wants Paxala for the North. He wants her to fight in his battles for him."

I shook my head in exasperation. It was a whole lot more familiar scenario than even I dared to let on. Hadn't I, myself, been sent to the Draconis Order not on the face of it, to honor some three-kingdom peace treaty, but instead to spy on the monks for my father? Didn't my father look at the world through the power and the threats that each person represented?

"Then we will keep her safe," I agreed. "But we also won't be far away from you. Ever."

"Skreeach!" Paxala agreed, her eyes flashing gold and silver in the night.

CHAPTER 12
WILD

"Hmm. Are you sure?" My brother Wurgan looked at me oddly, and I nodded once again, causing his suspicious frown to only deepen into his ruddy mustache. "Something's changed," my giant of a brother said. "Maybe the good mountain air is doing you good."

"Mount Hammal is also a mountain, you know," I replied, remembering how Sigrid had hated the cold mountain air, but I had claimed it was 'good for us.' I wonder how Sigrid is getting along, I thought with a shiver of apprehension. Neill didn't have time to tell me last night how he had managed to get away from the monastery, or in what state he had left the others. Would Lila the Raider have time to strengthen her bond with the young Blue? Would Maxal continue to help Dorf, Sigrid, and Lila with their studies into the origins of dragon magic? Would the Abbot, or Zaxx, take out his anger with us on them?

"Ah, spoke too soon," Wurgan grumbled in front of me. "There's that frown that I know and love so well," he teased, and I punched him on the shoulder.

"It's fine, Wurgan, get going with you. I can play nice daughter and entertain father's captains and counsellors and all the rest. It makes a change from learning dead languages," I said, wondering if I agreed with myself really or not. The truth was, it *was* a change from being in the monastery. Here, people actually smiled when they saw me coming, and almost a third maybe, of all of my father's troops were also light-haired mountain folk like me. I wasn't looked on as just 'the bastard' or the 'wild woman' or some other such insult. Here, I was Char, daughter of Prince Lander, of the clan of Nefrette. I was a good shot with a bow, and I was good with horses and with dogs. The people of my father's rough court knew me, and I didn't have to prove myself constantly to them. *But that didn't mean I was free.*

I wandered out of the tent behind Wurgan to see the guards standing to attention (not for me though, for my brother, a general in his own right). It was another cold day in Faldin's Bridge, but thankfully, today we were going to be heading north, to Queen's Keep, and leaving the world of barricades and reinforced positions behind.

Our father had left the sizable part of his troops at the bridge, as a brief, grey, and morose little ceremony had been held at first light, halfway across the bridge. Neither my father nor my uncle had been there, but Wurgan had, and he had told me all about it. A hand over of crates of gifts, and that was it. It made me think that all of this posturing on the part of my father was for show. He had just wanted to rattle some sabers to draw attention, to get me to go north with my dragon perhaps, and now that he had what he wanted, he was returning with his 'prize'--me–to his fortress. I felt stupid, and taken for a fool, though at least I had good reason to go the Queen's Keep myself.

"They're over there," Wurgan said. I rolled my eyes, before considering the band of mostly fat men, with a few gaunt and tall women amongst them. All were dressed in great animal pelts of bear, mountain lion, wolf, otter, (black, brown, or white) to signify their clan allegiances, and most had a mixture of robes, cloaks, and smaller furs like snow fox, beaver, or wolf sown into their garments. I recognized a few of the 'difficult' captains and counsellors in my father's court, most particularly Lady Bel of the River Fork and Captain Virk of the Otter Clan. My father needed their warriors and I, with my mixed heritage, would show them how the 'north could unify' as my father was always saying. He had won over the tribes of the wild people with such talk, as I supposed he must have won my own mother's heart.

And I was the result. The perfect union of Northlander and wild clans. Or so he thought.

"Greetings, ladies, gentlemen." I nodded at the assembled,

and elicited just a chorus of murmurs and dark looks. *Wonderful.* I sighed. "Let's get saddled up and start going, shall we?" I said, as there was a shout from across the courtyard. My brother, and most of the hosts of mounted warriors, took to their own steeds and clattered joyously out onto the road. I was stuck with this lot, the phalanxes of a few hundred foot warriors, and my father's own retinue and baggage trains.

It was supposed to be a great honor to be here, in the slow group with my father and these clan leaders but… My eyes sought out the dust on the road from my brother's force. I would much rather be out there, with them.

Or better yet, I would much rather be on the back of Paxala, and flying far above all this. I sighed, but even I was unable to completely dispel the brighter feeling that my brother had noticed in me. He was right, something *had* changed in the night – but it wasn't mountain air. It was the fact that I knew that Paxala and Neill were somewhere very close by, and all of this was just an act. At any moment, I could call on her to pluck me from this boredom.

"And Paxala would, little Char," her voice whispered into my ears, making me chuckle in delight. After having feared that I might never see or hear her mind again, having her so close was a balm to the troubles of my soul.

"Char? I mean – *princess,* do you find something amusing about your old allies?" Lady Bel asked, looking at me oddly. She was a thin, tall woman dressed in blue, with long fair-to-white hair scraped severely back over her head and falling straight as an arrow down the center of her back, and a large black bear pelt flung over her shoulders.

"Lady Bel," I greeted her. I knew her of old, when I was a kid and she would harangue my natural mother (Galetta) on behalf of my stepmother (Odette). She was a lady of the court, and was practically my 'aunt,' seeing how close she was to my step-mother. "Of course not, I was just remembering a friend, that was all."

"This was a friend from the Draconis Order, was it?" Lady Bel raised an eyebrow archly as she settled into the saddle of her pony. "I heard you had become friendly with the Torvald boy there?"

Where did she hear that? I looked at her in alarm, and now it was the Lady Bel's turn to smile as she continued.

"Oh, we all have friends and allies, princess," the woman said mysteriously. "Now, Malos Torvald, the Warden of the East is quite a good match indeed, good tracts of land, the ear of the Middle Kingdom listening to him, but he's no clan captain, is he?" Lady Bel said perfunctorily. "And as for his Sons of Torvald… The rumor has been that two of them are thugs, and the one at the monastery is a milkweed." She laughed, causing a chuckle from some of the other larger men and women around her.

Oh, I see why father wanted me to 'entertain' these people, I thought with despair. They are going to try and tell me how great this marriage idea was, I groaned.

This was going to be a long day indeed.

"So, meditation is thinking about *thinking*?" argued Captain Virk, a small, almost entirely round man who looked very comical on his horse, with a horned helmet and a cloak made of otter pelts. As the Otter Clan chief, he had accepted my father's calls to unify a decade or so ago, and had since moved to the rich lands surrounding Queen's Keep and had made himself very rich. He was an important lynchpin between mountain and kingdom relations

"I suppose so, Captain Virk." I shrugged. How was I supposed to explain what the Abbot's meditation was to someone who only thought deeply about wine vintages? "But it's a bit different. You would have to experience it for yourself to really understand."

So far, the day had been about as interesting as one of the Abbot's theory classes. So boring and slow, it made me want to do was go to sleep (which wouldn't be very noble of me at all).

"And this Abbot... He is a good man, is he?" the Lady Bel asked.

"Good stars, no," I blurted out before I could stop myself. He had tried to sacrifice me to Zaxx the Golden last year, and he had apparently been trying to hypnotize me as well, so that I would use my dragon abilities for his benefit alone. "But they say that he knows the most about dragons, more than anyone else at the monastery combined."

Lady Bel pulled a disgusted face. "It sounds like a sham to me. Just the sort of thing that the Dark Prince," she suddenly looked worried, "Prince Vincent, your uncle, I mean…" I shook my head that it was all right. I didn't care anymore for the Dark Prince than I did for the Abbot. They were both terrible people in my book.

"Anyway…" Lady Bel opened her mouth to speak again, just as a far-off screech split the air. It was an eerie, snarling howl of a call, and one that I knew could belong to only one thing.

"Dragons!" Captain Virk was shouting, immediately looking around for his trusted Otter Guard.

"Paxala?" I reached out with my mind, to be instantly flooded with her fast, excited, and energetic thoughts.

"Dragons! More like me. I smell them. But they are not like me. They are angry. Very angry. They smell like blood and winter and cold…"

"Wild dragons, Paxala. They are dangerous, get yourself away," I thought at her quickly, my hands gripping the reins in anxiousness. "Where are they?" I called out, standing on the stirrups to scan the horizon, many others in our troupe doing the same.

"They are coming. To the West," Paxala's answer breezed into my mind and I twisted to see shapes bounding down the barren rocks of the nearby peaks. Two, three, four maybe. They were long and sinuous like the Blue dragons of the Middle Kingdom, but they were nowhere near the size.

Instead, they held themselves low to the ground, and undulated like a snake, deadly and fast. I stood transfixed at the sight of them as they each in turns took to the air to coil through the air on leathery wings and spiraling midnight-colored bodies, flashing black, purple and blue in the cold northern sun.

They are kind of beautiful, in a way, I thought.

"Pssht! Little fierce dragons," came Paxala's immediate reply, and through our mental connection I sensed her excitement and unease. Distantly, on the far side of her mind I could even sense Neill's worried mutterings and anxious movements, as he sought to calm her down. This connection I had with her still amazed me, every moment. Did this connection only work between me and Paxala or could other people also hear and feel dragons in their heads. Was it even possible to feel *other* dragons' thoughts, like these wild ones?

"Princess, come on – no dawdling!" Lady Bel shouted, reaching to tug on the reins of my horse as she led us away with the other courtiers and captains, heading off the road to where the deep woods sat. It was an old tactic of the north: get underground, and if you can't do that, light fires, and if you cannot get underground or light a fire to keep away the wild dragons, then you will have to get into the woods.

It wouldn't stop them, I knew. Plenty of woods folk had been picked off by a hunting wild dragon in the past, but the trees would slow them, and we Northlanders knew that if you ran fast enough, and put enough obstacles in their way then these wild dragons would eventually give up their hunt for easier prey.

"People! Get to the woods," my father bellowed, drawing forth his long steel hand-and-a-half sword to bark orders at the rest of them.

"I have to stand with him," I cried, trying to fight against the Lady Bel's pulling and the sudden rush of people. I might be the only person in the North who had bonded with *any* dragon. I had even been part-trained at *the* Dragon Monastery, and if I couldn't help my father's people now, in their hour of need, then who could? The wild dragons were boiling across the sky now, getting larger and larger with every passing second.

"You will do no such thing, Princess Char," Lady Bel snapped. "Your father knows the risks of traveling in the open in the north."

Lady Bel was partly right, I thought in alarm. One of the many reasons why the northern kingdom was thought to be so uncouth was that the mountains were either infested with wild dragons or wild folk. You couldn't travel far in numbers like this without drawing the attention of one or the other.

But I couldn't leave him. He was my father, after all. As cold as he was, as horrible as he was, as much as I hated him for the way that he treated me like a tool – he was still my father. I would be a better daughter, and a better woman than one who would just abandon her family when they were in need. It didn't mean that I had to agree with them, just because

I didn't want to see them get ripped apart by dragons. "I have to," I said, allowing the Lady Bel to seize the reins of my pony as I slid from the saddle, and landed with a neat tumble to the floor of the road, my bow at my side, and already running and pressing through the throng of fleeing people.

"Char!" the lady shouted in outrage at my retreating back.

I ducked past the last wave of people who were fleeing into the woods for safety, just in time to see the first wild dragon land on the far side of the road. It came in screaming, landing with a running thud as its claws tore out great hanks of roots and boulders from the grip of the earth. Whereas that fast landing might hurt a larger and heavier dragon, these wild ones just rolled, uncoiled, and coiled again like an angered snake, moving with incredible speed as it finally came to a stop.

"Warriors, steady…" my father was shouting from ahead, clearly visible from where he stood behind a large defensive semicircle of warriors. I ran to his side, already releasing my bow from my shoulder as I did so.

"Char? What in all hell's name are you doing here?" My father barked in anger, sparing me a glance, but he was far too much the soldier to let family annoyance and anger upset his life and death plan. "Well, seeing as you *are* here – did that monastery teach you anything about how to deal with these wild dragons?" he snapped, looking straight on at the curious wild dragon, who was a few hundred meters away, and hissing at the air in our direction.

"Not a lot," I said truthfully, swallowing nervously.

"Excellent," my father cursed through gritted teeth, before raising his voice to shout to his men, "We use fire! Wurgan?" My father called to where my brother was marshalling his worried and almost-panicking horses.

"Wurgan!–Marshal the front ranks to hold them off," he called, and my brother obeyed immediately, sliding from his horse to start barking orders at the assembled warriors and forming them into defensive semicircles around the position of the prince.

"Rear ranks gets pitch, lamp oil, rags, and tinder boxes. Anything you can to make torches and fire pots, understood?" my father directed.

"Aye-aye, sire!" the various sergeants shouted, quickly organizing the men as yet another of the wild dragons screeched and screamed to a landing, this time farther down the roadway from us. We had dragons on two sides, the third could pick to land to our north or between us and the woods. Either way, we would be cut off.

"Char must stay safe! Char must stay safe!" Paxala was almost shrieking in my mind. I felt her stretching her long legs, unfolding her giant leathery wings, readying to pounce…

"No, Pax – don't get involved!" I begged her, shouting out loud and causing my father to shoot me a strange look.

"Pax? Isn't that your dragon, is one of these wild dragons her?" Around us were the sounds of running feet as soldiers quickly started emptying packs, pouring out lamp oil onto rags, and tying them to sticks, spears, even the heads of their weapons.

"No! Of course not, I was just…overexcited," I tried to explain but my father was already distracted by the screeching cry of the third wild dragon, as it landed behind us, between where we were huddled on the roadway, and the courtiers had fled into the trees. We were cut off, and so were they.

"No!" I shouted, as the wild dragon behind us hissed first at us, and then turned and tumbled towards the woods, clacking and grinding its rows of razor sharp teeth.

"Skreeyar! SKREEEYAR" The heavens were split by the sound of trumpeting shrieks as yet another giant shadow eclipsed us all. My father looked up in dismay, but it wasn't dismay that my heart felt. It was a wild and terrible hope. I didn't want Pax to get hurt, I didn't want to see Pax even in danger–but Pax was also my connection to the world of dragons. She might be able to convince these wild beasts to flee.

Swooping over our heads came Paxala the mighty Crimson Red, bigger than the wild mountain dragons, but younger. Her wingspan cast a shadow that covered the road, and each of her talons were the length of a man's sword. Her long neck speared the sun, and from her snout she snarled and gnashed teeth as large as the axes that were carried below her.

CHAPTER 13
MINE

"Paxala!" I shouted once more in alarm, as the Crimson Red swooped low over our heads, causing my father's warriors to duck and shout.

"Char? Is this your doing?" my father was shouting, trying to rally his troops – but I had no time to spare for him, as I broke from my father's side to run towards her.

"Sssss!" There was a loud hissing and a thud, as the wild mountain dragon between us and the forest lashed and thrashed its tail, splitting apart the stone and packed earth of the road in its fury. I stumbled and froze, as all about me warriors fell backwards.

"Mine!" said the Crimson Red's voice in my mind as her shadow fell over me. There was a mighty thump and the ground shook as Paxala landed with her forelegs protectively over me, her wings beating so furiously as to make a hurri-

cane. The Crimson Red was challenging the wild dragon for me, not letting the mountain reptile make any other movement towards me if it wanted to keep its claws.

Where's Neill? I thought looking up above me to Paxala's neck, fully expecting to see my friend hanging on. He was nowhere to be seen – had Paxala flung him off her back in her own attempt to get here the quicker? Oh, by the gods. I swore, slowly setting an arrow to my bow and crouching in the shadow of the red dragon's claws. In front of us the wild hissed and thrashed its tail, but it did not attack – it dared not, as Paxala, as young as she was, was still the larger of the two; and while Paxala stood here, the wild mountain dragon couldn't afford to detract its attention to go after the other humans. I watched as the two started to sway and bob their heads on long necks like serpents, about to strike.

"Paxala, no – please don't fight – you'll get hurt," I pleaded.

"Char fights. Paxala will fight," her words came back to me, laced with anger and aggression. *"Paxala needs to know how to fight, if she is to defeat Zaxx, yes?"* she argued. The terrible thing was that she was right – but how could I convince her not to take on three faster dragons than her? Especially when she had never engaged in dragon combat before?

"Sssss!" The hissing noise of another of the three wild dragons rattled through the air, as the slightly fatter wyrm that had landed on the road reared up suddenly, displaying its

breast and neck sacks before thumping with stocky feet onto the road below. It was challenging Paxala, I knew, and I watched as it started to stalk on heavy, stiff and proud legs towards the dragon we had in front of us.

"Sckrech!" Paxala croaked at it, raising a foot to pay deep furrows into the ground ahead of us. *"Come, look at my claws, brother dragon. Are they not sharp?"* I could hear her jeering and taunting the new arrival.

"Pax…" I said warningly, even as my father's horns could be heard coming towards us. He had managed to rally his soldiers, and was running up the road to join his daughter.

The wild dragons roared and chittered; two in front of us, one on the other side of my father now. I watched the two flickering and lashing their tails. They moved constantly, not like Paxala who was much more catlike – elegant and smooth, choosing precisely when and where to move. No, these wild dragons were like agitated serpents in the way that they coiled through themselves and even each other. They moved light-ning-fast, teeth flashing, claws ripping the ground.

"Pax – I have an idea." I breathed quickly. "They are quicker on the ground, but you have the larger wingspan. If you can out-fly them…"

"Flee? Run? Char wishes me to run?" Paxala said in anger. She was almost in full battle-mode now, I could tell. The muscles of her neck that helped pump whatever gasses or ichors produced her fire were full, and the larger, overlapping

plates around the back of her neck were fraying, angry, and challenging.

"Not run. Fly. We're faster in the air," I said to her, looking at the two dragons ahead of us, and the phalanx of northern soldiers rallying behind. I knew some of those soldiers. I didn't want any of them to get hurt, and I knew also that they wouldn't hold back from the bloodshed. What if their stray axe blows or spear throats found Paxala in the melee? *No. I couldn't allow her to get hurt.*

Thinking quickly, I dropped the arrow, turned and seized Paxala's elbow spike, and pulled myself up to the crook of her shoulder, the wing joint, and settled myself in behind her neck.

"Hsss! Paxala flinched a little in alarm at my sudden movements. She still had a way to go before she could accept humans to ride on her with ease.

But now she will have to, I thought in grim satisfaction, using my knees to squeeze her strong slabs of muscle at the crook of neck and shoulder. "Fly now, Paxala, we'll tire these little wyrms out, we'll show them what a *real* dragon can do!" I congratulated her, knowing that flattery was always the best way to Paxala's heart. She reared up, throwing back her head to roar triumphantly.

"Woah," I had to scramble to seize onto her neck spines and larger scale 'ruff' just to stay on. "But keep me onboard at the same time!" I yelled awkwardly, as Paxala leapt into the air above the wild dragon's lashing forms and into the air. With a flick of her broad and strong tail she whip-slapped the larger one across the snout, causing it to hiss and jump after her, as did its fellow.

Two down. "Yes!" I shouted, punching the air before my mind had a chance to catch up with what the rest of me could see, and my face fell. "Oh no."

I was on a dragon, and we were being chased by two very fast, very ferocious, wild mountain dragons known almost *definitively* for their ability to eviscerate and disembowel their prey.

"Pax...?" I murmured, as the wind whipped my hair around my head and tore the words from my lips. *"Fly!"*

The larger Crimson Red was slower to get up into the higher airs, I saw. Within moments the wild dragons had caught up with Paxala's tail, and were snapping at it with their rows of circular, serrated teeth.

Fly, Pax, fly... My breath caught in my throat; it was chill up here. The ground beneath us had become a green and brown blur, and the only sound that I could hear was the booming and crashing of the wind as it tore around us, and the sudden, bird-like shrieks and hisses of the dragons. My fear was a white-cold thing, as sharp as ice and as quick as lightning. It was beyond apprehension or terror, and somehow made my stomach turn and my jaw clench in a feeling that was close to exhilaration. How could I be excited about being so close to death?

I heard the clash of iron-hard teeth biting nothing but themselves as the Crimson Red once again lashed her tail out at one of their maws. My heart was thudding, as fast as a rainstorm as Paxala rose higher and higher into the air… No time to feel the frost. No time to hesitate as I hunkered lower and closer to the dragon's neck, willing her on with all of my might.

Slowly, with mighty wing-beats we drew away from the smaller dragons. It was simple physics. Paxala had the larger wingspan, so she would be faster. She *had* to be faster. The dragon underneath me surged forward, her wings moving faster and faster as her muscles warmed up and she found new reserves of strength. The two wild dragons fell away and we powered upward, upward, and upward until we broke through a haze of cloud and suddenly it seemed as though we had reached the top of the world.

"By the stars and stones…." I swore, blinking around us.

Paxala flared her wings wide, as the rivers of air currents that we had been fighting through had suddenly stopped. We were gliding over a hazy sea of gold, and white. Clouds that, leagues below had been barely visible as just white mists were, from this great height, a delicate blanket of strange hills and valleys. The sun was bright and higher still in the sky ahead of us, so bright that every time I turned my head in its direction my eyes swam and bright neon aftereffects glared across my vision. I had never seen anything so beautiful as this, just as I had never traveled so high on Paxala before.

Distantly to the West there were lines of shapes breaking the golden cloud-sea. Dark shapes with their own cloud-storms and waves piling up around them.

"The northern mountains," I breathed in awe. They were the gateway to the northern wastes' endless high plains of ice. I turned, blinking, looking at just how far and how clear everything was. I had never dreamed that the world was so big.

"This is all...*beautiful*," I breathed.

"Yes, it is." Paxala agreed, and for one, eternal moment we were locked together in silent awe at this world above the world. This dragon's playground. Our reverie was broken however, when darker shapes burst from the cloud layer below, I saw how their boiling shapes struggled with the thin air. The wild mountain dragons didn't have the wingspan to drag themselves against this windless place. I watched as below them the hazy gold of the cloud shook and rippled as their movements tore at it.

"Shall we?" I asked Paxala, my teeth chattering a little in the high and thin air and cold of the clouds.

In response, the Crimson Red let out a triumphant roar, turning expertly on her gliding wingtip and plummeting straight down, *towards* the two wilder dragons as fast as one of the arrows from my bow. The wind tore at my face and hair as I gripped with my knees and hands and gritted my teeth. My eyes squinted to just the tightest of slits as the wind howled and roared in my ears, rising in pitch as the wild dragons beneath us grew closer and closer…

Paxala folded her wings close to her body the way that a crow does, adding to the insane speed she was reaching as she reached out with her claws-

"Ssckreayar!" she roared as she slashed past them, the speed of her movement knocking them from around her like children's toys, her claws ripping through the heavy leather of wings. The two wild dragons snarled and snapped at her as she flashed past, but they didn't have the time to attack as she was there and gone in a second, and they were tumbling out of the sky.

"Wooohoooo!" I was shouting in enthusiasm, and below me the Crimson Red was also roaring her delight. For one, perfect moment we were no longer the princess and the outcast, or even the girl and dragon – we were one—a fierce hunting creature.

But the feeling dissipated as I saw with horror the greens and browns of the earth rushing towards us faster and faster. The large acres of green became forests, became trees and creeks and small clearings and bothies, just as the browns and greys became roads, fields, roadways, and my father's soldiers—

"Pax!" I screamed, as she unfurled her wings and changed her flight, sending us in a sickeningly fast curve down the roadway, just tens of feet over the head of the remaining wild dragon and the semicircle of my father's troops above it.

Below me, my eyes caught a glimpse of bodies lying on the floor, of thick blood here and there from the battle. It was hard to defeat just one wild dragon in battle, but my father's soldiers were well-trained, and had managed to drive it away from the road.

At the sudden darting flight of Paxala, however, and the confused and pained hoots and whistles of its fellows, the wild dragon took fright, bellowing and snarling at the few spear men who chased it, turning and tumbling through its coils as it jumped away from us, away from the road, and away from the battle.

"Yes, flee little dragon. These are my humans." Paxala flared her wings to slow her down, turning in an arc around the battlefield, and seeming to get ready to chase the dragons again.

"No, please, Paxala, don't," I begged her. We had won the day mostly out of surprise and luck, but I couldn't say how we would fare on *their* home territory, and possibly with other wild dragons nearby. "I couldn't," I said, feeling a little queasy. "Please, set me down – I am not used to such flying as you are." I made excuses, causing a pulse of amusement from the dragon beneath me.

"Then we shall have to train you, little Char, how to accompany a dragon when she is a-hunting." The idea seemed to amuse the dragon to no end, as I had been telling her that *they* needed to learn how to be ridden by humans for so long, when in reality it was all the other way around.

"Yes," I agreed, holding on to her scales as Paxala took another lazy circuit of her victorious battlefield, before making a big show of landing with large beats of her wings (which appeared entirely unnecessary to my eyes). *Show off.*

"My daughter, what a beast she is, what a magnificent, brave, and fierce creature," my father was congratulating us. Flattery, I thought. It comes so naturally to him. Not concern. Not asking how I was.

I slid unsteadily from Paxala's shoulders, to the crook of her front leg, and then climbed down to her ankle, and then staggered onto the ground.

My father was clapping his hands as he walked up to greet me, but his eyes were on Paxala above, admiring her curves, her muscles, and her strength. "Did you know that she was here? Or maybe she followed you? Does she come when you call?" My father was saying in wonder, only half interested in the answers as he beamed, finally, at me in particular. "She will make such a wonderful addition to the northern armies. Just look how she dispensed with those wild dragons! Imagine what she could do if we mounted some steel halberds on those claws of hers. Or blades on her tail," he marveled. Around us, soldiers warily picked themselves up and similarly looked in awe at the fighting dragon in front of them.

"And why not? Am I not strong? Am I not impressive?" Paxala crowed in my mind, holding her wings out in a half-fan.

Ugh, I thought. Great, all I needed was a pompous, arrogant show-off for a dragon friend. I would have found the whole situation funny, were it not for the look of delight on my father's face. He wanted her as some sort of war machine, like a cart or a catapult or a prize stallion. Not for herself.

"She'll not fight for you, father," I said quickly, trying to sound as fierce as the dragon was beside us.

"No, but she will fight for *you*, won't she, my princess?" my father said, not in a cruel way, but in that calculating tone that I knew meant that he was thinking about maps and tokens and strategies. I snorted in disgust, shaking my head at my father's ignorance.

"It doesn't work like that father, it *won't* work like that." I said heavily. Besides, this dragon and I had other things to do, not stay out here in the north – no matter how beautiful it was. My heart thought of Lila and her young Blue dragon, of my friend Sigrid, of little Maxal Ganna and Dorf and all of the other dragons in the crater. It was seeing the Mount Hammal from way up there above the clouds, seeing how it was so close in dragon terms, and also so big in human terms. It was the most important thing in all of this; I had a rare moment of insight.

The Three Kingdoms will rise and fall, but the dragons and the Dragon Mountain will still be there, I knew. We humans and dragons need to learn how to live together. No matter how many wars went on around us…

"We'll see about that, my daughter," father was saying, as Paxala sensed my unease and snuffed at the air over my head.

"Shall we fly away home now, Char? I left Neill in a tree not far away," she asked, and I was sorely tempted to say yes, but in order to do that I would also needed to be able to bring the old queen's crown to Zaxx. That was the deal that I had struck, and I knew instinctively that to break a contract with a dragon would have dire consequences indeed.

"No," I shook my head. *"Not yet, anyway."*

At that, Paxala leapt into the airs over our head, and, with a victorious squawk, she flapped lazily to the edges of the forests.

"Where is she going? Where is the dragon going?" my father asked, irritation lacing his words.

"Like I said earlier, father. You cannot order a dragon to do anything. No one commands them but themselves."

"Hm." My father stood on the roadside and looked calculatingly at the sight of the disappearing Crimson Red, and I didn't wish to know just what schemes and plans he was hatching, before he ordered the bodies buried and the rest of the caravan of people to assemble and resume our journey. Another day in the north, another skirmish.

CHAPTER 14
THE QUEEN'S KEEP

My father's keep was one of the great wonders of the Northern Kingdom. No need for gatehouses or guard towers, as the entire building was a dark and imposing tower, with deep crenulations across its top. Its ten stories rose high above the village clustered at its feet like one of those fairy tale giants that my mother used to scare me with stories about. Made from a heavy, pitted sort of black-red granite that was foreign to these hills, there had long been controversy over how the old queen had got the rock here to build the fortress.

It had taken us a day of careful trudging to get this far, with my brother Wurgan and his mounted troops clearing the road ahead of us of any impediments, merchants, wagons, or bandits. Now that we were finally here, it felt strange to be seeing the place of my birth once more.

"Good to be home, is it?" Wurgan said at my side, and I could only shrug in my seat. Actually, I was surprised at how little I reacted to seeing this place again, I thought, but I still nodded and gave him a wan smile.

I guess that it *did* feel good in a little way, to smell the same old smell of charcoal and roasting meat, with that hint of fresh pine and cedar sap that seemed omnipresent up here in the Northern Kingdom.

But it wasn't flying, I thought.

In fact, the entire keep seemed the antithesis of that freedom that I had experienced above the clouds. I had to find the old queen's crown, and once I had ensured the safety of my friends—then I would think about freedom.

I stared at the keep again, wondering if the secret to its construction was the Great Crown. Maybe the queen just conjured the rocks up here with nothing but her mind, I thought, scoffing only slightly. After all, I had seen— had been a part of— the Abbot's Draconis Mages in-training, and had helped him summon a mighty storm to drive away the Sons of Torvald when they had laid siege to the Order Monastery. If the Abbot could do that, who knows what the old queen could have done?

"Brother?" I asked Wurgan as we rode at a sedate pace (giving the people time to see the triumphant return of the daughter of Prince Lander, I suppose).

"Yes, sister?" he said, his face lowered in thought as we rose up through the gates and the packed-dirt streets beyond.

"Do you know anything about father's keep? Queen's Keep?" I asked lightly. "Being away from it has made me kind of look at it again in a new light."

"Huh? More impressive than the monastery, you mean?" Wurgan chuckled. "Not much. Father doesn't even use the half of it, but has it locked off."

"Really, why not use it?" I asked.

"Oh, he claims he doesn't have the guards, but every boy and girl in the town here would willingly give up anything to work in the keep as a prince's guard." Wurgan sighed, as if this matter had long been a bone of contention between the two of them. There was much I didn't know of what had been happening here in the north, in my home while I had been away.

"So, you mean to say that he just doesn't *want* to use parts of the keep?" I asked him. "It just seems a bit odd to me, that's all."

"You're telling me." Wurgan laughed. "We're on the verge of war with the Middle Kingdom, and we need every guard and soldier training that we can, and we could store weapons and armor, or stockpile food if we might need it, or run classes for the new recruits. It's better to be overprepared, as our father *used* to say."

I nodded. It was one of the many little sayings and quotes my father had handed out as if they were sweets when I was a child.

Not that they were ever particularly meant for me, I

thought, remembering how my father would let me learn horse riding or tracking or hunting along with Wurgan, but whenever I wanted to learn any of the more exciting skills: swordfighting or archery or close combat, then I would have to sneak off to my mother's people rather than to him or any of his guards.

Even so, the clans only ever let me learn how to use a bow, in case they angered my father. I sighed.

"Oh," my brother said gravely.

"What?" I frowned at him as we crossed the main plaza of the town, heading up through streets lined with houses, the old style thatched and wood-chipped long houses of the north, giving way to the stone and white-lime render style of the Middle Kingdom the closer we got to the Queen's Keep itself. I wondered what father thought of this new 'comfortable' trend of the south creeping up here to the north.

"Well, you may have been away to the south, living amongst Middle Kingdomers and learning monkish ways, but I still know when my sister is upset," Wurgan said. "I know that Father is difficult and that he has always been protective of you. But here's my advice, if you will hear it: let the past be the past, Char. Try to get on with Father as your own woman now. You will find that he's changed."

"He hasn't seemed it so far," I said. "Did you know that he was getting Lady Bel and the others to help arrange my marriage?"

"Ah." My older brother had the decency to look ashamed, at least.

"What? You pig!" I punched, hard, in the shoulder. "Why didn't you tell me? You know that's never going to happen, right? I won't be sold off like some prize piece of cattle, just because my father wills it."

All I wanted was to be back up there, flying on Pax. The memory of that freedom – as terrifying as it was to be in a fight with the wild dragons at the same time – was all that was keeping me civil right now.

How is Paxala doing? Where are they right now? How is Neill? I thought as we moved forward.

Our procession had crossed to the main gates which had been drawn back: a metal portcullis was winched up and locked in place, and double wooden doors had been pulled open to reveal the large cobbled entrance hall. We dismounted before going inside, Wurgan looking worriedly at the others around us.

"Keep your caterwauling to yourself, sister. You don't want the others thinking that there's trouble in the family," he said casually as he patted the horse.

"There bloody well is going to be trouble in his family, if you all expect me to marry some fat chieftain from the village!" I shouted, causing a tut from Lady Bel and a few amused chortles from some of the door guards.

"Sister!" Wurgan hissed in alarm. "Have you even met Tobin Tar yet?"

Tobin. So that was the name of the one they all wanted me to marry, was it? "No," I said, throwing off my cloak and thumping it into the waiting hands of a gate guard come to help (and to eavesdrop I imagine on what will be some prime gossip back in the mess hall). "And, quite frankly, brother mine? I don't want to either!" I said in a huff, turning to smartly walk around the guard and towards the doors into the inner rooms of the keep.

"Lady Nefrette!" one of the guards was saying, not one that I recognized, a look of urgent panic on his face. "You still have your weapon belt, lady, your father has planned a feast and a display…."

"I know where my old rooms are, thanks," I said tartly, ignoring his frantic looks as I ignored his advice and kept my weapons belt and my long boots on. If I was supposed to be a princess of this kingdom – even a bastard one – then I would have to start acting like it, I thought. And that meant that no one got to tell me what to wear – or whom to marry.

I was fuming as I followed my memories through the keep, up the stairs to a different gallery that overlooked an interior hall, past a row of gated-doors that had been sealed off with locks, and past some more guards to the area of the Queen's Keep where the royal rooms were. The tapestries got finer, the hallways grew a little grander, and even the guards seemed a bit sharper as they nodded, bowed, or saluted me as I stormed past.

"Char...?" said a voice from behind me, as a figure emerged from one of the royal rooms.

My heart did that little tumble that it did whenever I flew on Paxala, and somewhere, either far above me or in the depths of my mind I heard a chirrup of dragon call as Paxala shared my emotion. "Mother?" I said, turning to see my mother, the mountain-wife of Prince Lander; Galette Nefrette.

My mother wasn't a tall woman like my father's 'official' Northlander wife Odette. She also wasn't as thin-limbed as the scraped and pinched woman who shared my father's throne. She was small in the way that many of the mountain folk were, and she had hair that was the lightest blonde so as to be almost white (my platinum white was a little stronger than hers). She had a smattering of freckles across her face, and large, deep brown eyes that regarded me kindly. "Little Hawk," she murmured her baby name for me, and I found that I had crossed the intervening space and she was enfolding me with her strong arms.

She smelled of mountain heather and a touch of cedar – just like always, and, if her strong limbs, used to climbing and hunting and riding had become a little softer in the two years that I had been away, it only made her the warmer to me.

She wore a deep blue and green gown, which I knew that she must hate, as she had always preferred the sturdy breeches, jerkins and boots of the mountain folk, but she was also always good at fitting into court customs when she needed to.

"I'm so glad to see you," I said, my heart thumping in my chest. I had been worried that my mother wouldn't even be here, as she spent half of her time up in the mountains with her own people.

"There, now." My mother shushed me as we broke our embrace, and we regarded each other in that examining way people do when they haven't seen each other for a long time. "You'll have me crying – and we can't have that, can we?" my mother said, one of her easy smiles appearing over her features. My mother was always easy to get on with, everyone said so – even the more 'civilized' Northlanders.

"Mother – there is so much to tell you," I began, but my mother shook her head quickly. One abrupt nod that cut off my talking.

"We'll get to that later. Much later," she said, a hint of gravity to her voice. "I just wanted a moment to greet you as a mother *should* greet her child, before the court takes over."

The court. Ah yes, with her words, the thoughts of my impending marriage slammed home, upsetting my previous good mood. My mother must have seen my face drop, as she said quickly, "Now, Char... I know you have a temper on you – as my father said I had the same, if you would believe." She lowered her voice confidentially. "But at least take this advice: Take no decision, make no judgments of what you see and hear here, not yet. Not until the excitement of your dragon dies down."

What did she mean by that? I thought. *That I shouldn't*

marry Tobin Tar, or that I shouldn't speak out against it?
"Mother?" I started to ask, but once again she cut me off.

"These are trying times," she said. "Trying for everyone. Your father is trying his best to repel your uncle, and there is a lot of unrest. Just try to keep your own counsel, for the moment…" She gave me an encouraging smile, but it made me feel a little upset and annoyed. *Was my mother chiding me, straight away, the first time that I saw her?* I thought, as there was a sound of shuffling and another figure appeared in the corridor. A guard wearing heavy leathers.

"Greetings, daughter," my mother said more formally, and inclined her head. "It is so pleasing to have you here at last. Maybe one day soon we will go up into the mountains again."

"I hope so," I answered, feeling even more troubled as my mother took her leave, returning to her room and the guard, and leaving me to go the rest of the way to my old rooms.

Let's just hope that it isn't *my* rooms that father decided to block off as well, I thought, angry at my brother and my father both, but not angry enough so that I wasn't thinking about the mission I had to fulfill.

Father had sealed off parts of the keep. Could they be the same parts of the keep that might hide the Queen's crown?

My old suite was just as I had left it almost four years ago. The door was stiff, but the guard at the door dutifully unlocked it for me, as I walked into my stone rooms in the rear corner of the keep, with views of the mountains and the wilds beyond. They were three large, separate rooms: a bedroom, a lounge, and a study with all my old furniture and wall hangings. The black bear rug on the floor with its almost cute gawky snarl was still there, as was the old wooden writing desk where I had carefully graffitied arrows, mountains, and dragons. The rooms looked large compared to the tiny stone dormitory I shared with Sigrid at the monastery but they also strangely looked small to my eyes; as if all of the chairs, wardrobes and desks were now a size too small for me. As I looked at the hanging by the side of the small fireplace, a tapestry of a fantastical castle with long towers and with a sky whose clouds were perfect round blobs, it seemed to me childish and stupid. The world wasn't like that. Princesses might live in castles, but castles were boring places where you were married off to some warrior with a bit of a noble name. The world out there, outside the tapestry, had far better, exciting things like dragons and adventure.

With a kick and a shove I managed to barge open the lounge's large wooden shutters to reveal the old stone balcony on the far side. The breeze was cold as the high mountain airs washed off the ice plains and ravines above down and into the room – but it felt good at the same time, it reminded me of the air, and of being free as I breathed in deep.

CHAPTER 15
NEILL, ON THE OUTSIDE

"I know, Pax, I know…" I said wearily, looking down at the black square building that stood in the center of the town below. We were standing on a small escarpment that overlooked the town, with wooded hills on either side, and a thin trickle of a river that meandered towards a river gate below. Beneath us was spread out Queen's Keep and Lander's estate-town, with smoke rising from the rooftops, and the distant sounds of people calling and shouting as they went about their daily business.

The Crimson Red chirruped in a huffy sort of way. I didn't need to be connected to her mind in order to know that she was annoyed at having to be stuck out here with me, when she would much rather be with Char, wherever she was.

"Well, you and me both, Pax." I sighed wearily, kicking my heels on the dry ground. Paxala had picked me up from my tree perch where she had left me, heaving and huffing with exhilaration, so pleased with herself that it had been almost impossible to be angry with her. Still, I wish she wouldn't take it upon herself to fly off to Char's aid like that, without me.

"I know that you are a dragon, Pax, and a very mighty one at that," I nodded in her direction (and from her perch on the rocks I heard an answering, appreciative purr) "but you really do have to learn how to collaborate if we are ever to beat Zaxx," I informed her.

"Hsss!" the Crimson red made a rattling, annoyed sound and lashed her tail (breaking a small pine sapling behind her).

"It's true, Pax, I mean it," I lectured, knowing that she was probably not even going to spend a blind bit of difference, but that didn't stop me. "I know you just want to defend Char, but we have to work together," I said carefully. If there was one thing that I had learned from my father and my older brothers, then it was that you needed allies in order to win a campaign. You couldn't send one man into a battle alone, and we can't send one dragon to defeat Zaxx.

"Skreck-ayar…" Paxala said dismissively, before suddenly hissing over our shoulder, behind us.

There was a sound of cracking branches, and out of the trees stepped a man with wiry grey and white hair and beard, with skin as tanned as old oak. He wore the studded leathers of a guard and in his hand he carried a short bow, but he held it in front of him uselessly at the sight of the gigantic Crimson Red dragon perched on the rock behind him.

"Uh…" the man said in a thick, guttural accent. "You have to work together to do what?" He squinted at me, and then at the dragon. I saw from his clothes that he must be some kind of scout, as he wore soft moccasin shoes, and hanging from his belt and around his back were a myriad of small pelts and pouches.

"We mean you no harm," I said hurriedly.

"Of course you don't." the man growled. "The prince sent me looking for that big red there, to see if I could track down where the princess was keeping it. It turns out that it's not the only thing that the princess has been keeping hidden, right?" He squinted at me suspiciously.

"You're from Prince Lander?" I asked incredulously.

"'Course." The tracker nodded, relaxing his bow and moving to open one of his pouches. "We've been tracking the movements of that there red all morning now. The prince is going to be glad of this, he wanted to invite the dragon to the keep, you see, instead of being out here all alone…" I watched as he pulled out a bright orange and yellow stretch of cloth, before tying it to the end of his bow and stepping out from under the tree cover, and waving it high. In answer, saw the flashes of color all along the tree line from what must be other scouts.

Oh no. I felt some trepidation, as I had known, obviously, that Paxala had revealed her existence to Prince Lander, but from the scout's reaction it seemed that Char hadn't told her father about me. How was the prince of the Northern Kingdom going to react to one of the Sons of Torvald skulking around his town?

I am Char's friend. He will have to see that… I bit my lower lip and summoned a bit of courage. *I am here for her, not for the prince.*

"Now uh, you two aren't going to be causing us any trouble, are you?" he said a little carefully, eyeing Paxala.

"Well, I imagine that she'll just do whatever she wants to do, to be fair." I nodded at Pax, which caused the scout to grimace. "But I'll try to put in a good word for you, you know, in case she gets peckish."

Paxala spat a tiny puff of flame into the air, as if to say that she would be very happy to eat anyone who tried to hurt her. The scout backed away, waiting for the others of his colleagues to arrive.

"Well, Pax." I sighed under my breath. "It looks like you got your wish, and we're going to the keep after all."

"Look at the size of it!" I heard one of the townsfolk say as we walked through Lander's town to the gates.

It? She's not an it! I thought angrily, casting a scowl at the merchant, who didn't notice, being much more interested in what the giant Crimson Red dragon was doing beside me. A ripple of gasps and awed voices followed us as villagers opened windows and doors to gaze on the dragon entering their town.

"Now, Paxala, these people don't know about dragons," I tried to tell her, as she stalked through the streets.

"We do," said the scout ahead of us, "only the dragons that we all know about are the wild mountain ones, and none of them would ever get within a league of the Queen's Keep without getting shot out of the sky…"

Paxala growled in response.

"It's okay, Pax, he means that the wild dragons are like, well, they are a bit more like Zaxx. Violent and savage. As you have reason to know," I pointed out, but the Crimson Red was already paying more attention to other things. Namely, the fish stall.

"No, Pax, wait…" I tried to say, just as there was a scream from the people around us as the Crimson Red suddenly launched herself at the fish stall, exploding wood and ripping the simple tarpaulin cover, but also covering herself with fresh river fish.

"Ah, sorry," I said to the owner of the stall, who seemed to shrug in a bewildered way. "It's really is a great compliment, that a dragon thinks the contents of your stall are worth eating," I said, hoping Prince Lander had some means for compensating the fishmonger.

It took me a considerable amount of time to get the dragon to resume our procession through the town, during which time the streets filled with more people (many of whom made the sign to ward off bad luck, I saw). But eventually, we managed to get all of the way up to the Queen's Keep, where a line of the prince's guard stood on one side of the gate while on the other side was a line of warriors who looked a lot more like the scout. Char said that her mother's people were wild mountain folk, I thought, noticing how they had rougher, homespun clothes as well as large animal pelts on their backs.

In the center stood the thin, rugged form of Prince Lander himself, wearing deep blue. I sank to my knee, but Paxala just cocked her head.

"Mighty dragon, my name is Prince Lander, ruler of the Northern Kingdom," he said in a loud voice. "I welcome you to my home, and bid you to have everything you desire here!"

In response, the dragon just turned her head to one side, as if wondering what on earth the human was saying.

Not what, why, I thought, raising my head as a shadow crossed in front of me.

"Neill of Torvald, you, too, are welcome here," the prince said with a brittle smile and much cooler tone, I noted.

"Thank you, my prince." I nodded, rising at his gesture.

"Tell me, Neill, can you communicate with the dragon as well?" he asked me with bright eyes.

Immediately my stomach filled with ice. He wasn't as scary or as threatening as Prince Vincent of the Middle Kingdom, but there was something here that I didn't like. Something that reminded me of my brothers: harsh, and warlike (but not as loud or boisterous).

I shook my head. "No, sire," I said. "But she sometimes listens to people…"

"I see." The prince nodded. "Well, we have prepared a space for her on the very top of the keep, where there is room enough to land and to sleep and to sprawl or whatever else she might like to do. I have ordered wood and straw and sand and barrels of meat and water to be taken up there for her pleasure. Will that suffice, do you think?"

"You'd have better luck with fish," said a voice from the gates behind, as emerging from the keep came a figure that I didn't recognize, or hardly at all.

"Char?" I said in confusion, seeing not the young, light-haired girl who had always worn a utility belt under her black monks' robes, but instead a young princess, dressed in a blue and purple short riding jacket, above a voluminous powder blue skirt that swelled out from her hips as if she were a giant mushroom. "Oh my gosh." I tried to stop the grin from invading the lower part of my face (and failed, utterly).

"Don't you dare laugh," she hissed at me, striding forward to Paxala, who was making small leaping motions with her front feet before excitedly bumping the princess to the floor.

"Daughter?" The Prince of the North looked alarmed, but Char was laughing as she got up, her powder blue skirt now smudged with dirt as she caught a hold of the dragon's wide snout and gave her a playful wrestle.

The dragon purred loudly, and that appeared to be that, as the dragon accepted where she was as comfortably as if she had always been here. Within a few moments, the Crimson Red had enough of the adoring (and frightened) crowd of onlookers, and jumped into the air to circle the keep once, before alighting high up there on the roof and disappearing from view. After a moment, I heard scraping and the distant sounds of chirrups and calls as she settled herself in.

"Marvelous," Prince Lander was saying, looking up to the top of his keep with a look that could only be described as a gloat.

"Come on," Char whispered at me, nodding that I was to follow her inside. "I'll show you around," she said heavily, and I knew what she meant--that we had to get on with why we were really here.

CHAPTER 16
OBLIGATIONS

W atching Neill try to navigate his way through my father's court and the Queen's Keep was like watching one of my father's horses learn how to hold a knight for the first time. I had never been to the Eastern Marches of the Middle Kingdom, but I guessed now that they did not have the same finery or elaborate courts as the prince's kingdoms did at all. Neill was skittish and wary of those around him, even of those courtiers who would suddenly appear, offering him wine of food.

"Why?" I heard him ask one of the courtiers on the first night that he was there. My father had decided to call a 'dragon feast' in honor of 'his' dragon, and of course every clan chief and captain of the guard had been invited.

"Because you might be thirsty, young sir?" I overheard the courtier say with a smirk.

"No, I understand why I might want to drink," I heard Torvald say hotly, turning red as he must have felt embarrassed. "What I mean is, why are *you* offering me a drink? Can't I get my own?"

"Ah, that is not uh, that is not how we do things here…" The courtier frowned, just as I waltzed in to rescue Neill from further upset.

"Neill!" I smiled, taking his arm and pulling him away. He gladly hurried with me across the marble checkerboard floor, pulling at the tight-fitting blue and red jacket that they had put him in.

"I still don't know why I can't wear my traveling clothes," he grumbled. "They were much more comfortable – not that I'm not grateful to your father for the gift of course…" he said apologetically.

"Because you're meeting most of the nobility of the north here," I said in exasperation, even as I secretly shared his sentiments. My dresses had gotten more elaborate seams, and the fashion of the court itself had become closer to the Middle Kingdom decadence of Prince Vincent. *This is how he wages war with us, by making our people want the things that he has,* I thought, knowing that it was my mother's voice that I was recalling.

"You see those over there, in the furs and the sturdier clothes?" I nodded to a gaggle of people who stood around the great hearth, quaffing wine, singing songs, or otherwise arguing about things. Torvald nodded.

"They're representatives of my mother's people. The mountain folk. There are loads of clans--literally hundreds--up in the mountains, but these are the ones allied to my father, and most of that is because he took my mother as his mistress," I explained to him, before leading him around the grand hall.

The Grand Hall of the Queen's Keep was only one of a few such halls, but this was the longest so most feasts happened here. It was also where my father had his throne, with two slightly smaller thrones on either side of him (one for Odette, my stepmother and the other for Galetta, my mother). The fact that the two women got on at all was a mystery to most, and Neill seemed no exception as he looked in alarm at the two 'queens.' Odette was thin like my father, but older, with hair that fell in dark curls around a pale face. Her frame was thin--nothing at all like my shorter, rounder, and thoroughly more pleasant mother, the red and white frizzy-haired Galette. The two women were engaged deep in conversation over the empty middle thrown of my father, so I decided to leave them.

"They're not queens, though." I explained the situation to Neill. "But everyone calls them that. Odette couldn't have children, so she allowed my father, as is the mountain way, to take another wife."

Neill was nodding in confusion, reaching up to scratch at his scruffy hair and almost unbalancing one of the smoke censers in the room. "Oh, sorry," he said after seizing the large marble and bronze thing and, with several clangs, getting it to finally stop wobbling. It was clear to anyone that he was out of place – even when compared with the mountain clan people. The warlords, it seemed, were far more used to feasting and games of strength then they were of people singing sagas, poets, and fine clothes.

I guess that is why they are warlords, and my father's people are nobles, I thought in despair.

"Woah." Neill was looking around the upper galleries of the hall, seeing the tall, vaulted doorways that led to still more corridors and halls and banqueting rooms. The pillars that held up the balconies and galleries were carved with elaborate decorations, and the walls were hung with tapestries and mounted suits of armor. "And I thought that the Draconis Monastery was impressive," he said with a sigh, and I thumped him in the shoulder.

"It's not *that* rich. We don't have any statues, walled gardens or anything. Just wait until you see Prince Griffith's court, or Prince Vincent's." I laughed. "We Northlanders are considered pretty tame by comparison."

"Comparison to what?" Neill said, and I decided that it was probably for the best if I *didn't* answer 'well, *you* warlord families,' but he must have known. I suddenly felt very aware of how rich all of this was compared to the everyday people of the Three Kingdoms, and even to the sort of life that a successful warlord's son like Neill must have grown up in.

I was lucky. And yet, I bit my lip at the opulence, the

waste, the hollow laughter even here, in the rugged, harsher north, what I wouldn't give to be out there, flying high above the clouds again!

"I found something out," I whispered to Neill, telling him what my brother Wurgan had told me about parts of the Queen's Keep being sealed off by my father.

"Do you remember what it was like before leaving for the monastery?" Neill scratched at his collar once more. "What was in those rooms that are now sealed off? And what your father might be hiding in there?"

"I remember the keep of course, but I only ever saw the parts where I was allowed to go, as a daughter of a prince. I was young when I was sent off for the Order. Remember, it was a few years ago – and I always tried to spend more time with my mother's people anyway. But I do remember one thing… Where my father's old throne room was." I nodded to the three thrones that we had just walked past. "They never used to be here. This here used to be a throne room especially for the prince, which I guess could have been so old as to have been originally here, for the old queen herself," I said.

I had taken a walk around the keep just yesterday, trying to find any hiding places that my father could have used to stash the Great Crown of the Queen (if indeed, he was the brother to have it!) There were large areas of the keep where the heavy wooden doors remained locked, or even had been bricked up, all 'because the prince didn't have enough guards' as the excuse went.

"Well, the old throne room is one of those areas that are locked, *and* so is the stairwell to the old vaults, where my father is supposed to store the kingdom's gold," I said.

"Sounds as good a place as any to start looking for a crown!" Neill nodded, his eyes running to the doors. "Which way? Where are we headed?"

"We can't go now," I said in alarm, thinking of the eyes that were already on us, the princess and the oaf of a warlord's son.

"Char, we *have* to," Neill said in exasperation. "Just think of Lila, Sigrid and the others back at the monastery – think of the hatchlings in the crater. They are depending on us."

"Of course I know that," I whispered back. *Had he thought that I had forgotten?* "But we cannot go right now, everyone will see!" Did he really think that I didn't care at all about the others on Dragon Mountain?

"I hope that you're not planning something terrible with that dragon of yours?" said a man's voice from behind us, and we spun around to see none other than Lady Bel accompanied by a younger officer– a tall man at least a few years older than me, but what struck me first about him was that his lower jaw had been smashed--an old battle injury perhaps?—which also made him lisp terribly.

"Lady Nefrette, this is Captain Tobin Tar, whom I told you about?" the Lady Bel said through narrowed eyes. "The Princess Odette decided that it was about time that you two met," she said with a brittle smile, before looking severely at

Neill beside me. "Young master Torvald, can I interest you in a tour of the keep with me?" she asked, and even Neill, for all of his uncouth ways had the sense not to refuse a lady's request at a noble court.

But that left me with this man, Tobin Tar. The more I looked at him, the more I saw that he was grotesque in many ways. His arms appeared too spindly to even hold a sword, but even more, his hands appeared deformed with the fingers on his right hand crumpled and awkward. I hated to think it, but I felt horrified at his injuries: an animal reaction, perhaps, to seeing such devastation in another creature.

Char! You should be ashamed of yourself! I thought guiltily. His hair had fled from the front part of his head, leaving the longer locks to fall behind his ears in greasy strings, and I could not help but notice his eyes were bright and inquisitive as they regarded me, and he wore fine clothes of sensible deep greens and golds.

"Please, forgive me," (which I heard as *pleesh, fore-giff me* through the lisp of his broken lower jaw). "I know I am a fright to look at, especially for one so young as yourself." He made an awkward, shrugging movement.

"No, of course not, Sir Tar," I said quickly, wondering if my face had betrayed my horror. *Was this the man that my parents wanted me to marry?* Almost as soon as I had thought it, I felt a wave of shame. Why was I so shallow? There was nothing wrong with this man, only his physical form – and wasn't one of my best friends in the form of a dragon? *Did it only take a few nights back in my old life to suddenly become shallow and arrogant?* It reminded me of Prince Vincent on the few times that I had seen him–how he had seemed obsessed with his and his followers' appearances. I would not be anything like him.

"It was a hunting accident as a child," Tar said, waving his crooked hand in front of his crooked face. "I thought that I could chase down the boar, but the boar had other thoughts in mind! She leapt a creek I had not seen, causing me to fall in it, and leaving me in this state that you see now." Tar again made one of his awkward shrugs. "I thought that my life was over, until I realized that it wasn't."

I had to quell a momentary shiver of revulsion as he took my elbow in a perfectly courtier fashion, gliding me as effort-lessly as if he were handsomely formed across the marble floors.

"The Tars are a very successful clan now, princess," the man said, not in a boastful way, but merely as a statement of fact. "Our territories comprise almost the entire tracts of the Wisewood, down to the Tarl river, and up to the edge of the Fang Mountain."

I raised my eyebrows. That *was* a lot, in comparison to any of the other clans. Most of the mountain folk only controlled their own little mountain valley, or perhaps even just a trail and the few dotted settlements that it connected. But the Tars had managed to hold a large swathe of the low-lying areas around the mountains it seemed, making them, in effect, warlords.

But not as powerful as the Torvalds of the Middle Kingdom, I thought, hating myself as I even had started to think like my father. Why was he and Odette convinced that I would be better off living up here and marrying Tobin Tar, when at least if I were friends with Torvald, then we would have powerful allies in the Middle Kingdom?

"Your father is a good prince, Lady Char," Tobin said, scratching his chin. "If you are concerned about me trying to take his place, or usurp him…"

"No!" I said quickly, wondering how on earth I was going to get out of this one. "Of course not, Captain Tar, it's just…."

I watched as the expression on Tobin Tar's face, if anything, managed to get worse as he murmured. "Oh, I do beg your pardon, please, forgive me. Your father hasn't told you, has he?"

What now? I thought in dismay. "He hasn't told me what?"

"About the proposal?" Tar said awkwardly. "I was led to believe by your stepmother and the prince that, were I to offer my proposal for marriage, that they would be delighted to join the Tar Clan to their family." Tobin pulled an annoyed face, but I could tell that he wasn't annoyed at me, but at my family.

"I, uh, I am honored Captain Tar, it is just that…" I started to say, aware of how many eyes were glaring at me (some in hope, others in reproach).

"No, do not answer me now, princess," Tar said. "I will not

force you into a marriage or into answering a proposal at such short notice. I was led to believe that you knew of this, and even that you were looking forward to your life outside of the monastery here, with me!" he said through slurred lips.

"I'm sorry, Captain, but this is the first that I have heard of it," I said. Technically, it wasn't true, I thought with a grimace, as I had heard of the proposal just yesterday morning – but still… One day was hardly enough to wrap my mind around the idea of marriage, let alone consider the person who was offering it.

"Well, Lady Bel told me that you had been informed a year ago as to the Tar Clan's proposal," Tobin said slowly, attempting to smile but unable to hide his dismay.

A year? I thought. My stepmother and her band of cronies have been planning to marry me off for over a year now? I felt a sudden flash of white-hot anger. How dare they make such decisions about my life without consulting me? But then again, wasn't that always what they were doing? It hadn't been *my* idea to go to the Draconis Order so many years ago, it had been my father's.

Or had Odette been behind that one, as well? I thought in alarm. Maybe she wanted me out of the way so that she could concentrate on controlling all of my father's affections and power?

No. I curtseyed at the dismayed lord before me. I must be being paranoid, because my father never paid any attention to me anyway, and regarded me as little more than a playing piece on a chess set.

Only, I am now one with a dragon. I suddenly had a thought about how to smooth over his hurt feelings.

"Captain Tar, the problem is not of your doing, or of Lady Bel's-- it's just the situation has changed beyond all of our vision right now. I have found out that I am a dragon friend, and now I have her, the Crimson Red, to think about," not to mention all of the others, I thought but didn't say. "I'm not free to choose or accept any suitor without consulting my dragon-sister," I said, surprising myself as I said it. Paxala sometimes called me sister, and it had just fallen from my lips, as natural as stating that I had hair. It felt *right* as well somehow – the same way that when Monk Feodor called me a dragon friend, it had felt *right*.

"Oh, yes, of course, I understand completely," Tar said with a nod. I could see that he didn't believe me at all, but that he was willing to believe my excuse as long as it saved him from the hurt and embarrassment of being publicly rejected. "And then I shall leave you to consult with your dragon." Tar bowed his head sagely, and I felt as if I had only just managed to dodge an arrow. But Tar had something to tell his own courtiers and clan, and I had a little time. Not a lot, I thought as I looked up to see Lady Bel standing by the side of my step-mother's throne, both women glaring at me. How long did I have before they found out that I had (temporarily) refused Tar?

"Char?" It was Wurgan, arriving at my side, dressed not in his fineries, but instead in his battle armor. There was a stir of voices around him, as he clearly had a long ax and sword hanging at his side in the Great Hall where it was forbidden.

"Wurgan? What is it? What is wrong?" I said.

"It's the raiders again. They've attacked westward along the river from Faldin's Bridge, and father thinks that it has to be the Dark Prince's forces in disguise."

"Vincent was stationed at Faldin's Bridge when we came through there." I nodded. If it were his forces that were behind the raids, then it would make sense that the Dark Prince would take advantage of having so many of his soldiers there at once to keep them up.

"How bad is it?" I asked of him.

"Some of our southern farms. Livestock stolen or slaughtered in the fields," Wurgan growled. "That is why father isn't here at the dragon's feast – but he wanted to ask if we could take the dragon. Root out the raiders, and put the fear of the heavens into any of Prince Vincent's troops that might be thinking about crossing our borders!" Wurgan grinned.

"I, no...!" I said in alarmed amazement. *How could he ask this of me? Why was everyone trying to get me to do things that I didn't want to do?* "I've already told father that being a dragon friend doesn't work the way that he thinks it does. It doesn't mean that Paxala is just another beast of burden, for me to send out into battle! No – we barely know how even to ride her yet!" My voice rose high enough to earn some worried glances from the other courtiers around us.

"Well, father guessed that you would say something like that," Wurgan said darkly, "and that is why he is up on the top of the keep above us right now, trying to persuade your dragon to fight for us." Wurgan shook his head at our father's stubbornness. "That is why I am here, Char. I am here to *warn* you that if that dragon eats or hurts our father – well, then even *I* won't be able to stop the Northern Kingdom baying for its blood."

All of the blood drained from my face. "Father is seeking to what, employ Pax? On her own? Without even approaching me?"

I clenched my teeth in a grimace that made even my larger, warlike brother take a step back as I demanded, "Which is the quickest route to the battlements? Now, Wurgan – before father goes and insults a very young and temperamental Crimson Red dragon!" I stamped my foot.

It was just my father's style, to go behind my back and arrange things about my life without even talking to me. I'd had enough. Any illusions I had that we might be able to bring the dragons out here from Dragon Mountain, maybe start again far away from Zaxx, were now shattered. Even up here in the Northern Kingdom, things were still terrible. My father wanted a war, just the same as the Middle Kingdom and presumably the Southern Kingdom wanted. When were they ever going to learn?

Wurgan was nodding toward the nearest servant's door. "Follow me," he said, turning as servants and courtiers scattered out from our running feet.

～

Wurgan took the narrow steps three at a time, holding his weapons to his hip to avoid them from banging against the stone walls of the narrow stairwell. I could not be so fleet of foot, as I had to hike up my red ballooning dress to my knees in order to run. After we had crossed the second flight of stairs I paused to discard the ridiculous white heeled slippers Odette had wanted me to wear for tonight, and instead ran bare foot-- much faster than I ever could have in that strange footwear.

When did the northern court become like this? I wondered. When did it become more important who married who and what you wore, rather than what we said to each other and what we felt? It seemed that the decadent ways of the Middle Kingdom court, and of Prince Vincent, had infected all the realms, spreading like a poison through the top tiers of society, making everyone miserable underneath it.

This is not like my father, I considered as we ran past a third flight of stairs, panting and gasping for air.

"Odette," I wheezed, as we passed another bricked up doorway on a landing and kept on going up and up.

"What was that, sister?" Wurgan said above me, slowing

down as even his legs must be starting to feel the exhaustion of our madcap running.

"It's Odette," I repeated. "She's the one behind all of this." I pulled a face. "These masks. These fine clothes and balls and arranged marriages…" I had never really trusted my step-mother. Maybe that is a natural feeling for a stepdaughter to have, but now I wondered whether she was a baleful influence on my father, and the realm around him.

Wurgan said nothing to confirm this – but also nothing to deny it either. "Here." Wurgan reached the final narrow wooden door, thumping it open with his shoulder to let in a sudden blast of chill mountain air. It was fresh up on top of the keep, and we emerged onto the wide, flat flagstones marked with grasses and mosses and little else. The battlements were high with small stairs leading to walkways where once they would have been manned, but now stood empty. The only shapes in the entire plaza-like area of the roof were the large oak casks of salted and fresh fish, as well as the stacks and piles of straw and deadwood, a prince, and the dragon.

"Pax?" I said briefly, looking at how she was standing with her head held high over my father, who was imploring her to investigate the fish.

The Crimson Red made an annoyed *churring* sound, which I knew was the dragon equivalent of *tsking* or clicking a tongue. *"Little prince wants me to fight."* Her words came into my mind with sudden fierce anger. She was riled and annoyed, and was caught between whether she should take to the skies, or roar at him.

"No, please don't do that," I said, stepping forward across the battlements towards her. "It is okay, father just doesn't understand the ways of dragons…" I pointed out, but father, ever the astute strategist turned to look at me sharply.

"You can speak to her, can't you?" he demanded, his voice sharp, and his blue eyes cold. I squirmed, wondering if I could lie and say that I could read the dragon's body movements, but it was no use. "It's true, isn't it? You have a way of talking to her with your mind?" Father's eyes were lighting up in a glee that I found faintly disturbing.

"Char?" Even Wurgan was looking at me oddly, as if I had suddenly managed to grow horns. "Is this true?"

"Yes," I said, wondering what this would mean. No one knew that I had this connection to Pax other than Neill. "Yes, I can communicate with Paxala with my mind, in my thoughts," I said, looking at both of the men with uncertainty.

"I had thought it a legend," father said, his voice full of excitement. "This is excellent news, excellent!"

"It is?" I said awkwardly.

"Of course! Then you can be my Dragon Commander! You will be able to call to the dragons of the Middle Kingdom to come here, to leave the monastery, and no longer be held hanging over our heads as a threat!" My father was delighted. "You will be able to call the wild dragons, to get them to stop their ravages upon our people, and that will free up our guards and armies from fighting on two fronts...."

It was too much, I held my hands to my ears and shook my head. "No, no! It doesn't work like that, father, even if I wanted to – which I don't. I didn't come here just to be used by you!" I shouted.

"The little prince wants to be like the Abbot," Paxala growled, and I could only agree with her assessment.

"So, you are telling me that you will not ask your dragon to fight for me, to defend our kingdom with your brother Wurgan here?" my father said in a colder, flat tone of voice, the tone he reserved only for the gravest of violations of his code. "You do know that we are being attacked, every day, all along the coasts? Our people are dying, daughter."

I stared at my father, knowing that he was seeing me for the first time. I was no longer the little girl who he could order here and there on his giant chessboard of loyalties and threats. No, he would have to see me as I really was, for what I was.

And I was not the sort of person to send my friends so easily into war. Not unless our lives were threatened, or the lives of those we loved. There was every reason to assume that this was an overtly *strategical* skirmish between my Uncle Vincent and my father. It didn't need to happen, and any lives lost on either side would only exacerbate into a full-blown civil war. At least, that was my thinking at the moment. "No. I will not send or ask Paxala to fight for you," I said. "And that is that. You will just have to accept that about me, father."

I looked at him, and my father stared back at me incredulously. But then his eyes narrowed, and his mouth pursed. "I see," he said. "Then, if you will not become my Dragon Commander, you will have to marry Captain Tobin Tar, and secure his troops for my realm." He said this carefully, all trace of his earlier excitement and glee faded, replaced with cold calculation. "You will have to be of use here, Char, or else you will just be another bastard in the line of succession."

I opened and closed my mouth, stunned by my father's callous attitude as he turned and stalked past us both, leaving the dragon and the fish on top of the battlements.

"Wurgan, come with me. You have to ride out to confront the raiders immediately," he commanded, not turning to see if my older brother obeyed him or not. Wurgan looked at me, his face alarmed and his eyes full of reproach.

"Brother?" I said cautiously, unable to keep the hurt from my voice, but Wurgan just shook his head, his eyes wide as if he couldn't even see me anymore, but that I had become something else; a freak, a monster. He had spent most of his adult life fighting the wild mountain dragons and the people of the south. Now that he knew that his very own sister can communicate with at least one dragon – what did that do to him? Did he hate me now?

My father hates me now, for sure, I thought as the door clanged behind both of them, leaving me with my dragon on the cold rooftop, but probably because I refused to do what he told me, to let him use me, anymore.

"Oh Pax," I muttered. "What have I done?" Waves of self-pity rose up in me.

"You have become yourself. Do not be sad for that, little Char," my dragon purred gently in my thoughts in a surprisingly wise way, as she took slow steps towards me, heavily lying herself down, and coiling around me in a wall of scaled tail and legs until I was held in her warm and loving embrace.

"We should leave this place," Paxala nudged at my mind after I had stopped crying. How I felt at this very moment, I wasn't so sure that she was wrong.

CHAPTER 17
BLOOD AND BONES

"Neill, wake up!" I whispered as loud as I dared. It was night, and there was no way I wanted to alert the guard just at the end of the corridor to what I was doing. There were enough bad rumors flying around already about the returned bastard daughter of Prince Lander, without adding to them how she was caught trying to sneak into the Torvald boy's room.

But that was precisely what I was doing. I shook my head as I tapped on the door with my fingertips once again. "Neill. Torvald. Move your lazy behind," I hissed once again through the door, just as there was a muffled thump and a movement from the other side.

"Char? Am I glad to see you…" the boy opened the door a crack to reveal that he was already dressed, with his dark cloak wrapped around his shoulders and his short sword strapped to his belt. As for me, I was dressed in the functional clothes that I had arrived in (breeches, jerkins, and cloak) as all of the others that Odette had seen to leave for me were ridiculous ball gowns.

"You're up?" I said, a little surprised. I was expecting after the 'dragon feast' of last night that he would be hard to rouse.

"I have been for hours, wondering how to contact you," he said with a grimace, slowly closing the door behind him. "I couldn't wait any longer, not after what you told me about the vaults, and the old throne room, and then I heard the other servants and guests talking about attacks on the border, and your marriage to some clansman captain."

"Tobin," I said heavily, sensing a slight amount of awkwardness in the air around the subject. "The man from the feast last night. But don't worry – I'm not going to marry him. Another remarkable idea of my stepmother's I think."

"Oh." Neill nodded, following me as I indicated the direction that we had to go in to get to the hidden rooms. I could tell that something was bothering him.

"Out with it, Torvald. What is it? What's bothering you?" I asked, ducking back to the side of a hanging as we heard footsteps of the guards or servants slowly pacing the halls. It was after the middle of the night, but sometime before dawn, or at least I *thought* it was. The quietest part of the night, with only those awake who had work to do, or had no business being up and about – like us.

"It's just…" Neill whispered beside me in a voice that was

as low as a mouse's squeak. "I've never had this life you've had." He nodded at the giant and ornate tapestry, the flagstone floors, the wide corridors. "I'm not jealous, but I don't see why you would want to give it up. Maybe you *should* marry that Tobin guy..." he said, shrugging a little.

"You don't believe that," I said.

"No, I don't," Neill agreed. "But it's different for me. My brothers will never accept me anyway; I don't have a prince for a father. I can do whatever I like, in a way..."

"My father won't accept me, either," I said and then told Neill about the earlier altercation on the roof, and how my father had wanted to call Paxala off to war, and about how he seemed to want to start a new dragon training regime up here, in the north. I remembered how Wurgan, my own brother had looked at me with anger and fear on his face when he realized that I would choose the dragon over the kingdom, and could even hear dragons in my head. "We can't bring the dragons here because this isn't their home, and Zaxx would only follow them and destroy everything," I said. "And I would choose Paxala and my friends a hundred times over rather than marrying Tobin Tar," I said. It was clear to me now: my friends, Paxala– they had stayed with me through thick and thin. Neill had reached out to me at the monastery when I was still regarded as 'just a girl' and an anathema to the monastery, and a child of the mountains as well. My friends didn't like me for what marriage potential I had, or whose daughter I was. Paxala wasn't trying to use me to get anything other than fish, whereas I felt that if I started on this road of choosing kingdom over my friends, then I might never have any real friends again. I would be caught, lonely and isolated, with everyone only wanting to use me for their own agendas.

The footsteps at the end of the corridor paused, scuffed, and stopped. We froze, and I dared to peek from the tapestry to see two black-booted feet coming towards us.

"Excuse me," a voice slurred, and I realized that the voice and the feet coming towards us didn't belong to a servant or a guard, but instead belonged to no one other than Captain Tar himself.

Oh crap. I thought. Had he heard what I'd just said about marrying him?

"You might as well come out, I know that you are there, Char, Neill. I heard you," he lisped, pausing briefly.

The game was up. I had failed, I thought. What would father do now? Probably banish Neill. Lock me in my room. I stepped from behind the tapestry to see the mangled and ruined face of the clan's captain standing there, looking at me with the hang-dog eyes of a kicked puppy.

"Tobin, please forgive me," I hissed quickly. "I didn't mean it like that…"

"I understand." Tobin screwed up one side of his face in an approximation of a defeated grin. "I came to try and find the Torvald boy anyway, to ask him what his intentions were for you."

"My intentions?" Neill turned a bright beetroot, stammering as he looked frantically between Tobin and me. "I, I…"

"Tobin," I said quickly. "It is not what you think. We are involved in something that is so important, mightily important." I had enough of people looking at me like I had let them all down, or like I was a freak just as my brother had. I would no longer hide or lie or pretend to be someone's little girl or potential wife or anything else. I would just be me, and that meant that I had to be honest.

I told him. Not all of the information, granted, but enough for it to matter. About how I could communicate with Pax through my mind, and how the Draconis Order were not what they seemed. They farmed dragons, and they only barely had any sort of control over Zaxx the Golden, who killed whomever he wanted to.

Tobin Tar looked at us both for a long time. "So, you are telling me that you are doing all of this for your friend, the dragon up there, and the friends you left behind at the monastery?"

"Yes." I nodded, and Neill did the same beside me.

"And that Crimson Red is like you, an outcast from its nest?" Tobin said quietly – not really a question as he looked at the floor, and muttered. "I understand what that feels like. My own parents thought I was a weakling after the accident, and I know what it is like to always be pushed out, to be ignored, and to be feared." He raised his head to look directly at me. "For what it is worth, Char Nefrette – I never loved you. I didn't know you, but I was willing to go through with this marriage for the sake of the kingdom. Now I know that you are here to save a friend, another outsider like ourselves, then I will help. The Tar Clan will continue to support the prince because that is what we always do – but I see no need to marry myself to a young woman who doesn't want to marry me," he said with a lopsided grin, and the tension dissolved. I felt a wave of relief wash over me, as I knew that we could indeed be friends.

"And Tobin, I want you to know that I believe you to be a good man, and one worthy of marrying a princess," I said, and watched as he smiled.

"Come, Princess Char," Tobin said. "You and the Son of Torvald here have work to do, and I will say, if anyone asks, that I saw you riding north and away into the mountains. That should at least give you a day or two to make your escape."

"Thank you, Tobin," I said, and Neill echoed my words as we rushed past him, towards the steps that I had taken just earlier that day.

"He is a good man," Neill said when we had the chance to stop, and I nodded.

"Yes. We might need allies like him before this is over," I thought, finding the narrow stairwell that had taken me to the roof, but instead of climbing upward, I chose down. Something had occurred to me just this evening – that this stairwell seemed to be a shortcut used by my father and brother, and that might mean that it led to areas which had not been blocked off yet. I explained my thinking to Neill behind me as we crept through the keep. "And there might be a way to get to the old Throne Room from there. I seem to remember a small audience chamber that my father never used, saying that there wasn't enough light in there..."

As our steps descended, the air grew a little staler and dustier, but not cold. I wondered if we were near to the vast fires of the kitchens or the bath houses, as the walls felt vaguely warm.

"Blood! I smell blood." Paxala's thoughts suddenly burst into my mind, and I stumbled against the wall.

"Char? What is it?" Neill whispered from right beside me.

"It's Pax. She's saying that she can smell blood somehow, somewhere..." I paused, trying to collect my thoughts. When a dragon suddenly thinks *at* you and you are unprepared, it is a little like having a whirlwind piling through your home.

"Blood!"

"Where?" I breathed in the dark, wishing that I had thought to bring torches with me.

"You. Through you. Through that lump in the middle of your face you call a nose," the dragon scolded me.

Could she use my senses? I felt vaguely alarmed by the idea, until I remembered that was exactly what I could do with her thoughts, after all. Was our bond growing stronger, now? Were we becoming closer and closer in our thoughts some-how? There was so much that we still didn't know about the old legends of 'dragon friends' and the sorts of powers that they had, but it seemed to me that bits of the lore were coming true.

"So, Paxala can smell blood through my senses…?" I said out loud.

"It makes sense, she has a much better nose than humans." Neill said.

I relaxed, taking a deep breath and allowing the dragon that sat inside my mind to sense the environment around me. It was strange, like having her here beside me, but at the same time invisible.

"There," she said, and as I turned into the direction that she had been talking about, I could smell something acrid and bitter, but also spiced with something sooty and sharp, like cinnamon.

"What is that?" I murmured. If it was blood, then it wasn't any blood that I recognized.

"Dragon blood," Paxala said with a growl, and through our connection I could feel that she was shaking her wings out in frustration and agitation.

Yes. It was dragon blood, but old, ancient dragon blood, long since dried – and it was seeping out from one of the landing doors. "Down there." I indicated the door for Neill to try and open, but it wouldn't budge.

"Wait," Neill said, taking out his short sword and wedging it between the hinges and the doorframe. "Now stand back," he said, before throwing himself at the door. There was a loud thud, and a creak. It sounded deafening to me, and still the door hadn't budged. I watched as he limped back, rubbing his shoulder, and readjusted the wedged sword before trying again. On the third try the wood around one of the hinges splintered and sheared off, and the door sagged outwards towards us, revealing the smell of dust to my normal nose, but the strong smell of blood and decay to the dragon's senses I was connected to.

"What is this?" Paxala was starting to growl, I could tell that she was snuffing at the flagstones and battlements far above me, starting to scrabble at them.

"Easy, Pax, I don't know what this is, but whatever it is – I think it happened a long time ago," I said, taking a step forward past the ruined door to suddenly find myself bathed in an eerie bluish light.

"Earthstars!" Neill breathed in awe, and I could see that he was right. These rare crystals were the stuff of king's vaults and legends, and just a handful of them could probably buy a house – here, the shards of faintly glowing blue crystal were set into the walls on either side of the narrow and low passageway that extended down into the keep. "Where are we, Char?" Neill breathed, tapping at the blue stones that always glowed in the dark.

"I don't know," I confided, drawing my long knife to walk forward. "From my old memories of the keep when I was a child, I had thought that this would lead the way to the old throne room, but I think that we have gone past it, to underneath the old queen's throne room maybe. I've never been

214

down here before – I didn't even know that we owned any of these earthstar stones at all!"

"It must be a part of the old queen's residence when she built this keep," Neill said, trying to remove his short-sword from the door but failing. It was wedged tight. "Ah well. You'll have to do the fighting from now on, Char," he tried to joke, but the thought made me nervous. Neill was by far the better fighter than I was, so I quietly passed him my knife, and followed my nose.

The dragon's senses led us in the only direction that the corridor also took us, straight to a round, circular chamber with a line of the bluish glowing earthstar crystals set in the walls around the room.

"What is this place?" Neill breathed beside me.

"I don't know," I said, "But it looks pretty bad to me."

In fact, to me it looked like the little chapel spaces in the Draconis Order monastery – a rounded sort of hexagonal room whose walls rose like a tube to a point, all made of solid brick-work. Only instead of those walls having stained glass windows as they would in the monastery, here they were studded with the blue crystals that provided the only light in the room, pouring down to fill a narrow space with an eerie glow. In the center of the room, intricately carved flagstones merged on a slab of stone that was almost chest high and stained with blood. But that wasn't all.

"Uhm, Char?" Neill had walked around the stone and

suddenly frozen, looking at the other side of the strange slab of blood-rock.

I don't want to know what this is, I thought, taking a step around it to see there, a collection of long stones, each about as thick as my arm, with curious organic sort of curves and bumps on them. Beside them were chipped fragments of smaller stones – only they weren't stones at all.

"Oh no," I breathed. They were teeth, sharp dragon teeth about as long as my fingers, meaning that they were from a dragon that was younger even than Paxala above. *And that means that these other stones weren't stones at all...* I picked the nearest one up, hefted it in my hands to see it clearer in the blue light. They weren't stones but bones. Bones that were so old that they had calcified, becoming pale and rocklike in the way that ancient seashells at the beech also do.

"How old are they?" Neill breathed in horror, reaching down to pick up one of the dragon's teeth as I did the same. They were still sharp as a pin after all of these years.

"I don't know," I said. "But I think that they are older than you and me, older than even my father up there."

"The old queen." Neill breathed, and I nodded in the glow. He was right. These must belong to the old queen when she had built this place, and had even lived here for a little while. Or else they might have belonged to someone who worked for the queen, an advisor or a personal seer or...

A monk, I thought in horror. "Neill? What was it those scrolls said about the Great Crown, again?" I asked lightly.

Pleased for the distraction from this horrible sight as Neill rummaged around in his small carry-sack for the scroll fragments, which he read out.

"There. That bit. That the old queen asked for the rarest gems and metals to be mined, and then asked for the wisest of seers and priests to help her forge the Great Crown," I indicated. "Wasn't the Draconis Order around then as well? Wouldn't they be some of the wisest of priests and seers?" I asked of the room. "And wouldn't *they* be the only ones with access to young dragon bones?"

"What are trying to say, Char?" I could see Neill's wide eyes as he looked at me. "That the Draconis Order somehow did this?" I could hear in his voice that he didn't want to believe it, but he also knew that it was the truth. It had to be.

"I don't know, Neill," I said. "Either they were the ones who killed a young dragon here, or maybe not – but I am betting that they knew about it. Maybe the Draconis Order doesn't do this anymore, but this is how they started. And we heard the Abbot arguing with Zaxx over which dragon he wanted to die in the crater. What if this is all a part of the same thing…?" I said, feeling my own bones shiver at just how terrible and appalling it was. A deep and cold certainty settled in my heart.

"Neill? We don't only have to get the other hatchlings out of the crater--we have to save all of the dragons. We have to put a stop to the Draconis Order itself," I said, watching as Neill nudged the bones out of the way.

Neill looked at the small dragon bones in our hands. "Yes, I think you are right," he said gravely. A terrible quiet settled on his shoulders, and I realized that he was *furious.* I had seen Neill angry before of course, but this time it was a cold, quiet anger that I had not expected to see in him, usually. *But yes, it is right to be angry about this,* I thought. *It is right to be furious about what the Order have been doing to dragons.*

"Look," Neill said, pointing to the flagstone underneath them, at the foot of the alter stone. What had been hidden by the bones was now visible. On the flagstone was a carving of a flame over a circle… *A crown?*

"Hang on a minute." I knelt down to run my hand along the groove of the flagstone. Why was only this one carved, unlike any of the rest? "Neill – have you got that knife there?" I asked, as he saw what I had in mind and he leaned down to start prizing at the stone with the tip of my dagger. It was easier than I thought that it would be, as the groove around this carved stone was subtly wider than any of the other perfectly matching stones. Very carefully, with the aid of the knife and our fingertips we managed to scrape out the dust and dirt (*and who knows what else,* I couldn't stop from thinking) and the carved stone started to wiggle under our hands.

"Okay, 1, 2, 3…" We carefully lifted it up, fraction of an inch by fraction, raising it higher and higher until Neill could get a hand under one corner and we were creaking it from its bed, to reveal a hollow in the mortar and rock beneath.

"Char…?" Neill was whispering at what lay in the hollow.

It looked to be just a wrap of rubbish. A deep, mahogany leather binding rolled around and around itself in a wide sort of loaf of bread size. It was too small for a dragon skull, even a hatchling.

There was only one thing that it could be. I reached down into the hole to brush the fabric. It was slightly greasy, as it had been oiled or soaked in preserving fluids. You only did that with metal, I thought, as I lifted the object out to find that it was surprisingly heavy in my hands.

"Now what?" I looked at Neill, who was looking at me in wonder and alarm in equal measure. I knew what the object *could* be but for some reason I didn't even want to open it to find out. It was all too terrible. If this place belonged to the Old Queen Delia of the Three Kingdoms, before she split them off to give each to her sons, then there was a good chance that she herself had put this here, or had been in this room of dried dragon's blood and bones herself. She was still, despite the long and strange years that she had lived, technically my grandmother on my father's side, and my father himself was her son, the Prince of the Northern Realm. Didn't that make all of this my legacy, this terrible, horrible family secret was finally coming home to roost.

I flipped over the top flap of leather to reveal a round of metal. In fact, there were *two* rounds of metal, one over the other, with the larger 'inner' round being gold, and the outer band steel or silver. The crown was very heavy, and had fluting peaks at the front and the sides, ornately carved into tiny forms of arching dragons. At its front was a giant ruddy ruby the size of my fist, and two very faint blue earthstars on either side, that brightened as I brought them out into the glowing light of their brethren.

The Great Crown of the Three Kingdoms. We had found it.

~

For a long moment, we both just crouched there, staring at it, unable to believe our eyes.

"Char," Neill pointed to what else had been wrapped up in the rags with the Great Crown. Fragments of a book; cracked brown leather stitched onto thin pieces of board, with cobweb-thin pages moldering inside. I almost *didn't* want to open it. With all of these bones and blood soaked into the stone, what-ever was in that tiny grimoire couldn't be good. But I knew that I had to open it. We had to know what was the nature of the great crime that had been perpetrated by the Order, if we were ever going to address it. I carefully raised the book from its covering and gingerly pulled it open.

"Careful!" Neill said urgently, as half of the spine fell away. The book had already lost most of its pages to time, and even as I tried to leaf through what remained, more of them tore and curled, dissolving into fragments.

"Dammit," I swore, stopping my examination of the docu-ment at the only patch of surviving sheaths of yellowed and stained paper. "There's writing on it," I murmured, trying to work out the thin trails of the black spidery writing. It was dense, and filled the page like some species of spreading lichen. The only breaks visible were the ones left for strange symbols, carefully inked in, but now having lost all of their color and vibrancy.

Was that the crown? Or just another circle? "They look like some of the symbols that we were studying with the Abbot," I whispered.

"Do you think that it was written by the old queen herself?" Neill said.

"I don't know." It felt spooky to hold it in my hands, wondering if it had belonged to the very woman who had ordered this place built. "There – I can just make out…" Some of the words were intelligible, written in the same tongue as we read and wrote nowadays, but with stranger, dialect words. I attempted to read the passage out loud.

"Tayke the mightiest of the dracos, but none (Higher? Older? Younger?) *than three summers. The broode matriarch should be calmed, and the King of Dracos should be appeased… Gather the bloode of the chosen dracos, and…"*

A shiver ran over my body. Did that really just say what I thought it did? I looked over at Neill for confirmation, and yes, he had heard the gruesome practice. I couldn't stand it, I could feel the anger mixing in my belly with a deep disgust. I forced myself to read to the last legible word of the passage.

"…the bloode should be poured, sunwise, over the chapel stone, and the bones of the creature pounded until they crack,

and ground until fine. Thys powder will prevent disease and maintain health, and the correct meditations in the dracos-blessed chapel will inspire visions, and magyckal powers..."

"By the stars." I closed the book, my hands shaking as I did so. "They killed the baby dragons, and somehow they used their bodies and blood to power their magic. What monsters were they?"

What sort of monsters *are* they? I added silently. This had to be the secret that the Abbott was hiding. "The Order used dragon blood, and baby dragon bones, to power their magic."

"I heard the Abbot negotiating with Zaxx over which younger dragon he would be allowed to kill, that night in the cave by the side of the Dragon Monastery," Neill breathed, blanched in horror. "I managed to tell myself it was something to do with the Order being curators or guardians. I never in my wildest nightmares imagined this..." he said. "But they are still doing it. Otherwise, why would the Abbot be negotiating which dragon to have killed? They must be. That must be the secret of the dragon magic!" Neill looked pale with shock.

It all made sense, making me feel queasy and unwell. "But why do I have the power then?" I said, before my heart seemed to freeze. "Have they been feeding us dragon blood? Powdered dragon bones, in the hope that some of us develop magical powers?" I felt myself start to wretch and dry heave as my fear wanted to expel from my system any trace of the horror.

"I don't know, Char," Neill said awkwardly. "With you,

things might be different. You heard yourself how Feodor called you one of the old dragon friends. Maybe only some people develop the magical powers, and some people are closely aligned to dragons naturally?" He looked confused and as sick as I was. "But there are only a handful of people at the monastery with any magical talent," Neill suggested, "you said so yourself."

"Me, Maxal," I agreed.

"And we know that Jodreth and the Abbot can use magic," Neill whispered. "I think the monks don't know what causes the magic, but they know this… *concoction* prolongs life, at least. Remember that we thought that the Abbot himself might be hundreds of years old?"

Another sick shudder running through my body. I had called the dragon crater not a sanctuary before, but a zoo – now it was starting to look a whole lot more like the worst sort of farm. Zaxx the bull was even allowing it. He was even helping the Abbot get rid of the dragons that he doesn't like. It was horrible.

"The other students and the dragons have to know about this. We have to get them to listen to us." I said, sighing heavily and my breath sounding ragged and scared. What could you do against people who would murder innocent young dragons? Who would rip them from their mother's clutches, and out from under the brood mothers?

Before I could come up with an answer there was something else that I knew that we had to do, however. Without saying a word, I re-wrapped the Great Crown and the grimoire back into their protective rags and set them beside me on the floor. Next, I carefully put the bones of the poor creature into the hole where the crown had laid, and carefully put the carved flagstone back over it reverently.

"I'm sorry," I said to the bones, and to Paxala above. "But this will have to do as a burial for now." I picked out two of the dragon's teeth, giving one to Neill and holding the other between my thumb and forefinger, saving them from their crypt. "These we will take and bury on Dragon Mountain, so the long-lost soul of this poor creature can finally come home," I said carefully, and Neill nodded. In the back of my mind I even felt the quiet assurance from Paxala above that this was acceptable. This was how we honored the sacrifice of the dragon that had gone before.

As I turned to regard the old queen's Great Crown once more, a quiet rage filled me. My father must have known about this place, about these bones, and about what had happened here. How could he not?

I had never thought of my father as an evil man, but now I saw that he could be a cruel man if he wanted to be. Why didn't he tell me about this crown here? Or this chamber filled with dragon bones? Was it because he knew I would be horrified? Or was there some bigger scheme he had in mind that required such secrecy? Well, it didn't matter now. I was done sneaking around, and I was finished with pleasing anyone. There had been a terrible, dark, and evil thing performed here, and the old queen had conspired with the very Draconis Monks who were supposed to look after the dragons in their care. What was more, the monks were responsible for covering it up. Maxal and Dorf thought that not only had the Old Queen Delia lived for hundreds of years, but that there was a chance that the Abbot Ansall had himself. Weren't we all told at the start of our initiation there that he had created the monastery *with* the help from Queen Delia? Did that mean that Prince Vincent, Prince Griffith – even my father was much older than I had imagined? I realized with a kind of horror that I had never actually asked how old my father was. He had always seemed to be somewhere around an athletic late forties, or so I had previously thought.

But the Abbot had known all about this. And, if he was indeed that old then he might even have stood right here beside the old queen. I felt like we had been lied to all along about the purpose of the skills we were learning at the monastery, about what the monks were actually doing.

"Neill? We are leaving. Now. And we are going to put an end to whatever this dark sorcery is," I said, and even though I could not hear it, I felt the triumphant crowing of the Crimson Red dragon far, far above me.

PART III
THE RETURN

CHAPTER 18
A DRAGON-SHAPED HOLE

Creeping back out of the hidden chamber, we had made our way past the earthstar corridor and back to the door when something happened in my head.

"Char – are you okay?" Neill looked at me, and he was frowning even more than was usual. I wanted to ask him why his face had blanched in that nervous way, until I realized that I was slouched against the wall, and that my head was ringing. *What was wrong with me?* I felt feverish and nauseous, as if I might suddenly throw up.

"Char?" Neill's hands were on my shoulders, holding me up slightly. "Is it the crown? The dragon bones? What is it?"

Dragon bones. As much as I could, well, believe that it was that gruesome discovery that had me feeling sick, I knew that it wasn't. As I concentrated on the source of my unease, I could feel it like a bruise in the back of my mind. *Paxala.*

Where was Paxala? I couldn't feel her in my head any more. Quite frankly, I hadn't realized before that a part of my mind *was* 'the dragon' – and by that I meant that there was a part of me that always felt dragon-like.

I had thought that was just me, or that it was just normal. I gasped. I had always had a fascination for the winged creatures. I devoured every story that I could find about them, I would hunt the skies for signs of their passage. When I found the hatchling Paxala and started feeding her, it had been as instinctive to me as if I were one of those Great White brood mothers myself, fierce and loyal.

Now, I saw that was this part of me waking up. The part that was always hand-in-claw with the dragons, or with one particular dragon anyway.

"Neill?" I said, terrified in a way that I hadn't been even upon reading the Old Queen Delia's macabre grimoire. "I can't sense Paxala anymore," I hissed. There was an emptiness in my head, and it was shaped like a Crimson Red dragon, my friend, and my confidante.

"Okay," Neill said in what he must have thought was his 'calming' voice when in actual fact it was his 'I am really, really alarmed' voice. "We'll head straight up to the roof of the Queen's Keep. She must be there, right? Why would she leave?"

"She wouldn't." I shook my head, before instantly regretting it as the corridor spun.

"Breathe, Char, breathe." Neill took my elbow and guided

230

me back to the door that led out to the stone stairwell that ran through the keep like a main artery.

"Pax...? Are you there?" I once again reached into that dragon-shaped void in my heart, from which the feelings of sickness and nausea were emanating. Did I feel some sort of flicker of response coming back to me? Had there been an impression of a tail flicker? A thud of a heart the size of a dog? If it had been some impression of the dragon on the other side of the mental connection I had, then it was far away, and very weak. I tried to hurry, only to stumble and have to lean on Neill for support as we climbed.

CHAPTER 19
NEILL, JUST ANOTHER
WARLORD'S SON

We did our best to climb as fast as we could, but it was difficult going, especially since Char needed my support to even stay upright. I stumbled on the stairwell and knocked my shins for the third time since we'd started climbing. By the time that we had past the ninth or tenth floor I had just stopped counting, trusting instead that the architecture would end eventually. From the way that my thighs and back was feeling though – it seemed that might not actually be the case.

I was worried – again, not an entirely unusual state of affairs. I think I must have spent the entirety of my life frightened up to this point. I was worried for Char, for the weird and sudden way that she had gotten ill, and for what she was mumbling about Paxala--that the dragon had somehow 'disappeared' from inside her head.

I had known that the two were connected, girl and dragon, but I hadn't realized that it was this deep, this powerful. It made me a little scared because I had never encountered it before. I didn't know what it meant. Was it a threat to Char, as it was making her ill right now? I didn't know how to protect it, or whether it was something that I had to fight. I didn't know how to help Char, or what under all of the stars would help her through this strange affliction, and that made me feel weak.

Too weak to help even your best friend, a part of me thought.

Stop it. I berated myself. *Stop thinking like your brothers.* They saw everything as something either to own or to attack. They were soldiers, through and through, and everything nearest to them was either a threat or an ally. I didn't want that for me, or for my friends. I had discovered something else out there on Mount Hammal with Char and Paxala. Friendship. Fun, even. Another way of looking at the world that wasn't all enemies and war and politics.

"Woah." I caught Char as she wobbled again, almost bodily carrying her up the last remaining flights of stairs.

But Char had it no different from me, really, I thought. For all of our differences, from the rich keep that she grew up in to my simple, study leather jerkins, to the hours I had spent studying the weapons forms, and the hours that she must have spent learning history and art and dancing and whatever – we were still very similar, I thought. All of the people around her viewed her in the way that my soldier brothers thought about their armies. She was a tool on a chessboard. She was either a threat or an ally. She had to be used effectively.

Threats, danger and wars. Would it ever be simple for us? Why couldn't we just be left alone?

"Neill...?" Char woke me from my dark, worrisome thoughts. We had reached the top – all that was above us was a door.

And even I, insensitive Neill, could sense the lack of angry dragon on the other side of that door. It wasn't exactly a magical thing like Char's, instead it was a complete silence that registered in the animal parts of my mind. No huffing. No scraping. No loud sounds of snoring, huffling, whuffling, whistling or snaps.

"Either Paxala is sleeping very deeply indeed, or..." I said, my heart in my chest as I turned the heavy iron ring, and with a creak we both rushed out. I didn't want to say what the other option was, of course, not in front of Char. Maybe Paxala wasn't *finally* gone, but had instead flown further than she was used to. She was still only a very young dragon, after all...

I had half convinced myself of the fact that I wouldn't see any dragon up here on the straw-strewn roof, and that instead she would come to one of Char's calls, or whistles, surprising us all with her new trick – but no. The Crimson Red was indeed here, half curled and half sprawled at the end of the roof, collapsed into her belly, with her tongue lolling out.

"Pax!" Char screamed, rushing forward across the flat

tiles, but wobbling as she did so, stumbling, and falling heavily to her knees.

"Char, wait!" I called, my eyes taking in the details of the scene much clearer than she could at the moment. Paxala was breathing, shallow but insistent breaths. Her long, spiked tail flickered its hardened end weakly, and her mighty claws were tucked up under its reptilian belly as if to keep them warm. She didn't raise her head to regard us, but her breathing snorted suddenly, and plumes of warm steam rose from the Crimson Red's nostrils.

"She's ill," I said, as Char got to the dragon's side and laid her hands on her belly. Even from over here it looked to me as if the dragon was sitting awkwardly, holding her belly gingerly.

"Well done, my girl! I knew it! I knew that the dragon would be able to call to you when it was injured." A voice from the shadows of the fortifications called out. It was Char's father, the Prince of the Northern Realm, Prince Lander.

"What did you do to her?" Char gasped, clearly not even well enough to feel properly furious. I hurried to her aid, making sure that I was standing at her side if she needed me to act.

The prince hadn't been hiding in the shadows alone, however. He had brought with him half a dozen archers, as well as Char's brother Wurgan who stood to one side, looking deeply troubled. At a nod from the prince, the archers stepped forward, their bows pointing down but still strung with arrows, already notched. What was he doing? This was his own daughter! I was stunned, my hands moving to my large belt knife and wondering what – if anything – I could do.

Char paid little attention to the archers or even to her family though. Instead, she cradled Paxala's massive jaws, trying to get the dragon to open her eyes. This close to the Crimson Red, I would have expected to be bathed in a warm glow of the internal heat that the great lizard constantly generated. On our flight north following Char it had at first come as a surprise and then a welcome relief when I realized that I didn't need to wear my cloak and thick woolens most of the time. But now, however, the fire inside of the dragon had subsided to a dull glow, and I shivered under the rising northern winds.

"It was the fish. Laced with Amorant's Helper. You know the herb, don't you my girl?" Lander was saying in the same sort of tone that my father would use for an unruly pup: stern, but not unfriendly.

"Thank god," Char murmured distractedly.

He has no idea of the pain he is causing either the dragon or his daughter, I thought. Both physical and emotional. "Amorant's Helper?" I hissed at Char. "What is it? Is it deadly?"

"It's a mountain herb. Mothers use it to help with teething babies, and healers use it for fever. It sends them to sleep if you take a little, and unconscious if you use too much," she said to me quickly, before raising her voice to demand from her father. "How much did you use? She can barely open her eyes!"

"Oh, I left all of that up to Odette and Lady Bel. You know, I've never been particularly interested in herbalism. But you can trust them – they know their way with herbs."

Can we trust them? I looked at Char, who had gone pale, whether with fury or illness or fear, I couldn't tell. Did Char get on with Odette? Wasn't it Odette who wanted her married off against her will?

"Char – since you don't want to marry Clans Chief Tar, and you don't want to send this beast to attack our enemies, I decided to take the initiative for myself," Prince Lander explained with false patience, as if this was a necessary bitter medicine that Char had to swallow for her own good. "The Three Kingdoms are at war. No one talks about it, but that's what's going on, under the surface. There are soldiers dressed as bandits crossing the borders between Middle and North every month now, and I, the Prince of the North and rightful king of the Three Kingdoms will not allow it any longer."

"What about Prince Griffith?" I said. "I'm sure that he would have something to say about that, wouldn't he? He is one of the heirs to the old queen as well..." Although I didn't claim to know all of the ins and outs of the royal family politics, as far as I knew Lander here was the eldest child, with Prince Griffith being the youngest, and Vincent being the middle. That meant, although in normal succession the North-lander Prince here *should* be High King, his own mother had decreed that the realm should be split into three, each with their own prince. If Lander was to claim himself High King, then I was sure that his brothers Griffith and Vincent would both rise against him.

But Prince Lander gave a flick of his hand as if shooing away a pesky insect and ignored me, as if such a statement was so ludicrous it did not bear response

"Char, you have to understand that history is made by great deeds. Great deeds by great men. It cannot be squandered on the dreams of young girls," Prince Lander lectured, not even bothering to look at his daughter as he surveyed the drugged-up dragon in front of him. This was a speech that he had been thinking about, I see. "If you will not use the dragon for the north, then I will find a way to train it for myself. I will start with the Amorant's Helper, and then, your brother here will start to teach it to take to harnesses. It may take a long time, but we will get there in the end.... That is why the archers are here, of course. We will have to keep a close eye on the dragon for a while, until she understands that escape is unwise, and impossible."

"No, no, no!" Char suddenly spat, facing her father. I had never seen her so angry, and for a moment I thought that she was going to strike him. On the other side of the roof the archers stiffened at the outburst, looking to Wurgan for direction. Surely each one was wondering what they should be doing to protect their lord from the dragon, a Son of Torvald, and even their own princess. Wurgan shook his head before frowning at his own boots.

Yeah, I thought with an internal snarl. You should be ashamed. You're supposed to look after your little sister, not endanger her!

"It won't work. Dragon's don't work like that," Char was saying, her words a fast torrent. "I know. *I* know," she thumped her heart (swaying as she did so). "Dragons have to be free. They *have* to. They won't take harnesses or leads or saddles for you – no matter how much you drug them or offer them. The Draconis Order have tried! Stars protect me, but they are trying to do that even now-- I was there. The dragons just reacted angrily, jealously, viciously. You'll have to drug poor Paxala so much that she won't be able to fly or fight or walk for you anyway! How could you!" Char started to run out of steam, and I could see that she was on the verge of tears. "How could *you* be like them?"

Her father was silent for a moment, this time truly regarding his daughter. "Because I have to be, Char. One day you will realize that. And if I have to drug the dragon to keep her at my keep then I will do it."

"I won't let you," Char said hotly, still swaying on her feet from the mental bleed-over from the dragon's pain. "I'll stop you, you know."

"Oh, Char." Her father shook his head sadly. "You will do no such thing. But, if you will not marry Tobin Tar, then I suppose that I could send you back to that Dragon Monastery if you prefer. I am not an unreasonable man. Perhaps you could fetch me back another dragon?"

Char screamed in rage and moved towards her father, raising a hand to strike him. I didn't know what to do. Should I intervene? Wouldn't they just shoot me for it?

Before I could come to a decision, however – I was surprised by the sudden movement as Char's raised hand was caught by another. It was Wurgan, moving quickly to step in the way, and to hold his struggling sister to him. "Easy, little sister," he said in a deep growl. "That won't help matters."

"It would make me feel a whole lot better," Char spluttered, as the prince nodded to the archers once more.

"Yes, I see what has to happen now, Char. You will be sent back to that monastery of yours, and bring us back as many eggs as you can carry."

"Char…" I had an idea as the prince's eyes flickered at me, as if just considering me for the first time. If we couldn't stop Prince Lander, and we couldn't convince him, then my fathers' wisdom in me said that we had to negotiate. Negotiate until you can control the situation, my father had said many a time. Would it be better to try and bring the dragons up here to the North, free from the Order's influence and threat of being killed? "There is no Order here, no *Abbot*, and none of his *medicines*," I said, hoping that she would take my hint.

Char must've caught my drift, as her eyes widened, then narrowed, and then looked worried. Did she think that I was betraying her? "There is poison here instead," she muttered darkly, as her father cleared his throat loudly.

"Interesting. You are a Son of Torvald, aren't you?" he asked, tapping his chin.

"I am," I said, hoping that I might be able to sway the prince in some way. "We are the elected Wardens of the Western Marches, protectors of the western lands of the Middle Kingdom. Fierce in battle, our exploits are known far and wide…"

Prince Lander coughed once again. "I have armies, boy. And you are just another warlord's son, but I suppose that you may be a valuable one. Archers? Take him to the cells."

"Neill!" Char cried out. "No – I need him!" But her outburst did no good.

I shook my head. I had half been expecting something like this to happen since I even set foot in the Old Queen's Keep. I was a Middle Kingdomer, after all, and the son of a warlord as well. The prince would either view me as a dangerous spy, or as a valuable hostage.

Even so, none of that meant I had to accept it. If they wanted to tie up a Torvald and a friend of dragons, then they would have to work for it!

I struggled against their seizing hands, shoving, and writhing until one of the three of them managed to get a knee onto my back and stamp me down onto the cold floor of the keep.

CHAPTER 20
THE TRIALS OF WURGAN NEFRETTE

"Wurgan, you know this is wrong," I said as he dragged me through the shadowed corridors. At my hip sat the heavy collection of rags I had folded into my pouch, containing the Great Crown of the Queen. I had given up struggling after the first five floors, fearful that my brother would discover the crown on me, and also as every move that I had made had only increased my brother's grasp. Now, instead of clamping my arms to my sides, he had settled for holding my hand in a vice-like grip until I thought my hand was likely to fall off. Still, despite this pain, it was hard see my brother as my enemy.

Of course he was my enemy, he was effectively imprisoning me, dragging me through the castle with archers ahead and behind of us lest I try to run. Not only that, but he was helping my father to imprison both of my friends.

But some stubborn memory of our childhood together clung on, and I couldn't hate him. I could only pity him. He was my brother, so therefore he was being stupid. All I had to do was to make him see his stupidity for what it was and then he would surely come to his senses.

"This will go easier on you if you just keep your thoughts to yourself," he grumbled, but I had (of course) no intention of doing any such thing.

"How could you, Wurgan? How could you agree with Father like that?" I turned on him. "The pair of you, scheming and plotting your conquests in that audience chamber. It's a disgrace. You can't imprison Neill, either – he hasn't done anything wrong! He's saved my life, which is more than you can say, Wurgan. And Paxala? Father will kill her. He doesn't know anything about dragons, and I do. Paxala would never agree to anyone's commands."

"She agrees to yours," Wurgan grunted.

I almost kicked him in the shins (as I would have done a few years ago) but instead I chose to argue with him. "No, she *doesn't.* I don't give her orders and commands, I *ask* her to help me, just as I am *asking* you to help me right now," I said tartly as we turned a corner and started down another flight of stairs.

Wurgan remained stubbornly quiet the whole way down.

I had a thought it would be a low blow, but I wasn't above that at the moment. "Does Mother know you're doing this?" I asked.

Wurgan tensed beside me, before he grumbled. "It's not up to me to inform the prince's mistress of everything that he decides to do..."

"*The prince's mistress?*" I said, astounded. "Just who do you think you're talking about? That's our *mother,* Wurgan – or has Odette poisoned your head so much that even you have forgotten that?"

"Char!" he jolted to a stop, causing the archers to stumble and bunch into each other as his large, bearded face suddenly turned to hiss into mine. "You have to be more careful when you are talking about Princess Odette. *She's* the rightful wife of our father, and our mother is what she is. Another lady in waiting."

His eyes sparked with fury, but there was something else that was going on here, his forehead prickled with beads of sweat as he scolded me. He's worried? I thought. He's scared of speaking ill of Odette?

When had my brother ever been scared of anything? He wasn't one of those insane people who knew no fear, but he was big, and he was good at soldiering, and even when I had seen him look concerned over some riding challenge or upcoming skirmish – he had never let that fear stop him from speaking his mind before.

But even so, I thought. All of this 'rightful princess' and 'lady in waiting' nonsense made him sound more like a Middle Kingdomer than a true Northlander. Always before, the Northern Kingdom had a different, wilder attitude to the ways of the court than the Middle Kingdom. Not that I hadn't grown up surrounded by ballgowns and royal visits and what have you – but the prince would share his table with clansmen and warlords as much as he did courtiers and advisors.

"What is this?" I pointed it out to him. "You sound like Prince Vincent and his preening cronies. Since when has clanswoman Galetta Nefrette, daughter of a chief and moun-tain-wife of a prince, ever been a *lady in waiting*?"

"Since you went away, Char," Wurgan said, his tone turning sour, his mustaches downturned as he scowled. "Things have been changing for a long time up here, and when you went off to that accursed monastery…"

"It wasn't *my* choice, brother – father made me, remem-ber?" I pointed out, before feeling a spike of shame alongside the surge of dizziness that Paxala's mind was spreading through me. Another wave of nausea rolled through my stomach.

"Well, whatever the reason, sister. When you left, our mother went to stay with her parent's people in the mountains for a season, and when she returned she never took the same high place in the keep as she once had." Wurgan coughed into his beard, embarrassed at his own strength of feelings. *He's upset,* I saw, but my empathy for him only made me angrier. Angry at my father, at my brother for not doing anything, and angry at myself for being such a bad sister – and now it seems, a terrible daughter to our mother as well.

"It was her own fault," Wurgan said harshly, as if reading

my mind. My brother was never a very good one for emotions and empathy. "Our mother withdrew from the life of the court, preferring to spend more time with the mountain clans. In her place, Princess Odette rose to greater power. All of our father's clan advisors and allies, the sorts of people that our mother brought with her to the feasts and to live here, started to drift away or actively spurn the court. That is why father wanted you to marry Tar. It'll cement the relations again." Wurgan shook his head, grunting in frustration. "Mother always cared more for you anyway," he said thickly.

Ah. Is that it? I thought. He thinks that mother doesn't care for him?

But it was true, in a sense. I didn't think that our mother loved me more, but she understood me better. It was she who taught me many of the old clan ways, and who had fed my imagination stories of the terrifying wild dragons. As for Wurgan, he took much better to swords and riding and warfare and the camaraderie of the army life – and so our father understood him more.

As another wave of nausea made my head spin and I stumbled, my anger suddenly vanishing, leaving me gasping and defenseless like a fish on the shore. This was all so screwed up, I thought, reaching out a hand to lean against the wall.

"Char?" my brother's strong grip kept me standing upright, at least, as he steadied me and crouched a little so that he could look me in the face. "You're ill," he muttered, his eyes suddenly looking into mine. "Hm. If you were a horse, I'd confine you to stables and put you on the syrup."

Gee, thanks. I shook my head (gently). "I'm fine. I bet you would prefer it if I were a horse, right? Much easier to tell what to do," I snapped. It was nasty of me, but then again, he had just helped drug Paxala and drag my friend off to the dungeon. I made to push his steadying hand off of me, but I missed and stumbled.

"No, Char. You are *ill.* I don't say that lightly. What is wrong with you? Is it the dragon? Does it have diseases?" Wurgan said.

"It *is* the dragon, but not what you think," I was past caring right now. All I wanted to do was to sleep, and preferably curled up with my dragon. "Thanks to father, the drug seeping through Paxala's system is affecting me as well. It's the connection that I share with her…" I started to mumble, feeling very sleepy indeed.

"Char, this is – wrong." Wurgan was searching for the words, eventually settling on the one that would allow him to scold me some more.

"It's not wrong. It's natural. It is what friends do for each other. We share each other's pains and troubles." *It is what families are also supposed to do for each other as well…* I was too ill to say.

"But we have to keep the dragon dosed if we are to work with it – she damn near bit my arm off when I went to check on her!" Wurgan said, more to himself than to me.

"Well, maybe next time she'll bite your head off, you're not using it anyway…" I mumbled, rubbing my own free hand over my eyebrows.

"But if you get ill every time that the dragon gets its medicine…" My brother was thinking (not his best attribute).

"Poison…" I corrected. "And it's *she*, not *it*." Now that I knew what was happening above me, I wasn't as traumatized as before. I could sense the shape of the Crimson Red in my heart and head, just not the edges of her thoughts. That was still terrifying, but I knew that she was alive, at least. I could make out a faint feeling of nausea, dizziness, and aching bones – but it was something.

I'll get you better, I thought *at* the shape of Paxala in my head, although I had no idea how.

"Here." Wurgan led me into my room and set my down on my bed. "Guards? Bring fresh water and food. I want my sister to be the looked after, damn it!" he snapped as I collapsed into the soft furs and blankets.

"Sister?" Wurgan said a little softer to me, but I ignored him. It wasn't just the illness – I was mad as hell at him. With an awkward sigh, he turned back and left me in my room, his boots dragging on the heels. *Click-thunk* came the sound of my door being locked. From the outside.

I was running through the corridors of the Old Queen's Keep,

my home. Only it didn't look like my home at all. The corridors were tighter and narrower, and a lot darker than the ones that my father kept – and yet I knew it was the keep. I knew it was home.

But a home that was also different, alien-like, and strange.

"Pax?" I called out, but she didn't answer. Oh yes, I remembered. She couldn't answer because she was asleep at the moment.

"Neill?" I tried – but once again I got no answer. My father had him put in the dungeon – didn't that mean that he would be below me? I turned in my scramble and ran back the way that I had come, only to find that the stairs weren't there anymore. In fact, the entire section of corridor that I had just passed wasn't there, and instead there was a blank wall.

I was lost inside my own home, and I didn't know how to get to the people that I cared about.

Left, I'll try left, I thought, turning down an exactly similar narrow corridor, only to have my feet crunch over rough ground. Why was the ground so gritty? I thought, seeing that the entire passageway had seemingly been covered in fine, yellow-white grit.

"What is that, sand?" I murmured, crouching down to run my finger through the inch or so depth of crunching material. The granular pebbles poured through my hand, and, as I took out another handful, my hand brushed against something larger and solid buried in the sand. Curiously, my hand tried to feel around it, wondering what it could be. It was heavy,

and stiff with the compacted gravel but it came easily when I tugged at it.

A metal circle. A gold and steel double-circle, joined together by elaborate jewels...

"The Great Crown!" I gasped, tugging it out of the pebbles, but it was stuck. There was something stuck in it, I saw, and I brushed away the top layer of the pebbles to reveal the dark shadow of the eye socket, staring back at me.

It was a skull. A skull of a young dragon, wearing the Great Crown like it was the true queen of all of these lands. That was when I realized that the gritty, sandy pebbles weren't sand at all. They were the crushed and pulverized fragments of bone. Dragon bone. The whole keep--where I had played through its corridors and laughed and danced and sung-- was littered with bone fragments from murdered dragons.

"I'm so sorry. I'm so sorry," I was saying, over and over again as I held the skull and crown in my hands. There was the sudden thunk as the dragon's skull dropped to the floor, leaving just the crown in my hands. But the crown was glowing. Not only the blue earthstar rocks, but also the ruby as well. Without knowing quite what I was doing, I lifted the crown to set it on my head.

The sand around me shifted and swirled, as if pulled by a mighty wind faster and faster into a whirlpool. But I felt perfectly calm, and no air even disturbed a hair on my head. The dragon-sand flew away from me in ripples, leaving me in a perfect, calm circle.

I can do anything with this crown, my heart surged. Didn't the old legends say that the queen used dragons to build her oldest castles. I raised a hand and pointed at one of the paving slabs, and it cracked as if struck by a sledgehammer.

This was what they meant, it had to be. I felt strong and powerful as I pointed upwards above my head, to the roof where my dragon was. Stone after stone shattered and at the same time, I rose through the widening hole, until, like a hunting peregrine, I burst into the white light of the sky-

"Ach!" I coughed, falling out of my bed. "Ow." I rubbed my elbows where I had landed, looking around my room. I had spent most of the day asleep, if the light from the shuttered windows was anything to go by.

The windows! I thought, rushing to them to see that yes, they weren't locked. I opened them with a creak and a bang to see the cold and high vistas beyond. The map of the town beneath us just as it always had been, and the distant high mountains off my right, and the rolling greener fields, roads, meadows, and wildwoods of the left. I had used to love looking out at all of this, so long ago. I had imagined what might lie just over the horizon to the south down there, and I had hunted the sky for signs of dragons – torn clouds, black specks on the wind, sudden flames.

I had, of course, only rarely seen them, but even that

wasn't important really. What was important was imagining where they were, and what they might be doing, as well as what towns, magics, and stories lay out there. I had the classical training expected of the daughter of a prince, and so I could name the stars and all of the major cities, and knew just where places sat according to the maps. But that was nothing compared to actually traveling, and seeing for myself. I had yearned for adventure in the same way that my stepmother Odette yearned for power. It was in my lifeblood, either I was hopelessly addicted to it, or else I would starve without it.

"Well, Char Nefrette?" I had gone out and seen some of those places, but it seemed to me as if the rest of the world was just as petty and scandalous as the one in this keep. The only place that I had come close to falling in love with was the narrow lake and the cave under the waterfall, and the stony beach where I had kept Paxala hidden for the best part of a year.

That was the most like the mountain wilds, I nodded to myself as I took a deep sigh. I felt a little better after my rest, but my muscles still felt achy.

"Paxala?" I reached out to her in my mind, unsure if I might create a solid connection to her just with thought alone (it seemed a natural skill for the dragons, whereas I had to teach myself, or unlock some memory of how to do it). "Pax?" I tried again. "Are you there?"

"Char," a glimmer of a thought brushed against mine, and with it came the dragon's presence in my imagination. She

was weak, and she was weary, but it was the sort of weariness that I knew that she could recover from. What hurt worse, was that her thinking felt muzzled and confused. She didn't know what was going on around her.

"Paxala. You have to listen to me," I murmured as I concentrated on the words. "You can't eat the food they leave out for you. It's bad. Bad food, bad fish." I tried to say the words as steadily and as clearly as I could, but I still didn't know if she could understand me well or not.

"Bad food? But I am so hungry, Char..." I sensed it through her mind too: her belly was empty and she hadn't eaten as much as she should have over the last few days. And that was my fault, I cursed myself savagely. She had traveled north with Neill to rescue me, but she must have decided that flying was more important than eating, or else she still couldn't hunt well for herself.

"Hunt? Too weak for hunt. But there is hot fish, here?" she thought at me once more, and I had to steady my breathing as I thought I was going to faint with the echo of her dizziness.

"No, please don't eat that Paxala, it's bad. It will make you feel bad, I promise it will! It's... It's my father," I said, feeling ashamed. "He's put something into your food that will make you sleepy." I felt a sluggish annoyance from the dragon. She would listen to me for now, but in a few watches or by the end of the day when she was ravenously hungry, it might be a different situation entirely.

But I couldn't leave her up there to starve, either. How was

I going to get food to her? How was I going to get her healthy, without getting her drugged again? If Wurgan hadn't looked at me like I was a freak when he found out that I shared my mind with Paxala then I would have asked him – but no, I knew that I couldn't do that now. I would have to find another way to sneak out of the chamber, and get to her. *But that would leave Neill down below in the cells.* I bit my lip in frustration.

"Don't you dare make me choose," I whispered at the air, at Wurgan, at my father behind it all. I refused to choose which friend that I might help.

"Char is upset," Paxala was finally catching onto *my* emotions as well. This really was bad, as usually the Crimson Red would be able to sense what was happening to me, and what I was feeling much faster.

"Yes, I am, Paxala. But you don't have to worry about that right now. I want you to concentrate on getting stronger. Stretch your legs and tail and wings, and then rest again. Get this poison out of your body, but don't eat. Just rest!" I advised.

"Char is clever. Char looks after me." Paxala was thinking dopily, as she rested her aching head on her claws only managing to do half of what I had suggested.

"How my father, the Abbot, or anyone thinks that they can get away with ordering a dragon to do anything is beyond me," I muttered to the empty room. "I can't even get one dragon to look after itself!" The idea would have been laugh-able if it also wasn't so tragic, I turned back to my room, trying to work out what resources I had, and what use that I could turn them to.

~

As it turned out, I was only halfway through making a knotted-blanket rope by the time there was a knock on the door. I hurriedly stuffed it under the bed and hoped that whomever it was hadn't been counting blankets and covers whenever they were last in here!

Fortunately for me it was my brother Wurgan, so no need to worry about him paying too much attention to my well-being or comfort. But Wurgan was looking even more sheepish and awkward than he had before. What now? I thought. I bet he's come to tell me precisely how much I've messed everything up.

"Sister..." Wurgan closed the door gently after him, before hurriedly crossing into the room and looking out of the window. *Don't see the rope, brother!* I thought with a brief spike of alarm. He nodded to himself, turning back to me with a heavy sigh that was almost comical. "It's morning..."

"I can see that," I said. It must have been past midnight last night when I'd gotten ill – as worried as I was about Paxala on the roof. Now, the sun had risen over the mountains to the West and the early morning fogs that sat in the countless valleys around Queen's Keep were just starting to burn off. It took a long while for the sun to clear the distant peaks and allow 'morning' to happen out here in the foothills– so already I knew that the guards would be changing shifts, the kitchens would be clattering somewhere far below us, and the markets already starting to fill. My people in the Northern Kingdom were used to starting their day in the dark.

Wurgan flinched at the sharp tone in my voice. What did he expect – that I had forgiven him already? If ever?

"Yes, of course you do. Then you'll also know that this is one of the busiest times for the keep."

I nodded. "I haven't been away for *that* long, brother," I said tartly.

"Mother has called a great hunt, and is amassing the clan warriors and scouts who will want to go right now at the mountain gate," Wurgan said.

"Okaaay…" I gritted my teeth. My mother, the clanswoman, who hadn't even come to see Paxala when I had brought her here to the keep. That stung. I didn't want to admit it, but it did. It was what me and Wurgan had talked about just last night – I really was closer to our mother Galetta Nefrette than I was to father, or Wurgan was to her. *Does she even know what is happening to me?* I thought in dismay, before biting down and ignoring the bundle of hurt feelings. *I have to rescue Neill.* When was Wurgan going to get going out of here, so I could get back to my escape attempt?

"I thought you said that mother was retiring from court life?" I said, thinking that I had probably at least *try* to make some small talk with him, if only to allay any suspicions he might have.

"She is, and this morning she announced to the clan chiefs that she was about to retire to the mountain clans for the rest of the summer, and this great hunt is the last of her duties here at court," Wurgan explained in a not-so patient, pacing sort of way.

I knew that the great hunts were really a clans' tradition, but one that the staid Northlanders had taken to just as enthusiastically (what difference was there really between a clansman and a kingdomer, as the old saying goes). More than celebrations, the ad-hoc processions led by chosen clan chiefs and well-respected scouts, were a chance not just to take to the foothills and woods, beating out any prominent game, but also create an excuse for bonding-- and the sorts of negotiations between the clans and the court that happened because of it. *I used to look forward to them, on the few times that father let me attend.* I remembered with a sigh. *Although I never liked all the talking at the feasts.*

"And?" I shrugged. Currently, as wonderful as my mother was and as exciting as a great hunt could be – *my friend was imprisoned downstairs!*

"And so, the Lady Odette is beside herself. She is annoyed that Mother is calling half of the clans' chiefs away – Tobin Tar with them, I might add – at a time of national crisis."

"National crisis?" I asked, feeling vaguely offended. Was it my dragon which was the crisis?

"The bandits, Char!" Wurgan said, his voice almost rising to a shout. But although he was clearly frustrated with me, I wasn't the only source for his anger. "If only Father had brought you to the council meeting we've been having all night. But I suppose that you couldn't, as you were ill…"

I was still ill, to be honest. My head felt groggy and that made me tetchy; at least now I could feel the presence of Paxala in my head again. Even if it was just a dim shadow of what it usually was.

"Anyway. Father has decreed that, with the Prince Vincent's soldiers dressed as bandits harrying our borders, and now with a dragon living on our roof, and you back here safe--"

"Back here imprisoned, you mean?"

Wurgan had the decency to look uncomfortable at my interruption, but he didn't stop talking.

"--and the Torvald boy in the cells, that we are to stand prepared for any attack. There are scouts being sent to summon the levies, and the clans have been called to send their warriors to the keep."

"I see." I groaned. More politics. "So, Mother calling a great hunt now is not to celebrate my return, or even the dragon's arrival, it's really an excuse to mess with Father and Odette." I was sick of it. How had relations between Father and his two wives – one kingdomer, and one unofficial mountain woman – become so strained, and so politically fraught? There used to exist a good alliance between them. Stronger together, as the clan and kingdomer slogan always said. As it was, I wouldn't be surprised if Father chose to cast off our mother if she got more troublesome, and that would mean that we--Wurgan and I--would be nothing but noble bastards in the line of succession, and my father and Odette might even have call to seek for a new child, or find some other answer to the problem.

"But Father has his hands tied, you see." Wurgan had apparently been following my line of thinking. "Even though our mother is doing everything to throw a halt to our fathers' war, he won't label her a traitor, because of us." Wurgan looked even more awkward, as he mumbled through his mustaches. He didn't have to explain the details to me. Wurgan was the eldest and only male heir. He would be the successor, as Lady Odette hadn't produced any children for our father.

"So...?" I shrugged. As far as I was concerned, although it might be great to hear of Mother taking her stand, it meant very little compared to the fates of my human and my dragon friend. If Wurgan thought he was going to lure me into keep politics with all of this talk – he had another thing coming!

"Char, you're very slow-witted when you want to be!" Wurgan hissed. "Do I have to spell it out to you?"

"Apparently," I said.

"*I* told Mother about your illness, with the dragon. You were right, last night. She deserved to know. She was mad – and this is what she is doing to help *you*. To help *you*, Char."

"How does this help me?" I asked, making Wurgan roll his eyes and give an exasperated groan.

"It means that the keep and the town are in uproar. Mother gave no notice, of course – as she only found out about what was happening to you in the early hours of this morning. Half of the clans who are staying here are sending their best trackers or attending themselves, readying their mounts and asking the keep kitchens for food, our father's guard has had to draft more people in to help escort Mother to the great hunt. Market people are even now taking their goods to the mountain gate to sell food and equipment and what have you to the hunters. And the scribes, clerks, and counsellors are running around like a bear with a beesting trying to sort the mess out," Wurgan said in a rush. "The keep has never been in such disarray as it is, right now."

"Oh…" I started to get an inkling of what my brother was intimating, and what present my mother had given me. *Oh, Mother…* I thought, my heart wrenching.

"So," Wurgan took another of his deep breaths "So, I will be over here, looking very studiously out of your window for perhaps the next quarter of a watch, keeping an eye on the chaos below. *Nothing* will distract me from my watch, do you understand?"

I did.

"And if that pile of clothes that I left inside the door doesn't fit you, and looks more like a servant's cloak and hood then I am sure that is just because I was taking them to the laundry," Wurgan said. "And if I left the cell keys to the keep's dungeons in the cloak then it is because I am an idiot, just as my little sister has always told me so."

"Oh, Wurgan…" I said in a rush, my rage disappearing like water out of a hole in a bucket, leaving me feeling empty and nervous. I crossed the space between us and folded him into my arms in a fierce hug.

"Huh," Wurgan growled, tapping my back a little awkwardly. "Don't thank me, thank Mother. She's doing what she can."

"But *you* went and talked to her, brother," I said. "Thank you." A tear rolling down my cheek, but I couldn't think of what I was sad for. My brother was letting me go free, and providing me with the keys to get an influential hostage out of my father's keep. *Ah,* I thought, as I found the reason for the sadness. *Nothing might ever be the same again after this.* When Father found out what had happened, he would be furious, and our stepmother would be even angrier. They might disown us for this, or I might never be allowed to return home again.

"Char already has a home…" a faint, reptilian voice whispered in my heart. *"Char has a home with Paxala."*

Yes, I did. I sniffed, and stepped back from my brother. "Wurgan, tell Mother…" I started, but found that I couldn't find the words to express my love.

"She's your mother, Char. She already knows. As do I." Wurgan nodded, gruff and final. "Now go. I have a lot of very important watching to do, and then I might just have to have a loud and very public argument with one of father's guards that I never liked anyway," he said with a slight quiver of mustache-grin as he turned and strode to lean against the window.

I didn't waste any time, slipping on the oversized dirty tunic and the heavy, voluminous grey cloak that marked me as a scribe's errand-boy, pulling the hood over my head and feeling the reassuring jangle of the dungeon keys in my pocket. At my side was the pouch, with the Great Crown of my grandmother secretly stashed inside. I wondered idly if my brother Wurgan would be so eager to aid in my escape if he knew the importance of what I was taking with me.

But I have to take this, I reminded myself. Zaxx told me that if I did not bring the crown then he will take it out on either my human friends, or the young dragons. Their lives depended on this. With a final look at my taller, statuesque brother standing in the window, I nodded silently at his back.

"You're still a good brother, and a good man, Wurgan Nefrette-Lander," I said, but true to his word, he did not turn from his watch, only lifted a hand as if to wave goodbye, and I thought, but did not say how I wished I could get a better chance to know him again.

But time makes fools of us all, or so my mother once told me, and with the knowledge that she was busy stirring up a hornet's nest at the mountain gates and masking our escape, I stepped out of my old room, and stole away.

CHAPTER 21
THE ESCAPE

"Neill?" I whispered into the darkness.

The dungeon was dark, cramped, and without any light whatsoever. How could they do this to my friend? I thought dismally, before correcting it to how could my father do this to the boy whom he knew was my friend? 'You might as well learn that a prince, just as a princess will one day do, has to know how to control their enemies, traitors, and spies,' Father had said, adding in the cold and strategic way he had that, 'it's not all pretty ballgowns and dancing, Char.'

But Father had never showed me these cells down here, I thought. He had shown me the larger banks of rooms that were nearly half the size of my bedroom, with a barred window, and even a pallet bed and a spray of straw. The prisoners there had been petty thieves from the town markets, all bowing and scraping and terrified of Father, but none of them nasty or aggressive (unsurprisingly, considering the man who stood before them, perhaps).

I had found my way to the guard's station, where two of the largest guards I had ever seen stood. Sneaking through the keep had been relatively easy with the scribing apprentice's disguise – especially as there were so many counsellors and court advisors running back and forth, trying to sort out the diplomatic mess that was my mother's great hunt. I was just another errand boy, delivering urgent scrolls or proclamations on an already outrageously urgent and busy day, clearly.

But down here, I knew instinctively that my disguise would not hold. I had decided to shuck off my hood and let my pale hair curl and flow around my shoulders – my own badge of office, it seemed, as the guards had recognized me.

"Lady Char!" the largest and baldest one had said, unsure of whether to snap to attention or not. I had remembered what my father would have done in the situation, and waited, motionless. Seeing my apparent impatience, the guards saluted me. I was still a princess of the realm, after all. And one who knew a dragon!

I had told them that I was to see the Son of Torvald, and that my father and their liege lord realized that I will be able to get the most information out of him.

How had they fallen for that? I had silently thought in surprise, waiting for them to shout for my father or Wurgan to come and apprehend me. But of course, they hadn't. They didn't know that I was effectively a house-prisoner here at the

keep, and they were not privy to my near-treasonous argu-
ments with my father. As far as they were concerned, I was
just another member of the ruling family – albeit a side-lined,
barely-noble one.

"As you see fit," the guard said, and pointed me past the
'nice' cells, and down towards the next level, where these
lightless cells sat. The rock here was older and the stonework
ancient, too. I wondered if these cells dated right back to the
old queen's time.

In the darkness down here there were more prisoners,
more dark shuffling and groanings. A few muttered curse
words, following from barking shouts from the guards above.

"Neill?" I tried again, whispering into the dark.

"Char...?" a shadow moved in the small cell, and the
guttering torch from the corridor beyond illuminated a shape
coming towards me from the darkness. It was Neill, looking
wan and worried – his brow furrowed in despair.

"Neill – thank the stars, look..." I lifted out the set of
heavy iron keys and selected Wurgan's master.

"You talked to your father?" Neill whispered, his wary
face transforming into delight. "I never thought that he would
see sense..."

"Well, you were right then," I said with a grumble,
straining at the stiff key before, with a *click-thunk* it hit true,
and the mechanism opened. "We have my brother and mother
to thank for this, come – we're leaving."

"Yes!" Neill said with a grin that was very infectious. "I

knew you would come up with something! Even when all the torches had died, I said to myself that Nefrette girl will find a way around this."

I shushed him, but felt an odd lurch in my heart at the words, all the same. This was turning out to be a very emotional day for me. First Wurgan and mother, and now Neill. There were few people in my life who believed in me unconditionally.

"Char..." the same, faint pressure in my mind that was almost mournful from the ailing dragon above.

"Hold strong, my heart – I am coming!" Of course, Paxala always had believed in me. With friends and family like this, even despite our terrible surroundings – I felt just a little lucky.

"Wait here, in the shadows while I distract the guards," I whispered to Neill, after giving him the spare cloak that Wurgan had left. The boy nodded silently, and stepped back into blackness.

"Finished, my lady?" said the bald guard to me as I emerged from the lower cells. His fellow was a little younger, and stood to attention much straighter.

"Yes, thank you." I nodded, doing my best to once again assume the sort of posture and voice that I had seen my father use with servants. "Now, which of you is going to escort me back up to the keep's halls?" I said.

"Uh…" the larger, balder, and older one looked confused.

"The prince has decreed that we should always have two on duty down here, just in case, milady."

"Do you not have faith in my father's cells, guard? Am I in danger right now?" I said immediately, raising one eyebrow and waiting for him to answer me.

"No, I mean, yes – of course I believe in them. You are perfectly safe, my lady…" the younger one was the first to speak.

I sighed. "I see. Well, my father has also decreed that I should never travel alone without a guard, as these are trying times. The guard who was meant to escort me down here was ill, so he will be seeing the inside of a stockade I am sure – but which of you will escort me back up?"

The older looked at the younger, both torn in indecision. "But, your father's orders, miss…" the younger said.

"Which ones?" I demanded angrily. "The orders he gave to you and the ones that have never changed in all your years of guarding down here, or the ones that he gave to *me*, his daughter?" I was treading on thin ice here, I knew. I hadn't been at court or in the keep for a few years now; how much power did the newly arrived bastard daughter of the prince have anymore? I just had to hope that my father's tight rules and regulations would impel them to action…

"Okay, of course. Vargus?" The older one looked at the younger. "You will stay here on duty, while I run the lady up to the courts…" the larger one said, and I nodded as if that pleased me – but inside I was secretly worried.

One fewer guard for Neill to worry about – but now what was I supposed to do with this big one? It might not take long for my father to realize that I was gone from my room – despite my mother's and brother's tricks.

"Very well. Let us go then. Now," I said, walking ahead and expecting the larger guard to follow me. I heard a quick shuffle, then felt the looming presence of the guard at my shoulder as I marched. We went through the antechamber to the stairs, where I made my way quickly upwards with the large guard stamping heavily on the stairs behind me. At the first landing in the complicated array of stairs, I veered away from the main steps that led straight to the main entrance halls for the keep, even though it was the quicker route to the keep proper. Instead, my steps chose the smaller stairwell that ran the opposite direction, through the warren of service halls for the servants, kitchens, and storerooms.

"Miss…" the guard mumbled in concern at my change of direction.

"I have a question to ask of the cook for today's great hunt!" I demanded, not pausing as I thought I heard a distant, muffled yelp and a thud from behind us. I think that my escort heard the noise, as he suddenly stopped, but I wouldn't let him investigate.

"Come on, now! Hurry!" I took the steps two at a time, already half a landing space above him.

"Oh, heck," the guard muttered behind me as I went faster, taking three steps at a time, my brisk stride turning into a jog.

"Miss! Wait up?" I heard the guard gallantly ask behind me, but I was running now, darting into the first doorway and down the short hall filled with wine cellars, their wooden doors fitted with iron bolts. I tugged on the first, to find the bolts stiff and unmoving. The pounding feet of the guard were following closely up the stairs, and I might just have time...

There! The next door gave way a little easier, and I darted into the cellar, to find myself in a low-ceilinged room, where casks and barrels of wine, ale, and mead were stacked in the cool and dry dark, waiting to be rolled out to the halls. Selecting the darkest corner that I could find, I wedged myself between a barrel and a ceiling-high wine rack, and held my breath.

"My lady?" the muffled voice of the guard called outside in the corridor. Had he seen which one I had gone into?

"Miss? Lady Char?" there was a creak and a click as I heard him trying one door, and then another. "Hey – you! Wait!" There was a thud, a scuffle, and the banging of a door, followed by the sounds of scraping and kicking. My heart pounded. What could be happening? Was I about to be discovered? And by whom?

The door to my cellar clicked and then opened, light flooding into the dark.

"Char?" Neill whispered. Behind him came the banging and rattling of a very large guard stuck behind another bolted door.

"I'm here." I stood up grinning from ear to ear as I followed him through into the little hallway.

"At least the poor guard won't die of thirst," Neill said. "The other one is currently sitting in the same cell that he put me in, with a bang on his head and looking very sorry for himself." Neill grinned a little sheepishly.

"You did well," I congratulated him, earning a blush from the Son of Torvald before we were back out into the service stairwell once again, to head upwards this time. Even though I had been away for a long time, the layout of the keep hadn't changed. The service halls were connected to the warren of corridors and stairwells that tunneled their way through all parts of the Queen's Keep, behind the grander halls, libraries, audience chambers and living quarters. After several turns and many stairs, we had made our way once again to the internal central stairwell that ran straight to the roof, and down to the old queen's hidden rooms.

"We'll just have to hope that father hasn't placed a permanent guard on duty up there," I said.

"Why would he?" Neill asked. "Paxala is a dragon. No one's going to steal her, and if she decided that she wasn't staying, then I don't think that there is much that even Prince Lander can do to stop her." He looked at me with concern. "But – do you think Paxala is able to fly?"

It was a thought that had been worrying me as well. I had been trying to hold onto the shadow of awareness that I had of her now, but every now and again – I guess when the dragon dozed off – it would start to fade back into the terrifying dragon-shaped void that I could not penetrate.

"She is stronger now, in some sense," I said awkwardly as we climbed.

"In some sense...?" Neill didn't sound too convinced by that. I didn't blame him, as neither was I.

"She's much stronger in my mind than when she was last night, I mean, but she's hungry, and tired. I told her to not eat the food that my father had left out, nor drink any of the water that had been left. Paxala is hungry and thirsty, so she's sleeping a lot, but her sickness is starting to fade," I explained.

"You can hear her again? In your mind?" Neill sounded relieved. "That is good news. I was worried that..."

"Yes," I said, neither of us wanting to entertain the possibility that the connection that I had with Paxala might in any way be permanently damaged. Luckily, however, no matter how stupid my father had been, the mental connection I had with Paxala was returning, but not quick enough for my liking.

"Up ahead," Neill nodded, indicating that we were nearly at the top. It was a strange, almost lonely dreamy experience climbing up through the center of the Keep, not seeing or hearing any other soul apart from us two. I knew, rationally, that outside of these sturdy walls that there had to be my father and mother and the Lady Odette, and the guards, and Wurgan, the counsellors and all of the servants going about their lives but we were completely insulated from all of that in here. It was almost like the outside world had faded away, and all of my brothers' urgent talk of the chaos outside had just been a lurid nightmare.

But here we were at last, the last door. "I've got this," Neill said, and I watched as he sighed through his nose, relaxing his body as he crept to the door, waiting and listening on the other side.

"Neill?"

"Shhh. I've got this," he said. "I'm a Son of Torvald, remember? I was trained to be good at this sort of ambush tactics."

But, of course, we could just ask Paxala. I reached out to the dragon on the other side of the door. "My sister, how are you? We are here." I greeted the shadow of the dragon in my head warmly. "Are you guarded? Are there other humans with you?"

"Char. No. Just lots of food I am not allowed to eat, and water I am not allowed to drink." The Crimson Red sounded annoyed. She must be getting better, I thought with a smirk, as Neill carefully opened the door, raising the small short sword that he had managed to steal from the younger guard and rushing out.

"There's no one here," he said after a pause.

"I know," I sighed as I followed him out, crossing the space to where Paxala had lifted her great snout towards me mournfully. All along the side of the roof were different arrays of grilled, uncooked, or roasted fish (now starting to stink to the high stars, I should add) and giant wooden pails of water.

How could my father ever think this was a good idea? I shook my head angrily even as I leaned against the snout of my Paxala.

"Can I eat now?" she asked me morosely.

"After we fly far, far away from here," I said. "Are you strong enough to?"

"Of course Paxala is strong enough to fly!" The Crimson Red snorted suddenly, causing me to fall backwards against her shoulder. The warmth of her dragon body radiated up into my back. She was getting warmer again, her internal fires rekindled, and I knew that she must be on the mend. Even so, as she took to her four legs, I could still detect a wobble in her legs, and a slight cloudiness to her eyes that meant that she took longer to focus on what was around her.

I will have to be more careful how we treat her, I thought in alarm. She was only a young dragonet still, after all – for all of her great size!

"Char?" Neill called from where he was standing on the parapets of the keep. This high up, the wind was strong, pulling at his hair and his stolen scribe's robe. I joined him to look down onto my father's town below us.

"What is it?" I asked, and Neill pointed westwards, to where out bird's eye view afforded us a clear image of the chaos that my brother had been talking about.

Large throngs of people were clustering to the west of the town, and more were heading towards it every moment by the main road and streets that connected the marketplaces to the western mountain gate. In the large assembly square before the gate there were parked wagons and rearing horses, along with throngs and throngs of people; mostly the clans, but also a few kingdomers with their darker hair and generally more somber clothes. The streets were jam-packed with carts and carriages, and there seemed to be something like a rally happening, as people stood before circles of wagons and lectured, preached, or remonstrated.

"Yes, I know," I told Neill of my mother's and my brothers plan, to distract our father so that we could escape.

"Well, thank you, Nefrettes," Neill said awkwardly, "but it wasn't just the crowds that I was drawing your attention to." He pointed to the streets leading up to the mountain gate where lines of cavalry horsemen in my father's guards were pushing their way through the press. I could see one of the riders in the lead – definitely a soldier of some kind – raised his arm, holding a baton, and I saw it strike downwards with great speed.

"No!" I shouted. "What is that captain doing?" I demanded angrily. "Those are our Northern Kingdom people, our people."

"If I didn't know better, I would say that soldier and his knights have been told to stop that great hunt of your mother's from taking place," Neill surmised, and I could see his eyes darting for clues about the scene. There was something about the look that reminded me of my father; the way that the Sons of Torvald and Prince Lander both examined and understood battlefields. It made my skin shiver. The cavalry was met by jeers and shouts from the clans' warriors. I saw cups of water or ale chucked in their direction, and I wondered how long before it was going to be fists.

One impressively large clan chief (Ranuld, I think) had stepped out from the crowd of my mothers' clansmen and something bellowed back at the knights, and beside him formed up his own burly guard of bear-skin wearing sons.

"We have to stop this," I said quickly, turning back to rush to Paxala, who had turned to sniff the water suspiciously.

"No, Pax! Please, I will ask you to trust me – it is the water and the food that made you lose me, and feel so ill," I said, reaching her leg and looking up at her annoyed eyes. How did Neill get up onto her back? How come he had never taught me the secret to it?

But Paxala sensed what I wanted, kneeling down on her front legs, and allowing both me and Neill to clamber up her leg spurs to her shoulder, and then to settle in the depressions between her spines at the base of her neck.

"Can we go somewhere there is some real food, now?" Paxala turned her large head on its long, long neck to regard me with almost fevered eyes.

"Yes. But first, there is one more favor I have to ask of you, Paxala," I said quickly, as the sounds of shouts and jeering chants started up from the mountain gate below. "Please...." I added, knowing that the dragon had every right to refuse my request, seeing as I had been the one who had left her behind at the monastery, and that she had been poisoned all because of her connection to me. I wouldn't blame her if she just flew off to eat and left us there, to be honest (although I knew that Paxala would never do that).

"What is it this time?" Paxala said in my head to a small snort of flame.

~

"DIVE!" I hollered, as the dragon swooped high over the town.

"Char doesn't need to scream," Paxala advised me in my mind, immediately making me feel stupid.

"Of course, not, I'm sorry," I offered, but the giddiness of the sudden freedom and the feel of the dragon holding me had just been too great. I was flying again! It wasn't until I had felt that lurch of fear in my stomach as she had jumped from the tops of the keep, the sudden pull of the earth ahead of us and the *whoosh* of excitement as her giant, leathery wings had opened that I realized how envious I had been of Neill being the first to ride her, and in having the honor to ride her all the way north to find me.

Even though both Paxala and I still felt a little queasy, a little slow, the worries and concerns of my family lessened as soon as we were up in the air. Maybe it was seeing it all from such great height: it put the rest of my problems--my father's machinations, my stepmother's plotting-- all in perspective.

Why do we humans have to be so cruel and petty to each other? My heart called out. Why see the dragons as nothing more than trainable monsters? If I could get more people to fly like this, and if I could get more dragons to trust to hold human riders, then people would be less worried about borders and wars and struggling for power. Why worry about who controls what patch of river – if you can fly for countless leagues, to new adventures?

All of this musing flashed in my mind in a second, vanishing as I saw the bodies and the faces of the terrified humans below. I had meant to scare my father's knights a little, by asking Paxala to swoop over the marketplace and stop the riot. I had meant to make the people lift their heads up to see what a real dragon was, and could do.

Instead, the only impact we were having was terrifying everybody, Knight, civilian, and clans' warrior alike.

At least they weren't fighting each other anymore, but I felt more than a little guilty. Still, it had to be done if I wanted to keep either the kingdomers or the clans from attacking each other and ending a truce that stood in the form of my mother down there.

"*Skreeayar!*" Unable to contain her similar exultant joy to my own, Paxala snorted a breath of fire as she stretched out her wings to catch the thermals, swooping low over the marketplace and passing just meters over the rooftops of the nearest houses.

"Dragon! Dragon!"

"It's gone mad!"

Snatches of shouts and wails reached us as we passed, and people ducked, jumped, ran for cover by the side of buildings and carts. With a noise like the snap of sailcloth, we passed high above the mountain gate, our turn of speed incredible as we climbed high into the cold morning air.

"Neill?" I hazarded a look behind me, to see him grimly clinging on, his form low to the back of the Crimson Red. I hated to admit it, but he was a better rider than I was – but then again, he'd had a lot more time to brush up on his riding skills on the flight up here.

"Okay!" I saw him hold a thumbs-up more than I heard the shouted word, as the Crimson Red banked and banked in a slow, graceful arc in the air to return to my father's town.

"Again?" she asked, clearly enjoying herself. How could I refuse her?

"Char!" Neill was tugging at my robe as Pax beat her wings to gain speed as she carefully repositioned herself. I spared another glance over my shoulder to see that he was pointing frantically down towards the marketplace that I was trying to disrupt.

Well, it was certainly disrupted, I could see that. The central space was mostly cleared of people now, and the knights had broken their formation and scattered back to the side streets. The clans' warriors had taken, mostly, to surrounding my mother in a thick knot of people. There were arms gesturing, shouts, and a whole lot *more* chaos. But no fighting.

Paxala started to beat her wings faster, angling her snout downwards as a diver might buck their arms and body down into a pool.

"Char!" Neill was pulling again, as we started to tip towards the ground.

"What?" I shouted in frustration, but his words were stolen by the rising wind. All I could see was that he was pretty angry with me. Why? My father had tried first to marry me off, and then poison my dragon! Neill was the one my father had imprisoned. As we started to dive once more, I saw Neill pointing frantically at the market square below, and I finally saw what he was referring to.

The civilians. Not my father's knights or the proud warriors of the clans, but the everyday mix of both, who had either come to send off the clans or to sell their wares at the mountain gate. They were cowering in fear at the sides of their stalls, just as they would if there were ever a mountain dragon attack.

Instantly, my enthusiasm chilled. How could I take out my anger with my father against them?

"Paxala, no. Please, no – pull up," I asked her quickly, but it seemed as though it was too late.

"Why?" I could sense the anger and frustration like a hot coal inside the dragon beneath me. Even though she had not made me privy to her thoughts this time, I could still sense the

shape of them, like seeing the shapes of fish underwater. They poisoned her. They trapped her, they trapped her friends. What do we owe them?

"Because they are my people too…" I tried, as we dived faster and faster, screaming towards the marketplace as fast as a hunting eagle.

"I thought we were family, Char and Paxala?" the Crimson Red said with a sudden cough of angry flame, before she beat her wings to suddenly correct her flight. Instead of careening into a low dive-bomb of the market (like we had done the first time) we were veering much higher over the houses, past the Queen's Keep itself.

"Thank you, thank you, Pax." I breathed a sigh of relief, but I could still feel the dragon's skepticism at my change of heart, and now her weariness, as one of her wings shook under the immense strain of the speeds we were traveling. She was still a little groggy, a little ill as I was – and I guess that was why we had both been so eager to listen to our anger first, rather than to Neill.

"I will make it up to you," I said to Paxala, although I had no idea how, apart from landing soon to let her eat her fill. And I would make it up to Neill, as well, somehow. I felt smaller and weaker than I had done just a little while ago. I may be Lady Char Nefrette, one of the few dragon friends left in the world, but sometimes I felt as though I was still just as foolish as I had been when I was younger. I should never have believed that my father would look after the Crimson Red, I scolded myself, as we banked over the town. We were right in front of the keep itself now, and we were turning southwards, back towards Mount Hammal.

There was a sinister low whistle and a narrow shadow shot along the earth below us. I saw a dark arrow-like log falling away to the rooftops and streets below, splintering as it struck beams and walls. What was it?

PHEWT! PHEWT! Another, and another. Was my father firing at us? I thought, as Paxala screeched in rage and beat her wings faster. Looking behind, I could see that from the forward turrets of the Queen's Keep there were some of the largest-looking bows that I had ever seen being readied and fired. They were more like harpoons, each one pulled back on a winch by two men, and standing almost as wide as I was tall.

"They're firing at us? At me?" I said in alarm as we cleared the town and then the southern gates. More black darts cut into the air behind, but the powerful beats of wings and swishes of tail disrupted their flight, causing them to tumble from their trajectory, and splinter against buildings and street. I didn't see any injuries, but I was still shocked by the callousness that my father displayed.

Would he kill me, just to bring down this dragon? Had my father learned nothing about dragons since seeing Paxala up close?

Feeling disheartened, we screamed over the walls and the wide road, sending flocks of sheep and goats scattering as we fled my father's keep. Even though I was happy to be free, I wondered now if I had just managed to make everything worse for the dragons of Mount Hammal. How would anyone in the north ever see them with admiration and fondness, now?

Beneath me, whatever Paxala thought about my human worries she kept locked in her mind.

CHAPTER 22
NEILL, WHAT WE TORVALDS DO

The flight back was not as glorious as I thought it was going to be. It wasn't being on a dragon (*riding a dragon,* I had to pinch myself to realize every time) or the flying that was upsetting. In fact, I found that being in the air always helped to lift my spirits and to make me feel alive again.

No, I hated to admit it, but it was Char.

She appeared pensive and upset, and didn't talk much about what we had just done – nor what we had seen back there at her home. Not that I could blame her; last year I had got myself screwed up into knots thinking about what my father wanted of me, and how my brothers viewed me.

It was a terrible thing, finding out how different you are from your family, to realize you didn't belong where you thought you did. I wondered what I could do to help her.

We had passed the town of Faldin's Bridge yesterday evening before making camp for the night. This would be our second day of flying. Char had wanted to fly fast and far (and how could I blame her for wanting to get away from the Queen's Keep?) but despite that, she had suggested we stop several times to let Paxala rest, and to fish. By my reckoning we were about another day away from Mount Hammal.

The Crimson Red also seemed subdued on her flight, and I wasn't sure if it was all to do with the poison that Char's father had given her. She appeared less affectionate than she usually did with Char, which wasn't something that I was expecting. Even standoffish, in fact (although that was gradually lessening as we spent more time together, and traveled farther south).

"How do you know?" Char yawned as she stamped down the little scratch of a fire that we had made last night. We had camped on a rocky bluff overlooking a river, and down below the dragon was, predictably, fishing.

"How far we've got?" I said, deciding now was as good a time as any to broach the subject, since Char was bringing it up and all. "Well, I don't know exactly, but I've been thinking about this on the way up and back," I said, by way of introduction. As Char had been so silent, I had a lot of time to think. She looked at me, eyes wide. "And, well – we want the other students to ride the dragons, right?" I stated.

"To make friends with them," Char clarified.

"Yes, of course. But to do what we do – to work *with* the dragons together," I pointed out.

"Uh-huh," Char said.

"Well, when we were flying up here, all I had to rely on was Paxala's connection to you. I just had to trust that she didn't lose the scent," I said.

"Or get sick, like at the keep," Char agreed.

"Precisely. So – I think that we need a way for the human riders to navigate up there. How do they do it on ships?"

"The stars, I think. My father once told me about the sea convoy he made as a young man. They used the stars and the winds." Char thought for a moment. "Actually, it's the same thing that we use in the mountains. We navigate at night, not during the day."

"Well, that's all well and good, but remember when we were so high up there in the sky? So high that we could see the stub of Mount Hammal above the clouds?"

Char nodded.

"Well, I was trying to measure how far we'd come by using vantage points. How much we travel in a day compared to how far away some landmark is," I said. "And that got me thinking about having lots of humans on dragons in the sky."

"Lots...?" Char asked dubiously.

"Well, you and me, Lila, Sigrid maybe, Dorf, Maxal..." I thought of all of the likely candidates amongst the students who might be able to bond with a dragon. "If you think they could, I mean."

"I don't see why not," Char said. "They seem eager to get to know the dragons, on their own terms, as well."

"Great! Well – we're going to need some way for the riders to communicate with each other whilst we're flying, not just letting the dragons take us wherever they want to go, but to actually work together." I thought of watching my brothers at their war games and practices, mounted on the tough little ponies they could wheel about and flank each other as if each rider formed a graceful whole together with the others.

"It's a good idea," Char said, a little distantly.

"But you're not convinced?" I said.

"No, it's not that– I just…" I watched as Char struggled with her own despondency. "I keep thinking about the crown, and the strange dream that I had about it. It was like the crown could break apart walls, could command the stones them- selves…. And all of it comes from dragon blood. From baby dragons."

"Skreyar!" A sudden shriek came from below, as Paxala burst from the river, shaking herself off and stalking around in circles, like a worried cat. I waited for Char to continue.

"It's bad magic, Neill," she said at last. "That's what I think. And we're going to give it straight to Zaxx, because if we don't, someone's going to die." She sounded depressed. "What good will come of that? How does that change anything at the Order? Won't Zaxx just be more powerful? And the Abbot Ansall too?"

"We can't let that happen," I said quickly, and fiercely. I

was just as horrified as Char about our grisly discovery of the source of the Draconis Order's magic. How could we let that continue?

"But how can we stop it?" Char said. "I guess part of me was hoping we *could* use my father's position to help us defeat the Draconis Order. Maybe reveal to all the lords just how cruel they were – but now that I know my own father only wants the dragons for himself, and how we escaped..." Char shook her head. "It seems that I'm failing everyone. I'll fail the dragons by bringing Zaxx the Great Crown and making him stronger, I'll fail the other students, and I've even failed my family."

"You haven't failed me," I pointed out. "I might have rotted down there in your father's cells if you weren't brave enough to break me out of there. There was no one else with you. Just you. And I saw you argue for Paxala and defy your brother, your king. I wouldn't call that failing at all, Char," I said, wondering at how differently she saw what she'd done. To me, our escape from the Queen's Keep had been a success – a difficult success, granted, especially as I had to remind Char of the civilians – but it was a success. Maybe because I had been raised to war, and strategy. Successes could be hard-won, and complicated.

"Do you really think so?" Char asked.

"I do." I nodded, before another thought struck me. "And we are going to expose the Draconis Order for what they are.

And we won't let anyone stand in our way," I said with great finality.

"But how?" Char asked, her mood already darkening.

"I am going to teach you how to fight," I said. "It is what we Torvalds do, after all."

~

It would take longer to get back to Mount Hammal, but I figured that considering that the Abbot was used to having his messengers and news travel by horse or by foot, and that Paxala was a fast flier, then we had at least a handful of extra days to train, before the rumors reached the monastery that we had flown.

We started by sparring on the ground, first after the morning campfire, our noon meal, and last thing at night. It was something that my father had made me, Rik, and Rubin all do as young lads to teach us not only the different ways to block, attack, and win a fight – but also how to toughen our bodies, and learn to 'think with our bodies' as he had put it. Prolonged exercise built memory into your actions, it allowed you to be strong no matter if you were tired, hungry, or your vision diminished because it was night time.

"Ow!" Char said, as my wooden branch swung first high, and then low to take out her legs. It wasn't that strong a strike (not like the beatings I took from my brothers, that left me black and blue), but Char flinched all the same, making me feel terrible.

"Point," I said miserably, stepping back out of the practice circle to allow her a chance to get her breath back.

"H'yargh!" Char jumped at me, clobbering me over the shoulders with her thin branch so hard that the branch snapped.

"Hey!" I lurched and stumbled, rubbing my aching back. "What did you do that for? I had stepped out of the practice ring!" I pointed to the rough circle that I had made in the clearing with leaves and twigs.

"Maybe you should have been paying more attention," Char said with a gleeful smile. "I am betting that there won't be any nice practice circles if I ever have to fight for real."

She was right. Damn. She's better than I had thought. I couldn't very well continue to be angry at her if she was right. Wasn't that also something that father said? 'Fierceness wins a fight. As does cunning, but fierceness will always win.'

The training continued on, with Char growing in confidence at her own abilities with every passing league. It helped that she had already had a good, strong basis in hunting from spending time with her mountain kin. It was that dedicated mindset, the willingness to be rough and to have scrapes. By the time we started sparring and training, Char was already a passable fighter from learning it on her mother's side, all I did was hone her skills.

What surprised me the most was, on the eve of the second

day after our noon sparring, Paxala reared her head from where she had sat, curled up on a large slab of rock.

Char looked first at the dragon, and then at me in a sort of wonder as I felt that pressure behind my eyes that I felt every time the girl shared thoughts with the dragon.

"What is it?" I asked, eyeing the Crimson Red slowly unfolding herself from her coil, and look over at me with expectation.

"She says that it looks fun. She wants to join in," Char said. "Is that even possible?"

That was when it clicked within me, I think. All of my thoughts about how to navigate and organize a team of humans on dragons. "Yes!" I said, the image of flights of dragons with their human knights flashing through the sky in my mind. I could almost *hear* them, it was so clear.

"Remember at the Queen's Keep? The way that you asked Paxala to fly?" I said, imitating the gestures with my hands, back and forth, downward sweep, upward climb...

"Yeah, I was there, remember?" Char smiled at my enthusiasm.

"That is how we do it!" I said. "How bird's fight! A dragon and their rider could dart and dodge like that, but if they added long, sweeping climbs, curves, and dives—" I held my hands out as if they were wings, imitating what I saw in my mind. "The dragon has to turn *away* from the fight to gain height and momentum, but the human riders can advise it what is happening behind it, can suggest better angles to take, when to turn. So, say I'm a dragon and I see something there—" I pointed out a place on our practice circle-- "and I swoop in, it gives my rider a chance to shoot, or to call allies, or change tactics, or whatever..."

I flapped my wings and made a tight turn at the apex of the arc. "We attack, we turn, we flip around so that the rider can reload, or observe the enemy..." I was almost giddy with excitement. "What if we had two humans and one dragon, each other calling out suggestions and making improvements all at the same time. Six eyes are better than two. That's how we can fight Zaxx, and how we can keep the other dragon's safe!" I said, before hurrying to Paxala's back. "Come on, we need to get these movements down exactly, if we are to stand a chance!"

By the end of the long afternoon we were all weary and bone-tired, but we had also succeeded. Paxala listened to Char's suggestions – *most* of the time. She could also turn on the head of a pin, it seemed, and astonished us and amazed us with ever faster and more dangerous aerial maneuvers. It was pretty shaky, and not precise flying – but it was good enough for me. This can work, I thought. If a pair of dragon friends and their dragon can work together, and they can fight together.

And Paxala was fast. Paxala was faster than I could have imagined. Faster than any of my father's horses. As fast as an arrow? I wondered, imagining what might be waiting for us when we got to the monastery.

We tarried in the wilds. Despite Char's eagerness to get back, I was adamant that we had to train. On some days it rained, but never for long, and every morning we would awake to the fogs and mists of chill early mornings. We hunted in the mountain rivers and streams until I grew sick of eating fish (Pax never did, of course), until Char eventually said that she had enough of my moaning and decided to 'take a lesson from her mother's people' and hunt. Armed only with a sharpened stake fashioned with an ash sapling, some twine gleaned from her robe, and her knife, she returned with a brace of rabbits. She was, indeed, a far better hunter than I was.

In the mornings, I spent a little while trying to think and talk through the problems that we might face. It was hard to not be worried about what might be waiting for us though. If my calculations were wrong, then that meant that a messenger on a fast horse, or one of the Prince Vincent's spies might reach the monastery before we returned. That would mean that the monks would be expecting an angry Crimson Red and two students to approach by air. How could we get around that? They might have the monks armed with bows on the walls. They could use the dragon pipes to hurt Paxala's sensitive ears before we got a chance to confront Zaxx.

"You only get good by putting in the hours," my father had said, and in this, he had been right. I remembered, too, one of the more generous comments that my father had given me during fighting practice: "It doesn't matter how good you are, or how good you think you are – just do the work, and you'll get better! Just do the work!"

On the fifth or sixth day, however, as Char's anxious urging that we get back to the dragon crater reached a fever pitch, I finally found the missing element that I hadn't even known that I had been waiting for. I was standing on the ground of a clearing, high in the wooded hills of the wilds, and watching as Char and Pax spun, turned, and swooped through the air. I had taken to using my old cream tunic as a sort of flag, raising it to signal to the flying pair that they should change direction immediately. It wasn't as good as if we had a training partner in the air as well, I knew, but it was a way to tell them: *Turn now! Now! You are under attack – duck! Dive!*

I raised my cream tunic on its stick in the air as Char and Paxala swept past. The dragon was powering forward, daring herself to fly as fast as possible when I raised the tunic-flag. Char turned her head, seeing my sign, but *instead* of what usually happened – Char using her knees and shouting suggestions into the dragon's ears, I felt that pressure inside my head once again that I knew meant that Char was conversing to Paxala with her mind. The dragon flared her wings, opening one up higher than the other so that one half of her body caught the wind much faster than the other.

Pzow! The dragon turned faster than thought, spinning on an axis and keeping her momentum as she changed direction. It was like a catapult, and Paxala roared in delight at the speed. After a moment, I raised the tunic-flag again, and again, and every time I felt that pressure and saw the girl-and-dragon team move as fast as thought.

"Did you see how fast we were going?" Char told me after she had landed. She was breathless with excitement.

"You didn't shout to Pax?" I said. "When you made the maneuvers?"

"No – I didn't need to. She was already in my mind, and I barely even had time to *see* you waving the flag, when Paxala picked up on my thought, and knew what she had to do. It felt..." I saw Char almost lost for words. "It felt like we were one thing. One being."

"Skrip-ip," the Crimson Red chirruped, her forked tongue lolling from her wide jaws in clear enthusiasm. All signs of the dragon being annoyed at Char for not letting her fight their attackers in the Queen's Keep were gone, I saw. The flying as one had bonded them. It was at that moment that I knew that we were as ready as we were ever going to be.

"Tomorrow we fly for Mount Hammal," I said, and watched as Char grinned at my side. Without needing to say it, I knew that Char felt the same way as I: we might be able to beat Zaxx if we all, humans and dragons, worked together as one.

CHAPTER 23
THE CROWN

It was around mid-afternoon as we reached the Dragon Mountain, and I urged the Crimson Red to fly low over the trees, and follow the rivers to stay out of sight. Several times I saw the spires of the Dragon Monastery above off to our left – but there was no squeal and scream of the dragon pipes. If the Draconis Order had seen our approach, then they were making no sign to us that they had.

"There, the lake," I said for Neill's benefit as much as Paxala's. Already, the great dragon was angling her wings down, and I could feel the immense forces of her muscles as they took the strain of the rushing air. Every time that I thought of how the dragon flew I was impressed. She did it all so effortlessly and easily, despite the pressures, tensions, and winds that her body was subject to.

I've had so little time to really pay attention to her, I

thought a little sadly, watching how the broad leather of her wings snapped and shook in the wind. Every scale was a marvel, really; every part of her body was covered except her eyes of course, from the tiny finger-nail sized soft lighter-colored scales around her delicate nose, to the great plates of her sides and back – some growing as large as a human shield! Even though her breed was a Crimson Red, the colors of her scales changed, too, from the deep, almost inky red of the largest scales on her side to the sunburst ruddy oranges and lighter rose as they grew smaller.

And now I was asking her to face Zaxx with me, I thought in dismay.

"Paxala can beat Zaxx." The dragon read my mind with shocking ease. *"Zaxx is old. Paxala is young."*

"But Zaxx the Golden is also cunning, and likely knows a lot of tricks," I murmured, feeling the anxiety mount as the silvery waters of Paxala's lake appeared ahead of us.

"Sckrech!" the dragon couldn't help delivering a small chirrup of delight at seeing her home again and I felt it too, now that Queen's Keep didn't feel like a home at all anymore. This was her home, of course, this lake, the waterfall, and the secluded river valley it sat upon. Not the crater up above. For a moment, all of my fears intensified – why was I asking her to challenge the Bull of the Crater if she had a home here, but the answer was immediate and obvious: because of the newts and the hatchlings. They needed to be given a future just as I had given the dragon beneath me. Paxala understood this, and

I could feel her tacit agreement as a warm wall of confidence against my thoughts. And besides, it wasn't as if Zaxx would let the Crimson Red survive out here, so close to his territory. We were flying on borrowed time, waiting until the bull got too territorial to stomach a free dragon so near.

I guess this is the closest thing that I have to a home now, too, I thought. Whilst I should have been unhappy at the thought, with the dragon holding me up, and with my friend Neill sitting behind me – I actually felt good about that.

Paxala flared her wings and stretched out her legs as I had seen her land on the lake before – though never with a rider on her back. I held my breath, excited and terrified to be the first dragon friend to ride a water landing.

Woosh! A sudden, great spray of water as she sheared through and along the surface, beating her wings to encourage her to half-fly, and half-float, before she could tuck her legs up underneath her and paddle along the cold waters of the lake to the shingle beach at the far end.

"Woo!" Neill was laughing behind me, and, for just the briefest moment, I had to agree. We were soaked, but we were together.

~

"We have to challenge Zaxx," Neill said, his tone certain. "As soon as Zaxx knows that the Draconis Order is based on the blood of his young, then surely even Zaxx has to see what should happen?" Something had changed in him since being in my father's dungeons, I thought. It was like the man in him was coming out, and he wasn't so much the gangly youth that he had been before. What made him so confident now? Was it seeing us working together as a team? Was it being forced to rely upon himself and not on his brothers or family name? Whatever it was, it made him believe, apparently, that we could perform impossible things.

"Isn't Zaxx in on it too?" I asked. Neill himself had been the one to tell me that he had overheard the Abbot and Zaxx talking about which crater dragons to cull?

"Then we let the other dragons know, and the students, and the monks, just what the Draconis Order has been up to," Neill said triumphantly, but I couldn't bring myself to share his enthusiasm. *Killing baby dragons,* my heart reminded me, and I heard a low, answering grumble from Paxala beside us.

"But first, there's something that we have to do," I said, turning to rummage in my pack as Neill looked at me wonderingly.

"What?" he said, already impatient until he saw the delicate handkerchief that I brought out, the same one that I had wrapped the baby dragon teeth that we had collected in the Queen's Keep. Standing with her long neck arching over us, Paxala started to make a high, keening noise.

"I know, girl, I know… we're going to put this right," I murmured to her as I took out my dagger, and started to dig a small pit in the earth at the edge of the tree line, overlooking the cool lake and the slopes of Mount Hammal below. After just a few moments, I was joined by Neill, using his own dagger to help me dig and clawing out stones.

"Skee-rip." an impatient sound from Paxala behind us, and suddenly she was nudging us gently out of the way with her snout, before making a few clawing pulls at the same patch of ground, drawing out more rocks and earth in just those two motions than we ever could. I nodded, yes, this felt right too, as the dragon withdrew and sat just behind us on her haunches.

Very gently, I placed the handkerchief and the baby dragon teeth into the hole, before standing up and looking down. Something needed to be said, I knew, but I didn't know what. What poetry mourned dragons? What would the spirits of the dragons – if they existed – be pleased with?

"Gone before us, but not forgotten," Neill surprised me by suddenly saying in a clear voice. *"Your memory guides us, your life honors us,"* he said, before falling silent. The air was still, and the light was sharp over the lake. At last, I found the words that I wanted to say.

"Sleep well," I murmured, just before Paxala let out a singular gout of flame into the air. A sudden smell of soot, before she started to nudge the rocks and stones back over the baby teeth. It was done, and I looked over at Neill with a tear in my eye.

"I hope that you don't mind," he said, looking at me

gravely. "They're Torvald Clan words spoken at a funeral, they were all that I know…"

"They were perfect," I shushed him, shaking myself. The desire to put an end to this travesty was stronger than ever in me now. "Okay, let's do this," I said, still unable to shake my feeling of despair, despite the optimism expressed by my friend.

We walked up to the ridge in the late afternoon light, as I didn't want to risk setting off the dragon pipes. Still, I knew that the monks might see us at any moment. Beside me, Neill went silent and watchful as a look of determined concentration took over his face.

What if Zaxx decides to kill all of the young after we refuse to give him the crown? I thought. What if Zaxx attacks my beloved Paxala? Should we just give him the crown, I thought, before being horrified at my own defeatism.

"Pfft. Char is not thinking right." The voice of the Crimson Red suddenly appeared in my head. I nodded that I knew, but was still unable to shake the feeling of despair that we were walking to our doom, and that life would be so much easier if we just gave in…

"Char, look!" It was Neill, hunkering down behind one of the many boulders that littered the other side of the mountain, above the crater itself. He was pointing down towards the broad circular space, down to the green foliage of the hot-loving plants and the rising steams.

"What am I supposed to be looking at?" I asked Neill. As far as I could see, there didn't seem to be anything wrong or different at all.

Neill frowned at me, as if I had sworn at him or was being deliberately obtuse. "No dragons, Char. No dragons on the resting-rocks."

He was right. At various points around the insides of the crater there were large slabs of rock that must have been thrown up by the volcano long ago, or else fallen in from the tall sides. They acted as natural sun traps and heated slabs from the many steams and hot pools that bubbled up down there. And all dragons loved them. They were the place to sun themselves or to sleep, and the biggest and largest dragons commanded the best spots throughout the day.

But this time, there were no dragons in sight at all – not even the smaller Messenger dragons that usually flitted and darted through the trees like swallows, constantly chittering.

"Where are they all?" I asked. "Pax?"

In answer to my question, the Crimson Red carefully sniffed the air, breathing in and out to let the scents of the other dragons run over her forked tongue. *"Below ground,"* she informed me. *"And afraid."*

Oh no, I thought, as we hurried down towards the lip of the crater. Had we taken too long in coming back to the mountain? Had Zaxx already started fulfilling his promise to me, that he would start to kill the younger dragons and the students – any one I loved, really-- as a punishment for not bringing him the Great Crown?

"Remember Char: we have something that he wants…" Neill whispered as we got to the lip, all three of us standing side by side and looking down into the crater. I could feel a burning ball of anger rising in the Crimson Red at my side as her claws extended from their sheaths to clutch onto the rocky walls of the ridge. Zaxx had killed her parents and smashed the brood eggs of her brothers and sisters. Paxala could never forgive him. If it weren't for me and Neill, then Paxala probably would have thrown herself down into the crater already and challenged Zaxx alone.

It's not only Neill who has grown confident in his abilities while we've been away, but Paxala too, I thought. So then, why did I feel so terrible? I bit my lip as I looked at my colleagues, to see Neill watching me expectantly. This was my fight to start, I saw. I was the one who had saved Paxala and raised her first, so I was her guardian.

"Zaxx…?" I called out, my voice sounding weak and fearful – probably because that was precisely how I was feeling at that moment as well.

What was wrong with me? My fear grew. Wasn't this precisely the moment that I had been waiting for? The chance to confront Zaxx?

"Zaxx the Golden…" I coughed, "I call you…" my voice sounded small and far away, and Neill glanced at me in alarm.

"Char? Are you feeling alright?" he said. "We're here, right beside you."

"I'm fine," I lied, knowing that both he and the Crimson Red could see right through it.

"*Zaxx!*" This time, with the support of my friends, my voice carried down into the crater, and this time, something answered.

"*RuuaarghhK!*" came a grumbling, rumbling sound-- not from the crater itself – but from behind us. The ground shook, and rocks fell into the crater and at our feet as we stumbled back from the edge. At my side, Paxala hissed and lashed her tail in frustration, her head whipping this way and that as she sought to identify the bull dragon's location.

"*Ruaaaarghhkk!*" The sound grew larger and closer, and it was undeniably coming from the training tunnel Monk Feodor had taken us to. As the ground cracked and shook, my sense of fear and terror only increased. *We can't do this. This is madness. This is impossible.*

"*Char. This is not you. These are not your thoughts,*" Paxala said into my mind, and leapt in front of me, half shielding me with her wings.

"But… but what do you mean?" I shook my head, looking down to see that my hands were already untying the knot in the bundle of rags that held the crown. When had I decided to do that? I knew that I wanted to give the crown to the great and mighty Zaxx – but why?

"*Char is thinking with Zaxx's thoughts,*" Paxala snarled as the ground in front of us heaved, as if something giant was tunneling its way out of the earth below…

Of course. The Abbot had managed to hypnotize us students with his meditations – was it possible for a dragon to do the same? A dragon that was as powerful and as ancient as Zaxx was?

"Child." This time, the voice of the dragon in my mind wasn't that of Paxala – it was the mighty gold dragon Zaxx himself, and rocks and debris flew everywhere, as he exploded out of the training tunnel like a fat worm.

The fear and terror that I had been feeling fell upon me in waves, and it was all coming from this dragon in front of us. I even saw Neill quailing beside me, his face draining, and his eyes going wide.

"Skrechyar!" Zaxx had no hold over Paxala, however, as the Crimson Red made a small half-jump, challenging the much larger Gold. Paxala was mad–we all were--to challenge him.

The wyrm clawed itself out of the earth, and hissed. *"That feels better,"* he said, taking time to turn his alligator-like head to snap at offending dregs of dead skin and scales, ripping them off with teeth that were as ancient and yellowed as old bones. Zaxx was showing us how nonchalant he was about our presence, exposing the long wattles and folds of his skin to Paxala

She hissed in frustration and eagerness to challenge him,

narrowing her gold-green eyes at the one that had killed her parents.

"My child," Zaxx said again, lifting his great head to regard us all with apparent amusement. *"What a pleasure to see you again. Have you brought what I asked you for?"* I could feel Zaxx's words in my mind, and with every breath came the pulse of fear and anxiety. If I had thought that there was a window in my mind that was a place where Paxala and I intertwined, then now I knew that through that window could also peer this monster, pouring fear and self-doubt into my being.

"No," I said, as much to Zaxx in my mind as to my fears. "Paxala was right. These doubts and thoughts are not mine – they are yours!" With the revelation came my own flood of confidence. I *should* be proud at having saved Paxala, and standing up to my father, and turning down Tobin Tar, and how close I and Paxala had bonded. We *were* fast, and we were young, and we were strong.

"You mean the crown?" I asked, my voice hissing with Paxala's.

Zaxx blinked slowly, turning his gold-filled gaze to look directly at me, and me alone. It was hard to meet the dragon's unblinking stare, but I did so.

"Girl. What gives you the impression that I was ever, that I would ever, be talking to you?" Zaxx hissed maliciously, and I recoiled.

"But you called me child," I said in horror, as the full enormity of what Zaxx was suggesting settled on my shoulders.

"Child. Return to me," Zaxx hissed once more, his great and heavy tail flopping to one side and cracking rocks. Zaxx wasn't talking to me. He was talking to Paxala.

CHAPTER 24
REVELATIONS

"**Y**ou are my child. Come home," Zaxx hissed at my friend, my dragon-sister, the Crimson Red.

Paxala roared in defiance, unwilling to accept whatever Zaxx had to say, as my mind raced.

Could it be true? Could Zaxx the Golden be Paxala's father? It made perfect sense in some horrible way. Zaxx was the breeding bull of the crater. Any other male dragon in the Crater had to be subordinate, secondary, to Zaxx's wishes and whims. Would the Bull Golden dragon allow or even tolerate a male Crimson Red, full grown at half the size of him, to even exist, let alone breed within the crater?

Of course, he wouldn't. So Paxala had to be child of the only bull with enough authority: Zaxx.

"Yes, Paxala. You are my child, and that is why I have suffered your existence out there by the lake, and the

pandering of the humans." Neill looked at me in consternation and worry. He had already drawn his short sword – which wasn't even as big as one of the bull's claws. He would be ripped apart in moments.

"*Ssssss…*" Paxala's tail whipped with the sound like snapping twigs.

"*Did you believe that you had hidden from me? I, the greatest wyrm left in the world? I – who can see for a hundred leagues, and smell for a hundred more? I – who was young when this crater still belched fire? I – who flew between the Three Mountains of our race at the head of his own clutch?*"

Three Mountains? What Three Mountains? I thought.

"*Ssss,*" Zaxx the Mighty hissed. "*You can hear the humans chatter too, can you not, Paxala? There is so much that you and they do not know about our race. So much forgotten. So much that I can teach you.*"

Paxala snarled in disgust at her father.

"*There used to be many more dragon friends when I was young. It was not so unusual for dragons to share their thoughts with humans, but now, so few dragons can do it – just as so few humans can hear us. That is how you know that you are truly my daughter, Paxala, daughter of Zaxx. You have the gifts that I do. You will make a mighty Brood-Queen, one century…*"

"*Skreckh! Skrekh!*" Paxala spoke in pure dragon-tongue, but still I could discern her meaning easily. She was having none of whatever her father wanted to offer her. *And why should she? Zaxx killed her mother, and left her to die as a barely-hatched newt out in the wilds.* Only now we had something that Zaxx wanted, was he being 'nice' to her.

"The crown belongs to us, my daughter. Yours and mine. It was made from the blood of our kin, and it traps within it the power of our noble blood. Give me the crown, Paxala. Tell your human to return it to us."

My hands shook as I held the heavy burden, and now Paxala herself had turned her head to look at it, her eyes flaring in anger.

"I didn't know the secret of the Order, before…" I promised her, suddenly terrified that Paxala would take Zaxx's side and hate *me* for the sins of the other, long-dead humans.

"Once we have that crown, all of that power will return to us, my daughter. Think of the generations of dragons you will avenging. Think of your place in the world: at the top of it!" Zaxx had lowered his head to hiss sibilantly at her.

Paxala made a sort of short, clucking noise that I hadn't heard her make before. Had I judged everything so wrong? Why had I never stopped to ask the Crimson Red what *she* wanted to do with this crown, and this knowledge?

"Open," Paxala's voice echoed in my head, but it was not the warm feminine voice that she usually reserved for our inter-thought communications. It was harsh and strong, and full of fire.

Unwilling or unable to disobey her, I let the wrappings fall away to reveal the double steel and gold crown of the old queen, glittering with its large egg-shaped flame-red ruby, and two flanking blue earthstar gems on either side.

"Char...?" Neill said warningly, but how could I refuse Paxala? This monstrosity of metal that I held in my hands did, after all, belong to her in the end. It contained the blood of so many of her kin – not mine. I held it aloft, not knowing what I should do next.

"Throw me the crown," the Crimson Red said to me, her voice laden with outrage and hatred.

"Char...?" Neill was crossing the space between us, a look of alarm on his face. But I knew that we were defeated. We had tried to confront Zaxx, but the Gold Bull was far wilier and wiser than any of us here. He had outfoxed us and had laid this trap for us, all the while knowing that Paxala was his child, and knowing that Paxala would be furious over what the humans had done to her family. A part of me wondered how long that Zaxx the Golden had been planning this moment. Had he suffered Paxala to live, just so that she could be the one to fly to my father's keep, retrieving the accursed Great Crown of the dead Queen Delia? Had Zaxx even somehow planned that it would be me, the child of the Northern Prince who would bond with his daughter? Zaxx the Golden had lived for centuries, if not millennia. I had no idea how complicated and deep some of his plans and schemes might be.

"Pax, please – we cannot let Zaxx take this crown. It is too much bad power..." I pleaded with the Crimson Red, but her tail lashed and thumped on the floor impatiently.

"Throw the crown, Char," the Crimson Red demanded again.

And so I did.

~

With a cry of anguish, I threw the Great Crown of the dead queen high into the air between us, and in that moment, I threw all of my frustration, despair, and stubbornness at the cruelty of fate. I did not know what would happen next – only that we were all pawns in a game played by dragons and princes.

All I wished was to have Paxala back at my side, with Neill on the other. *I don't even want this crown. I don't want anything coming between me and my friends. Maybe now Zaxx will leave us alone--*

"Char – no!" Neill reached me, but it was too late. The double-crown arched high over our heads.

Paxala screeched and moved as fast as a striking snake, a tremor running up the entire length of her body as the fire-sacs at the sides of her neck filled and bulged. She roared a precise jet of molten dragon fire that engulfed the Great Crown, blasting it into the rocks of the mountain with sizzling, boiling clouds of black, acrid smoke.

Purple and blue sparks were released into the depths of the firestorm, there was the sound of shattering gemstones and the crack of pressure-heated rocks as the ground boiled-

A shockwave lifted me and Neill from our feet, and slammed us backwards, tumbling us head over heels until we finally came to rest, our bodies entangled a few hundred meters away. The world whirled, my head ached, I felt sick as I looked back up the slopes to where Zaxx the Golden and Paxala had managed to stand their ground.

"What have you done! You idiot! You ungrateful, selfish, human-tainted idiot!" Zaxx roared in disbelief, liquid fire falling from his jaws in hissing drops.

But something strange was happening amidst the dark smokes and destruction. Where the smoke wavered clear for a brief moment, I could see a crater as big as a horse cart, black with melted minerals and burnt rock. Small, shinier bits of metal glittered around the crater as the Great Crown bubbled and hissed. And in the steams of the crater, there escaped the hisses and whines of a hundred voices, screeches and chirrups, sharp calls and haunting shrieks of dragon voices. It sounded like a terrible, rising wind, and the clouds overhead started to darken and lower.

"Paxala will never call Zaxx father," the Crimson Red thundered with her young and noble voice. *"Paxala has her family."* With that, the Crimson Red leapt into the air and rode the thermals down the mountain slope straight towards us. I was crying in joy and relief, and Neill shaking himself to his feet as the claws of our friend snatched us from the earth, as fast and as quick as a fishing eagle, as she carried us off, towards the monastery...

CHAPTER 25
CONFRONTATIONS

"*Skreayar!*" Paxala shouted as we swept over the black rocks, the dark stone walls of the Dragon Monastery rose up to meet us. There ahead, was the tall spire of the Abbot's tower, matched in height only by the Astrographer's Tower with its strange collection of brass and gold-looking ornaments. Between them the Great Hall; several stories high, with windows like narrow tombstones (only filled with glass, not stone) – and everywhere on the battlements, monks running.

"They've seen us," Neill stated the obvious, his brow furrowed. I could tell that he was thinking exactly the same as I was. What was going to happen next? Had we misjudged this so badly?

"*Pax...*" I reached out to the dragon beneath me in my mind, and I felt in return a hot incandescence – a fire like that which I hadn't felt before. Was she angry with me? With all of us humans for what we had done to her kin? "Paxala, I am so sorry, about everything," I thought. "I just wanted to keep you safe. I didn't know that Zaxx was your father..." Even though Zaxx was terrible; a brute, even—I didn't want to ask Paxala to fight him. How could I ask a daughter to fight her father, when I knew just what turmoil and hurt was in my own heart?

Again, fiery rage, hurtful feelings, and anger from the dragon. But she was flying towards the monastery, and she wasn't throwing us off of her back (which she could easily do if she wanted, I realized).

Behind us, the ridgeline of the mountain was engulfed in smoke and flame as Zaxx the Golden roared in rage at what his daughter had done. I had never seen the bull fully enraged, and sounds of his thundering calls were booming down the mountain. *What will he do now?* I was terrified that the Gold would take out his rage against the smaller dragons. He had promised me that if I did not return the crown to him he would take his revenge against the younger dragons, against the students, against everyone.

"I will stop him." Paxala's voice in my mind.

How? I thought back at her, but I could feel from the white-hot fury of the Crimson Red that she would brook no argument.

Ahead of us, on the battlement walls, the older black-clad monks of the Draconis Order were assembling, directed by a figure that I recognized even from this distance: the hunched and gangly form of Monk Olan.

"Archers! I need archers!" the little man was baying, as four or five monks raised short bows towards us.

There was a convulsion from inside the dragon beneath us, as once again she poured fire out – but not towards her attackers, but instead, towards the walls below them. With a plume of smoke and steam, the walls were engulfed – we heard shouts, and the monks fell back as Paxala used the rising thermal to catch her wings and land as gracefully as a bird of prey. She suddenly swung her head at the fleeing monks, bellowing her rage and hatred at what they had been complicit in. One of them jumped from the walls, to land on the stacked straw and hay carts below.

"The dragon's gone mad! It'll kill us all!" I heard Olan wail in terror (from the far safety of the next section of wall, I saw) and run in the direction of the dragon pipes.

"Don't worry about Paxala!" Neill shouted angrily, already clambering from her back to leap onto the walls of the monastery. "It's *that* dragon up there that you really have to worry about." He gestured above us all, up to the ridge where Zaxx was thrashing in frenzy and fire. Neill strode towards the nearest monks, his short sword lowered but clearly warning them not to attack.

That's the dragon that we all have to worry about, I thought, unwilling to get down from Paxala's neck.

"Leave me, Char. This is something that I have to do." Paxala's voice in my mind was sharp, and I felt hurt by her sudden insistence on independence. Immediately, however, I

felt bad for thinking this. Hadn't I been feeling hurt over my own father's insistence to see me as a tool? Didn't I want to be the one to confront him, alone?

"But I don't want you to be hurt," I thought at her, dismayed. *"How can I let you do this alone?"*

"Because I am fast. Very fast. I will travel to the crater to tell the other dragons what I have learned. That the Draconis Order of old has been using their eggs for their foul magics. They will need to hear it from me in person, or else they will not believe me. This is dragon business, Char, and I must do this. They will rise up against Zaxx, I am sure," Paxala said. *"It will take too long to introduce you as well, and get the brood mothers to respect you..."* She flicked her wings in impatience.

"But what if Zaxx comes for you?" I said.

"When he comes for me," the Crimson Red corrected. *"I will lead him away from the crater. As you said: I am faster than the bull. I can out-fly him."* And then the Crimson Red said something that went straight through me, straight to my heart. *"Trust me, sister-Char. Just as I have trusted you to guide me, so you will have to trust me."*

"And if you need me, Paxala? Will you call?" I asked, my heart in my chest.

"That is what friends do." There was another roar from the mountain top, and a sound like a snap of thunder as a giant shape emerged from the smoke heading downwards towards

us. *"Now get off me, sister-Char. I must put right what my father has done wrong."*

This time, I did as the Crimson Red had asked of me, and I slid from her neck to her shoulder, elbow, foot-claws and to the stone beneath. A sudden wave of dizziness as my body once again was on solid ground after all of that frantic flying, and then a rush of wind-blast as Paxala leapt from the battlements behind me. She shot as fast as an arrow towards the crater, the smoke rolling around her wings.

"Char!" Neill was calling, pointing back towards the monastery grounds, where a large delegation of Draconis Monks headed towards us across the courtyard, and, at their head was the Abbot Ansall.

"I see him," I said, wondering what I was going to say, just as the air shook with the sound of the dragon pipes being played from the Astrographer's Tower.

The pipes were so raucously loud that they even hurt *my* ears, and several of the monks below us flinched.

"Neill?" I called in alarm, thinking of how the monks used the dragon pipes to try and subdue the dragons in the crater – their ears were so sensitive that the monks had found a way to use the brass pipes to drive them back when it was feeding time. "We need to direct the pipes on Zaxx – but somehow not distract Paxala!" I shouted.

"I got it, Char." Neill was nodding as he ran down the battlements towards the Astrographer's Tower. I had no idea *how* he was going to separate out the pipe blasts, but as I saw him running away from me – I knew that I could trust him. Just as I could trust Paxala to do what she said she would. Once again, I had that brief feeling of connection that I had whilst we were flying together; that I and the Crimson Red were one, and together with Neill we were all a part of one, larger, working unit.

Together, I thought.

"Together," echoed in my mind from the distant Paxala.

"Char Nefrette!" shouted a voice from below me. Looking down, I saw that it was the Abbot below me. "What have you done? Zaxx the Golden has arisen from his crater! He is marching on the monastery, even now!"

From the sounds of the thundering roars and scraping claws like steel on shields, I knew full well what Zaxx the Golden was about to do. He was climbing down the mountain side towards us like a slow avalanche of muscle, claws, and talons. But he wasn't flying, I saw, his wings barely more than weakened stubs from centuries of worming his way through the mountain. *He can't fly. The Gold can't fly.* I thought in sudden hope. It would take him a little while to get down here. Not enough time to lay traps or set defenses perhaps, but enough time to raise the warning. I turned back to the Abbot, and as my eyes fell on him I was filled with rage and disgust.

"I know what you are, Abbot. I know what you have done!" I shouted down to him, pointing an accusing figure at the thin leader of the monastery. "The Draconis Order is built on the blood of dead dragons! You used their blood for your terrible rituals and magics – that is the secret of the Draconis Order!"

"Bah!" The Abbot snarled back, raising one hand like a claw towards me. "The magic that you yourself have been trained in? The very same magic that courses through your veins?" His face flushed an angry pinkish-red, and his eyes glittered in fury. "How dare you stand there and defy me. After all that I have taught you?"

"I will never use your tainted magic, old man," I spat back, looking at his fellow monks who stood around him. "Do the rest of you know where his power comes from? Newts. Hatchlings. Dragon's blood. Don't any of you care for the dragons in that crater?"

I saw the ripple of unease spread through the other black-clad Dragon Monks as my words hit home. After all, they had only ever seen the Abbot actually use his magic. And they had been taught to believe that the dragons were nearly godlike, and noble. They knew the truth of what I was saying, they had to!

"Shut up, child. You have no idea of what you speak," the Abbot snapped at me, and he flexed his hand in the air as his lips curled around the strange words. *"Draco Hamba Silencio..."*

Something hit me like a cold wave. A feeling of having a heavy blanket thrown over my face as I staggered back from the edge of the parapet, opening and closing my mouth like a landed, gasping fish.

When I tried to call out to the monks, to Neill, no sound escaped my mouth except a brief wheeze of air. I could still breathe, but it was as if my voice became caught in a net any time that I tried to talk. I gasped, panted, and tried again but to no avail.

"There. Now no one has to listen to your treason," the Abbot said triumphantly, as the sounds of Zaxx's thunder and roaring only drew closer.

"Monks – get up there and get her, now!"

I had failed again, failed everyone – the students, the monastery—just as I had feared. Everyone was going to die here because of me.

But then, hope kindled as I heard one of the monks say, "What did the student mean, that we've been using dragon blood?"

One of the black-robed monks had stopped in front of the Abbot, refusing to follow the others that were even now running up the stone steps towards me.

"I never signed up to butcher dragons," the monk, a tall, broad man with a long nose said. No one I recognized, but one who clearly knew his right from wrong.

"Idiot!" the Abbot snarled, making another gesture with his crooked-finger hands, and uttering a short, sharp curse. *"Flamos!"*

I watched in horror as a ball of fiery energy flew from the Abbot's seemingly empty hands, engulfing the questioning monk's head as he screamed and staggered back, on fire.

There were gasps around him, but the Abbot didn't stop his tirade. "Obey me!" Ansall shouted. "You will obey me! Do you think that it is easy to control dragons? Do you think that there would not be a price?"

There were gasps and murmurs from around the Abbot, as many more of the elder Draconis Monks arrived in the court-yard, and with them, the students. I saw Dorf and Sigrid standing there, Lila, Maxal – even Terrence. The older Dragon Monks who were running towards me paused, suddenly shocked by what their master had done below. Unable to speak, I drew my knife and crouched, ready to face them if I had to.

"What the girl says is true," a voice shouted – it was the rich, deep baritone of Monk Feodor, the dragon 'handler', striding from the crowd of onlookers as the sky filled with Zaxx's smoke. "You all know me. And I was there, as well as a number of you, on the last time that the Abbot ordered one of the young taken to the caves beneath the monastery." I could see the large dragon handler monk slowly raise his arm, for all there to see the white rivers of scars that ran down it like thick cords of rope.

"He did what?" Terrence said, looking in horrified awe at Feodor and Ansall.

"The Abbot had negotiated with Zaxx for the young ones to be taken away for his experiments. I was stupid, and I followed his orders…" Feodor hung his head in shame. The tension between Feodor and the Abbot crackled, as I could see

Ansall carefully judging the mood of the gathering crowd around him.

"But Zaxx sought to break the deal. He charged at the Abbot, and I got in the way, seeking to defend him – although I wish I hadn't now. Zaxx almost gutted me and left me for dead, and if it wasn't for the Abbot's magic and the dragon pipes, I would be dead," the chief handler said gravely.

"Aha! So you see?" the Abbot Ansall crowed. "You have to admit that what I did was right. I saved you, you ungrateful wretch. I am the only one standing between those monsters out there and all of your deaths!"

But the growling and howling of the fierce and angered Zaxx was close now, so close that I felt the stone of the walls under my feet shake and tremble. In the face of such a terrible beast, I could see the older monks and even some of the students starting to side nervously with the Abbot. The Abbot might have questionable tactics – but they were all going to be obliterated any moment by an angry bull dragon if they didn't support him, and use his magic.

"They are not monsters," Feodor said solemnly, lowering his hand slowly as he faced off against the Abbot. "Even Zaxx is no monster. They are creatures, and they are angry at what you have done to them, *sir* Abbot." The larger monk stalked towards the Abbot, rolling his shoulders as he did so. Feodor was a far larger man that the Abbot, and it was like watching a mountain decide to snap a sapling.

"Traitor!" Ansall screeched, once again extending his

claw-like hands, this time towards Feodor himself. *"Flamos!"* the Abbot shouted as I opened my mouth to shout, to tell the kinder monk to duck, to jump, to get out of the way. *"Flamos! Flamos!"* Ansall repeated, firing from out of nowhere wave after wave of rolling fire, engulfing the larger man.

I watched helplessly as Feodor screamed, stumbled, his entire body one pillar of fire, before he took a mighty, staggering step forward towards the Abbot, and then another.

Oh my god. He's still alive, I thought, as we all--students and ordained monks-- watched in silence. The flaming man staggered another step, and then another towards the Abbot, until the black smoke swirled around both men – was he going to make it? Was he going to kill the Abbot with his own magic?

But with a small sound like a sigh amidst the flaming roar, Feodor collapsed to his knees, and then to the ground, dead. We all stood, watching at what the Abbot had done, fear spreading through the crowd. The dragon handler Feodor might have been brusque, he might not have suffered fools – but everyone knew him as an honest and hardworking man. Loyal. He would die for his brothers and sisters here at the monastery. And, I guess he had. I was sure that everyone who stood in the courtyard of the Dragon Monastery was thinking the same thing: Who was the real monster now?

CHAPTER 26
NEILL, CHOICES

T he dragon pipes were deafening at this close range, as I hurled myself through the door of the Astrographer's Tower and up the stone stairs beyond. I felt a pop and my hearing was replaced with a high pitched, tinny whine that I guess was my ears screaming in pain from the reverberations of the pipes.

How on earth did the monks ever operate them? I thought, as I rounded the set of spiral stairs onto the first landing, to see a stone archway and the stairs continuing upwards once more.

What was that? Through the stone archway I could see long, floor to ceiling cylinders of brass-colored metal, filling the room entirely. They had to be some part of the pipe mechanism – but there were no monks here 'playing it.' In fact, I couldn't even see any way for the monks to 'play' them here, as I stuck my head in to see that the room was entirely comprised of pipes, as well as canvas-and-wood bellow systems. Pipes made of more metal disappeared up into the floors above.

They'd turned the entire tower into a musical weapon. No wonder the dragons were so hurt by it!

I ran farther up the stairs as the tower wobbled and shook. Was it Zaxx? Was the Gold bull here already? I had no time to waste – although I still had no idea what I was going to do once I got there. Another floor landing passed, and another room full of the pipes and bellows equipment. My legs burned, and I wished that I could be out there in the courtyard, facing off the Abbot as Char was surely doing, when I smelled smoke and fire coming from somewhere. No time! No time!

Past another floor, until finally the stairs widened out and I burst into the center of a wide, circular room with more of the strange, fluting apparatus clogging the walls and floor. Bronze pipes ran everywhere, coiling back upon themselves like serpents, rattling and hissing as the alarm calls were broadcast.

Up here though, the sound wasn't so intense, and I could see the three people who worked the machinery each wore a tight-fitting leather cap over their skulls and ears. They were working something like a bellows, with one person sitting in a chair and pulling on sticks and levers, whilst another pulled on large cogs to pump the bellows. My mind registered that seemed to even be different settings for the bellows, and the person in the 'chair' could turn the pipes on the outer walls to direct at various parts of the mountain or sky.

"You!" cried a voice-- muffled to my poor ears, but still audible. It was none other than Monk Olan – the younger, cruel sidekick to the old Quartermaster Greer. Olan sneered, dropped the wheel that he had been pulling, and took up his staff for the charge towards me.

Olan was a young monk, but still a lot older than me. However, I was already taller and broader than he was. I squared my shoulders and drew my short sword, ready to meet his attack.

"Fool!" Olan sneered, hesitating before he attacked (I think that it was seeing my sword being held casually and ready, while he only had a stick). Behind him the two other monks – one in the chair, one at the bellows – looked terrified.

"It's over. Your little rebellion has been crushed just like all the others. You are nothing, Torvald. A bastard child of greater men. The Abbot has discovered your treachery, and he will come and cleanse you both with fire!" Olan said savagely, echoing almost exactly the same sentiments as his mentor, Greer, and I snarled at him.

"No, Olan, it is you who are the fool here. Zaxx is coming, and he will put an end to all of this, all of you – all because of what the Draconis Order has been up to. Sacrificing baby dragons! Ripping them from their brood mother's clutches!" I shouted, hearing the gasp of horror from the two other working monks.

"Enough of your lies and treachery!" Olan said, his voice pitched toward desperation. "You riled Zaxx up, that is what happened – you and that Crimson Red of yours riled him up and now he's come looking for you!"

"Really?" I said, feeling strangely calm as I started to circle around him. "You really think that Char, another dragon and I would make the mighty Zaxx seek to go to war with the entire monastery? A relationship that he has been cultivating for generations?" I laughed, finding the idea ridiculous. This time when I spoke, I did not bother to argue with the fanatical Olan. Instead, I glanced over to the other two working monks. "When have Char or I ever been known to hurt a dragon? Why would we enrage Zaxx? Why would Zaxx care so much about us?"

The other two worker-monks were scared, looking back and forth between Olan and me. I seized upon their indecision. "You know that I speak truth. You must have seen hints, rumors, had suspicions. Why does the Abbot have so much power? Where does it come from? Why does Zaxx even bother to listen to him? Because the Abbot has found a way to make magic from dragon blood!"

The two other monks startled and shivered at the dread of it, and well I could understand why. Every monk brought or sent here as a recruit did so because they were in love with dragons, not because they wanted to farm them like cattle.

The monk at the bellows took a small step away from his mechanism.

"Get back to your post! Or we'll all be killed!" Olan screamed at him, and looked appalled as the other monk got up from the harness-chair and stood awkwardly next to his friend. "No. I cannot condone this either, Olan," he said warily.

"Uch. Cowards." Olan swung his stick around in a wide arc, destined to catch the nearest of his fellow workers in a stunning blow that would probably have killed him, but I was already moving, leaping forward to bring up my short sword in an arc that caught the stave square in the middle of its length.

The staff collapsed into a shower of splinters as the dragon pipes continued to sound around us, and Olan fell back, defenseless. He looked at me in fear as I held up my short sword level with his eyes.

"I won't kill you without a weapon in your hands," I said, remembering what my father would have said: there's no honor in killing weaklings. "Get yourself a blade, or get out of this tower, and this monastery as well. If I ever see you again…" I said, but Olan didn't wait around to hear what would inevitably happen. Screeching and whimpering, he turned and ran back down the steps, as I slumped, taking a deep breath.

From outside, Zaxx's roar was very close now, his voice even louder than the screeching of the pipes above. The tower was starting to wobble with the thunder of his charging claws.

"Quickly," I said to the other two monks as I sheathed my blade. "You have nothing to fear from me. Is there a way to use the pipes only against one dragon? Not against others?"

"They're designed to subdue every dragon nearby, but sometimes we've had to concentrate on particular rogues in the past," the original detractor said. "There are baffles that we can install, we can change the tone and the frequency" --I had no idea what he was talking about at this point-- "and we can also direct the pipes towards one area – but it won't completely protect the others..."

"Okay." I nodded. "Just so long as we can give Zaxx a much harder time than our friends out there..." We set to work, the monks telling me which pipes to stuff with rags, with wheels to freeze in place on wooden wedges, and which lever to pull which would swing the pipes on the outer side of the Astrographer's Tower straight at the coming bull dragon.

CHAPTER 27
DESTRUCTION, JUDGEMENT

He had killed Monk Feodor. The Abbot just killed Feodor and another monk for doing nothing other than questioning him – right there in front of all of us! That was what I was thinking, and, as I looked up at my would-be monk attackers silently, I could tell that was what they were thinking as well.

They were wide-eyed in fear, and the crowd around the Abbot looked half fearful, half furious.

"He killed him for no reason," I heard someone shout from the crowd.

"No reason at all!" another monk called.

"Feodor was right!" shouted none other than Dorf Lesser, my friend, standing proud of the others.

"Dorf – be careful!" I gasped instinctively, suddenly aware that my voice had come back. It must have been that as the

Abbot concentrated his magic on killing Feodor, he had no time to maintain his enchantment of me as well.

"The Abbot is a tyrant!" I shouted, and there was a ragged, angry yell from below as the crowd started to close in around the thin, evil little man...

"Stand back, you fools." There was another glimmer of fire, as the Abbot held aloft a ball of burning flame as he stood over the smoking and blackened bodies of two of his most loyal monks. "You're all going to die without me, you know that, don't you?"

"You took *baby* dragons from their nests, and sacrificed them for your magic," I accused him. "And you dare call us stupid? You killed two monks who sought to question you. What sort of future will you give us? Will you give the Order? The dragons out there?"

Much to my surprise, there was a cheer from the other monks down below as they heard my words. I felt inspired to push on.

"Get out," I demanded. "Get out of the monastery and never return... You, and your wicked ways..."

The Abbot raised the flaming ball above his head, ready to hurl it at me, but there was a sudden rush of air from behind me, like a giant intake of breath – and then the world turned orange. Flames roared up the sides of the walls and the air behind me.

Monks screamed and fled—we all did. The air smelt of soot and acrid, burning smoke. My eyes stung and watered.

But as I stumbled back from the edge I caught an image of a vast, worm-like body humping over the rocks at the base of the walls, a vast alligator-like head hissing and clicking with reptilian malevolence. Zaxx was here. Zaxx the Golden, the greatest dragon left in existence had arrived.

~

In the terrified commotion as the monks sought to run for cover or run to the armory, I lost track of the Abbot. His fire had winked out, and his form disappeared into the throng. Where was he going? Was he fleeing, as I had told him too?

"Zaxx is here! Zaxx is here!" the monks were shouting, as flames once more soared up the sides of the battlements, and claws the size of swords scratched at mortar and stone.

Thud-thud-thud-thud, came a sound like successive lightning strikes, as I realized that the grounded lizard was digging at the roots of the walls, tunneling as fast and as ferociously as a mole through damp earth. Gouts of pulverized rock dust and smoke billowed outside the walls as the battlements that I stood on shook, and started to crack.

"Get back! Get off of the walls!" I shouted at the older Dragon Monks who had, until so recently, been the exact same ones ordered to capture me by the Abbot. In their fear and shock at everything that they had witnessed and heard this evening, they did so, clattering to the courtyard below just as the first building blocks cracked and crumbled below me.

Whump! Whump! The bull golden dragon hurled his tail and shoulders against the cracked outer wall of the Dragon Monastery, causing it to surge and buckle.

Oh no – how am **I** going to get down? I thought for a moment, as the entire walkway wobbled and wavered in the air.

"Char!" Someone was screaming, and I looked down to see Lila and Sigrid, breaking free from the gaggle of panicking monks to race *towards* the collapsing walls.

"No – get back!" I shouted feebly at them, as the mortar between the buildings stones cracked and burst with puffs of dust.

"Get some rope." Lila was looking scared but still moving with that grace of one who was used to leaping from ship to ship. Sigrid turned and sprinted for the nearest storehouse, as Lila gestured me back, towards the part where the wall was still only wobbling, not cracking. "Easy, Char, easy…" she called.

"Recharrgh!" Below me on the other side of the wall the Gold had managed to break the slabs of rock that sat at the foot of the wall's base, and soot was streaming from its mouth.

The dragon pipes sounded, but they were much quieter, and they seemed directed straight at the base of the walls, causing Zaxx to writhe and hiss in agony. Neill had done it! He had found a way to direct the pipes! I thought in glee as another chorus of discordant pipe-songs hit the Gold. The bull seemed unable to summon his fire as he was struck, again and again by the waves of sound.

Zaxx roared, furiously sending up gobbets of rock and earth as he resumed his battering of the walls.

"Here, here!" Sigrid was returning with a heavy coil of rope as the wall shook and wavered. I gritted my teeth. I didn't want to die like this. I wanted to see Paxala one last time. I wanted to see Neill one last time. I looked down to my friends below, just as a black-clad monk raced towards Sigrid, an ugly-looking club in his hands. He must be one of those still loyal to the Abbot.

"Sigrid – look out!" I screamed, as suddenly a shape hit her, and she was rolling onto the floor. It was Dorf! He had leapt to push her out of the way, both of them tumbling to the floor. Below me, Lila growled, drew her belt knife and ran to the defense of her two friends who now lay defenseless under the attacking monk. The exchange was short and swift, Lila, despite being half the man's size and about a third of his age, was a far better fighter than he was. The man hit the dirt as the walls shook underneath me, and I saw them turn to look up at me-

"Skreayar!" All of a sudden, there was a screeching in the air as something as red as fresh blood flashed from above the crater. It was Paxala! But she had to be with the other dragons now, she had to tell them--

"I have told them, silly. How long do you think it takes a dragon to think?" Paxala said as she swept past the battle-

ments once more, as, suddenly, she was joined by other roars of anger and defiance as other shapes, of all sizes, swooped through the smoke.

The dragons. Paxala had managed to raise the dragons.

"The dragons have risen!" I shouted, as the sky filled not just with the smokes and roars of the terrible Zaxx, but also with the cawing, shrieking, whooping calls of the other dragons. In the sky there were the sturdy Greens, swooping and rushing through the air; the Sinuous Blues flashing and zipping across the sky – even the Great Whites soaring high above it all, like elegant, graceful, dreadful herons or eagles. And everywhere came the Messenger dragons; tiny, falcon-sized dragons that flew in flocks and swarms, screaming over the battlements, alighting on the monasteries rooftops, darting down to harry and peck at the Gold bull's tail and back before zipping away again. It was a storm.

I was awestruck. I had never seen so many dragons flying at once – I had no idea what Paxala said to win them over, but it was clear to me that she had. The Greens and the Blues were following her lead, swooping at her side to dive bomb the olden bull as he thrashed his tail, and tried to catch them. He couldn't use his fire thanks to Neill's directed dragon pipes, and every time he swiped his tail – he missed my Crimson Red friend!

He couldn't hit any of them – they were too fast-- and I was delighted that my reptilian sister had been right.

"Children! Ingrates! Pests!" Zaxx the mighty dragon bellowed, over and over again as he thrashed and twitched on the floor, the dragons falling from the sky upon him like vultures.

I would have stood there watching until it was all over, but the fight was happening right below my feet, and the gigantic beast's body was hitting the sides of the walls where I was standing. The battlements bowed, and then gigantic blocks toppled forward as the wall gave way, sliding as if I were standing on the decks of a ship in a stormy sea, falling down to the thrashing golden body of Zaxx below.

"Pax!" I screamed, as claws as red as blood reached up to grab me.

CHAPTER 28
END, BEGINNING

T he dragon pipes blared once more, waking me up from my dark dreams. But this time, the pipes did not sound harsh or hurtful to the ears. Instead, they had a sweeter, almost melodic tone like a whistle. I blinked as bright sunlight flooded my eyes.

"Ow," I groaned. Everywhere hurt. I was lying in a cot bed, swaddled in soft linen blankets, underneath a round window.

"Skrip-ip?" Something chittered from the window, and, as I looked, one of the smaller blue and white Messenger dragons appeared, its claws clutching the stone work as it looked inside the room curiously, before returning to peck at the stone nonchalantly.

The dragon pipes peeled again, but the Messenger dragon didn't appear fussed by the noise, and certainly not in pain.

Someone had changed them so they didn't hurt the dragon's ears. I wondered why the Abbot would have done that.

"Oh yeah..." memories came flooding back to me about when I had last seen the Abbot. The monastery had turned against him when they had found out what he had been doing to the dragons, and he had fled. Or at least, I hoped that he had fled.

"Skreeayar!" Whistling screams of joy came from outside my window, as large shadows blocked the bright sun for a moment, before flashing past.

"What...?" I said, pushing myself up to look out of the window as the Messenger dragon hopped down into the room to investigate a wooden tray covered with a linen cloth. "Hey!" I said to it, as it had discovered a bowl of cold porridge, and some corners of bread, hunks of cheese, and fruit. The small dragonet delightedly started stealing my cheese – but I sighed, smiling. At least the little thing wasn't terrified of me.

In fact, none of the dragons outside of the window seemed terrified of the humans. Their shapes filled the sky, swooping and flying as they chased each other in quick aerial dogfights. There were dragons *everywhere,* even, I saw with a start, a long Sinuous Blue draped along the line of the battlements as Dragon Monks tried to creep around it. As I watched, it thwapped its tail and hissed at them, sending the older Dragon Monks scurrying off.

"So, they haven't completely accepted us humans yet," I murmured, as a voice answered me from the open door.

"No, but things are much better now that Zaxx and the Abbot have gone." It was Neill, looking pale but happy, smiling as he sat down on the corner of my bed and tried to shoo the feral Messenger dragon away from my breakfast.

"Leave it. I imagine I'll have to get used to that from now on," I said. "Sharing my life with dragons."

"*You already have,*" a voice said in my mind, and I threw my affection and thanks at Paxala, who I could sense was sunning herself on the roof of the Great Hall above where I was resting. She had saved me as I had fallen from the walls, flying as fast as thought, to catch me in her red claws.

"When the wall fell, we all thought Zaxx would be crushed under the rubble." Neill nodded to one entire third section of the Dragon Monastery wall, which was completely open to the elements. The snout of a Great White could clearly be seen snuffing and pawing at the masonry blocks, some as large as a house. "But when the Whites dug down into it--" Neill shook his head. "Zaxx had broken into the cellars, and then into the tunnels that honeycomb Mount Hammal. We think that he must have crawled out to the wilds, as we followed his trail right through the mountains to the near foothills before we lost it."

A chill rushed through me. "So, Zaxx is still out there then?" I thought. "He'll want revenge for this."

"Yes, he will. But not as much as the Abbot will, I think,"

Neill said gravely, shaking his head again at my questioning glance. "No sign of him either, although one of the other monks thinks he saw Monk Olan stealing a cart and horses from the stables, just as the walls were going down and dragons were everywhere. My money's on Olan rescuing the Abbot, and them both fleeing the monastery to some hide out somewhere."

"We'll have to find them," I thought, remembering the terrible infernos that I had seen the Abbot command.

"We will, Char, we will…" Neill said, reaching down to pick up one of the apples from my dragon-ravaged breakfast. "But for now – we should enjoy the fact that we are here, we are alive, and the dragons have a real home again." He nodded out of the window, where the flights of dragons raced and soared through the skies above the Dragon Monastery.

END OF DRAGON DREAMS

THE FIRST DRAGON RIDER BOOK TWO

Keep reading for an exclusive extract from **Dragon Mage,** the third and final book in The First Dragon Rider Trilogy.

THANK YOU!

I hope you enjoyed joining Char and Neill on their epic journey – I certainly enjoyed writing it! If you'd like to let other readers know this is a book they won't want to miss out on, please leave a review :)

Receive free books, exclusive excerpts and be kept up to date on all of my new releases, when you sign up to my mailing list at AvaRichardsonBooks.com/mailing-list

Stay in touch! I'd also love to connect with you on:

Facebook: www.facebook.com/AvaRichardsonBooks

Goodreads:
www.goodreads.com/author/show/8167514.Ava_Richardson

THE FIRST DRAGON RIDER

DRAGON MAGE

AVA RICHARDSON

BLURB

To unite a fractured kingdom, a reluctant hero must rise.

Neill has been charged with the impossible task of bringing the Middle Kingdom together to fight the burgeoning threat posed by the rogue sorcerer Ansall and his dragon Zaxx. Neill longs for his old life as a mere foot soldier for his father responsible only for his family's wellbeing, and is unsure about whether he is fit to lead an army. Neill's contemplative nature forces him to consider every aspect of the problems he faces, but often makes it difficult for him to take action—and failure to act could mean the deaths of many.

Now, echoing Char and their dragon Paxala, his duty beckons him to lead the Dragon Riders—and take his rightful place as king—but with doubt and new enemies creeping in, his resolve will be tested. When the mysterious Dark Prince arrives with an offer, Neill will have to make a decision that could change the course of history.

As Ansall grows in strength by harnessing black magic, Neill must choose between his own desires and the welfare of the entire kingdom. Can he rise to the challenge before it's too late?

Get your copy of **Dragon Mage** at
AvaRichardsonBooks.com

EXCERPT

We left the Fort, the center of the Torvald Clan lands before evening – we hadn't even stayed a whole day, but we had made sure that at least Garf knew of the coming refugees from Sheerlake. He had promised us solemnly that they would be looked after, and that it would give the Sons of Torvald a mission to learn some of the ways of chieftainship.

But I was glad to be flying westwards again, returning to the Dragon Monastery, and I could tell that Neill was happy too.

"There – down there!" He pointed at the glint of large shapes, blue and green against the darker sprawl of the forest. It was the dragons of our flight that had come to help defeat the Blood Baron, and, somewhere down there also would be our friends Sigrid on Socolia, Terence and Lila on Morax, and the crowd of prisoners and refugees.

Neill seemed fresher and brighter after having been home, I realized as I watched his face darting at the signs of our friends below. I didn't think that it was having seen home that had made him more assured and confident, and neither was it merely fact that we were now flying towards *our* home as well. I remembered how I had felt at being back at my father's fortress; even in my old chambers once again with their cutesy-princess decoration.

It had made me realize who I was now. That I wasn't who I had been, and that I had already outgrown the worries and fears of my youth. My father, the Prince Lander's fortress, had seemed small to me, and confining, and that had only increased my desire to be a Dragon Rider – whatever that would mean! And so, it seemed to me that Neill must have had the same experience as well. He now flew more confidently, he moved more confidently, he was no longer so deeply troubled by the ugly feelings as he had been before going to honor his father's passing.

But we would still have a lot to do, I was thinking, before Neill poked me in the back. "Ow!" I said.

"Haven't you been listening to a word that I've been saying?" Neill said in exasperation. The wind was low, and Paxala beneath us wasn't particularly flying very fast so I couldn't pretend that I just couldn't hear him. "There's something wrong down there!" He pointed once more down at the crowd of prisoners, refugees, and dragons.

"Is there?" I looked. The central gaggle of prisoners was trudging alone, the two groups of refugees in front and behind, as well as walking alongside the gaggle. Flying in a circling pattern were the riderless Green and Blue, and, farther away I could see the quick movements of the Sinuous Blue that must be Morax.

"I can't see what's wrong…" I began, before I registered what it had to be. *Three dragons. There were only three dragons down there.* "Where's Sigrid and Socolia?" I asked.

"I know, right?" Neill was already scanning the horizon and land I joined him in looking for the telltale silhouette of dragon wings against the sky, or the flash of green that could be Socolia... Nothing.

"Pax?" I reached out to Paxala with both my voice and mind, my sudden nervousness giving speed to my thoughts. "Can you sense where Socolia is?"

"Of course. To the west, and south, following the hot currents there," Paxala said to me, a pleasing feeling accompanying the thought of warmer winds. From my long time spent with Paxala, I knew that the dragons often thought of the airs of the world in *currents*; rivers of warmer, colder, sharp or slow airs that blew across the world, bringing with them all of the scents and noises of the lands that they crossed.

"What is she doing there?" Neill asked when I told him, as we sped down towards where the Blue Morax was circling. Morax's flight was erratic, flapping his great wings quickly and awkwardly as he attempted to hover and make turns quickly.

"Socolia is upset," Paxala said to me, a note of urgency in her voice. *"She is unsure of what her rider wants, she is struggling against the girl who rides her, and that is causing more anguish for Morax and his riders."*

Oh no. This was what I had feared could happen. The dragons had only been bonded to their riders (if bonded was even the right word for the tentative friendship that they had

349

with their riders) for such a short time – had Sigrid done something to upset the dragon?

"Can you reach her – Socolia, I mean? Can you talk to her?" I said.

"Dragons can speak with tongues that humans cannot, it is true," Paxala informed me, and I nodded. This was what I would call speaking with our minds, telepathy, but Paxala thought of it much differently. *"But we cannot talk to every dragon, everywhere. It is stronger if we are closer, physically, and closer, by friendship."* Paxala grumbled, making a worried clicking noise in her long throat. *"I can sense that Socolia is upset, but her confusion and struggle with her rider makes it difficult for me to reach her..."*

"We have to get to her," I told Paxala, as Neill was waving in alarm to Terence and Lila.

"We heard a roar from this direction, a dragon's roar – and then Socolia and Sigrid just took off! As fast as an arrow – and we're trying to find out the reason why!" Terence hollered across the slow-moving winds as we hovered near them. He was pointing southwards, and I saw him trying once again to shift his weight on the neck of the Blue Morax, using his knees and hips to try and encourage the Blue to follow the Green Socolia. But Morax couldn't – or wouldn't follow, caught in a moment of indecision, the Blue dragon was turning in circles towards the south, then seemingly getting fritted, and turning back once more.

"What is wrong?" Neill shouted, looking devastated at the

haphazard riding and flying of the dragons with whom he wanted to change the world. I knew what he must be thinking: if we cannot even work with the younger dragons effectively – then how could we ever become what we needed to be?

"It's Socolia, she's worried about something – and Sigrid cannot control her, I think," I relayed to him, before it suddenly became abundantly clear what had upset the green dragon so much.

Get your copy of **Dragon Mage** at
AvaRichardsonBooks.com

35601450R00200

Made in the USA
Columbia, SC
22 November 2018